KEVIN BALDEOSINGH is the autho
Paras P. A former teacher and journal
a freelance writer. Born in 1963, he w
the West Indies, where he also got his

The author says he likes squash, volleyball, tennis and the women who play them. Describing himself as young and single, he admits that he hopes to get older one day.

KEVIN BALDEOSINGH

VIRGIN'S TRIANGLE

Heinemann

For Cindy

Heinemann Educational Publishers
Halley Court, Jordan Hill, Oxford OX2 8EJ
A Division of Reed Educational & Professional Publishing Limited

Heinemann: A Division of Reed Publishing (USA) Inc.
361 Hanover Street, Portsmouth, NH 03801–3912, USA

Heinemann Educational Books (Nigeria) Ltd
PMB 5205, Ibadan

Heinemann Educational Botswana Publishers (Pty) Ltd
PO Box 10103, Village Post Office, Gaborone, Botswana

FLORENCE   PRAGUE   MADRID   ATHENS
MELBOURNE   AUCKLAND   KUALA LUMPUR   TOKYO
SINGAPORE   MEXICO CITY   CHICAGO   SÃO PAULO
JOHANNESBURG   KAMPALA   NAIROBI

First published by Heinemann Educational Publishers in 1997

British Library Cataloguing in Publication Data
A catalogue record for this book is available from the British Library.

ISBN 0 435 98947 2

Cover design by Touchpaper
Cover illustration by Andrew Holmes

Phototypeset by CentraCet Ltd, Cambridge
Printed and bound in Great Britain
by Cox & Wyman Ltd, Reading, Berkshire

97 98 99 10 9 8 7 6 5 4 3 2 1

Chapter One

Thinking about sex and money, Giselle Karan stood at the gate of
the construction yard of the new Caribbean Media Company waiting
for a truck to finish dumping a load of gravel. It was seven o'clock
on a Tuesday morning and only a few white clouds, which served
no purpose except to be picturesque, floated overhead in the clear
blue sky. The tropical sun shone like the gold which had never
been found in these islands. Across the road, calypso music blared
from large speakers set on the pavement in front of a small snackette.
All in all, it was the kind of day which makes the writers of
Caribbean tourist brochures feel, albeit temporarily, like honest
hacks.

Giselle cut a casually elegant figure as she stood waiting. She wore
straight black trousers, a short-sleeved top of cream-coloured silky
material, and low-heeled leather shoes. A simple black purse was
slung over her shoulder. Her jewellery, understated but unusual,
added to her appearance. She wore four bangles of flat, weirdly
twisted metal on her left wrist, bought from a private designer, and a
round bracelet of heavy silver with bud-like ends on her right wrist.
This was a traditional Indian bracelet, called a *bera*, which Giselle
had received from her mother exactly eight years and one day ago,
when she was eighteen. It had been passed down by Giselle's great-
grandmother who had come from India nearly a hundred and fifty
years ago. Giselle preferred modern avant-garde designs. She didn't
wear rings. Around her neck, she had a very fine silver choker chain
and, hanging outside her blouse, a milky-green stone in a stainless
steel setting strung on a black shoelace. When anybody asked her
what kind of jewellery she liked, Giselle usually said, 'Cheap.'

But Giselle's jewellery matched her exotic looks. She was a mixture
of bloods rarely found outside the Caribbean. Her maternal great-
grandmother may have come from India, but by the time Giselle's
generation was born into this world on the small, ethnically complex

1

island of Trinidad, her ancestry also included African, Chinese, Spanish, Syrian and Amerindian. A slim, brown young woman of medium height, she had slanted, honey-brown eyes with a very steady gaze. Giselle's jet-black hair naturally had the twisted curl that other women spend hours at beauty salons trying to achieve. Now, heading into work, she had it pulled tightly back and held in place by hair pins and a clip of dark polished wood. Giselle would have looked severe except for a pouting, smiley mouth which sat oddly, but attractively, on the longish lines of her face. All in all, she didn't look like a person who thought about sex and money at the same time.

In fact, Giselle's thoughts about sex on this fine morning were rather vague – she thought she wanted it, but she wasn't sure. On the other hand, her thoughts about money were quite definite: she had in the bank a total of sixty-two thousand, four hundred and thirty-four dollars and seventeen cents, and it was the first time in years that she had felt financially secure. Her advance cheque from the CMC had been deposited yesterday afternoon (a nice birthday present), and Giselle had awoken this morning with the unpleasant realization that she was twenty-six years old, it was six weeks till Carnival, and she was still a virgin. As a good Catholic girl of Hindu ancestry, Giselle knew she ought to feel proud, not worried. She knew she should be thinking of Ash Wednesday, not the two-day bacchanal which preceded it. She also knew she ought not to be feeling as horny as she was.

I must have the mentality of a prostitute, she thought guiltily and, being Catholic, felt a little better for her guilt. But she still couldn't help feeling that her horniness was written all over her face and was reflected even in her most casual movements as she shifted her weight from one leg to the other. Also, this year's favoured Road March calypso kept running through her head – a song called 'Looking to See Paul'. Though, like all Road March contenders, it was a dance tune, it also referred to an actual incident where the female Speaker of the Parliament – the third woman to be appointed to that position in any Commonwealth country – had been asked to resign by the government after being involved in a court case where her evidence proved contradictory. Of course, since the essence of calypso is *double entendre*, the words appeared to refer to acts that were rather less

2

political. At any rate, the Speaker, whose name was Occah Seapaul, refused to resign and the government eventually declared a state of emergency and put her under house arrest, after which she declared herself to be the light of the nation.

The Mighty Amazon was the sobriquet of the calypsonian who sang the song. (In Trinidad, calypsonians are better known by their sobriquets than their real names and, even when their real names *are* known, as in the case of top calypsonians, everyone, including the calypsonians themselves, still uses their sobriquets.) Amazon was the first woman privileged to win the Road March competition, with 'Looking to See Paul' proving to be the most popular tune this Carnival season. This was not because of the public's interest in politics: and, as the song began blasting from the snackette across the road, Giselle knew she wasn't remembering the lyrics for political reasons, either. In fact, humming the song to herself as she listened, she had to restrain herself from swaying her hips on the spot. Almost unconsciously, she began to sing in an undertone the words which, like any true calypso lover, she knew by heart:

> I was lying in bed last night with my Bajan man
> Listening to the crapauds' call
> And I turn to he and in Bajan say,
> 'Oi cah see Paul at all.'

> He say, 'But yer see Paul this evening from seven
> And you loime with he till ten.'
> And I tell he, 'Yes, but I like the lime so much
> Oi need a Bajan invasion again.'

As she sang along, Giselle noticed one man working by himself a little way in front of her, away from the central activity. He was swinging a sledgehammer on a pile of concrete slabs, breaking them into smaller pieces. He did not look like the other workers. He was not wearing a helmet, for one thing, and his hair was tied in a ponytail which flipped every time he swung the sledgehammer. Also, he was stripped to the waist, wearing only a baggy pair of rough trousers and chunky workman's boots. She watched him at work and continued singing. Even under her breath, Giselle had a good voice, rather deep for a woman, with a reasonable range:

3

I say, 'Oi want to see Paul run,
Oi want to see Paul play,
Oi want to see Paul stand up and wine,
Oi want to see Paul ramajay.
Man, you hear the call, you hearing me bawl
But is like Oi cah see Paul
at all, at all, at all.'

Well, he get up and turn on the light
'Cause he didn' want to get mih mad,
But while the crapaud singing love song in the night
Inside the going just wasn't going hard.

Sweat glistened on the man's brown body and Giselle, almost unconsciously, began watching him. He was thin, but muscular. She liked
the way his lats flexed as he stretched up to swing the hammer, the
little triangular muscles under his arms standing out, and the flat
planes of his stomach. The hammer was held poised for a moment,
then came the sudden violent surge as he swung, the hammer an
extension of his body.

My Bajan man say, 'Give me a chance, darlin',
It late, Oi tired, and it cold.'
I say, 'Like yer constitution need fixin',
I better give you some bois bande to plug the loophole.'

He tell me, 'Well, play ah over with Bas and Ramesh,
Dem boys have balls for everyone;
And while yer do that tell me something slack in moi
  ears
Because only if yer have no standards you will see Paul
  come.'

The man swung his hammer and the slab cracked as the iron head hit.
Giselle suddenly found the tropical morning becoming a little warmer
– his coordination was beautiful to watch. As a little girl, Giselle had
read all about the Norse god Thor and his hammer Mjolnir, and she
almost expected to hear the rumble of thunder, or at least a round of
applause. But, though this didn't happen, the song played on:

4

So I start to talk sexy in he ear
And I get so nasty and rude
That as soon as Paul start to hear
I see Paul get attitude, see Paul want to intrude.

I tell he, 'Put a Maraj in mih garage,
Put some Manning in mih planning,
Put your organ in mih Morgan
'Cause Oi know you's a man of good standing.'

The truck dumped its last pile of gravel and moved off. Giselle, walking across the yard, found her hips trying to move in a smooth circular motion – or 'wine', in the Trinidadian slang – in time with the pumping beat which floated loudly on the morning air. She restrained this embarrassing impulse, making sure her walk was still that confident stride that belongs peculiarly to professional women who are carving their way into the man's working world, and not the walk of another type of professional woman who is part of the working man's world. That Giselle was able to do this and continue singing to herself made her feel as accomplished as a person who can rub his belly and pat his head at the same time:

I say, 'Oi cah see Paul movin' at all,
What de 'ell is dis?'
He tell me, 'You wouldn' see Paul move
Until yer give an emergency kiss.'

Well, I do it and he say, 'See Paul, the engine eh stall,
And he wasn't trying to hide.'
I reply, 'Well, put your key in my ignition
And let we go for a roide!'

So I bawl, 'Oi cah see Paul
Even though he is the light.
But that is all right, I don't mind at all,
'Cause I feelin', Oi say Oi feelin', Oi feelin' NOT to see
    Paul tonight!'

I tell him, 'Oi want to see Paul run,
Oi want to see Paul play,
Oi want to see Paul stand up and wine,

Oi want to see Paul ramajay.
You hear the call, you hear me bawl
And Oi cah (Oi cah, Oi cah!) see Paul at all, at all, at
all!'

As the song ended a relative silence fell. Giselle became aware of the sun kissing her cheeks gently with its morning heat and, because she was in that kind of mood, she thought that if ever she found a man who could kiss even half so nicely she would marry him at once.

Marriage might only be a euphemism for what I really want, she admitted to herself, still vaguely, though she did know for sure that she wanted a husband with a middle-range income and the endurance of Paul. Her mind's voice suddenly became that of Jack Palance: *Giselle Karan, twenty-six, attractive, untouched: believe it . . . or not.*

Giselle, looking across at the labourer, saw his ponytail flip as he swung the hammer again, and she smiled to herself as she recalled another mythical god, from Hindu culture: Hanuman, the monkey god. The labourer paused for a moment, wiping the sweat off his forehead with the back of his hand. The sledgehammer's handle leaned on his thigh, anchored to the ground by its iron head. His eyes were closed and Giselle read in his expression a simple pleasure in his physical exertion and the feel of the morning sun on his face. He wasn't good-looking – his face was rather rough-hewn – but he had a nice mouth. Then he opened his eyes and caught her looking at him.

Giselle blushed. His eyes were very dark and smoky, resting coolly on her. To her surprise, Giselle found her automatic reflex to look away had been arrested. The man's face – he could have been anywhere between mid- to late twenties – did not change expression at first. Then he smiled. It was a smile of pure happiness, as if he was inviting her to share his pleasure in the morning and working in the open air and just being alive. His teeth were very white. Giselle could not help it: she smiled back. Then she turned and went up the stairs. She felt very embarrassed now, and the fact that the steps had apparently grown to twice their normal size did nothing to ease her awkwardness. Giselle had three flights to mount and she was sure the man's eyes were on her all the way. But when she risked a backward glance from the top, he was drinking from a bottle of water, his back towards her. She opened the grey metal door and went into the air-conditioned corridor. Discovering she had had no reason to be self-conscious, she now felt a little disappointed.

I shouldn't have kept looking at him, she thought. *He probably thinks I was coming on to him.*

Giselle shrugged mentally. *Men*, she told herself, *stared at women as a form of intimidation.* She had held his gaze to show she could not be intimidated. But, even after she had inwardly repeated this three times, Giselle still hadn't convinced herself.

Face it, Giselle my dear, she thought. *You liked the man's body and you were scoping him out. That's the long and short of it.*

She reached the end of the corridor and went into the newsroom. The room was divided in two by an area of open space. On one side, the obsolete generation of word processors sat on desks covered with papers, markers, books and the occasional coffee mug. This was where the newspaper staff worked while the newsroom was gradually converted to the new Macintosh computers. These machines were on the other side of the room, resting on clean, shiny desks. A few of the Macs were still covered with plastic wrapping and Giselle, who sometimes felt computers were alive in some manner, thought those Macs seemed rather smug in their newness. There were the small desktop models and the large-screen ones for the sub-editors who laid out the pages. Giselle's job, along with four other programmers/ graphic artists, was to work with the company's computer department to oversee the installation and programming of the new system.

The CMC was actually the bastard child of the *Colony News* newspaper, which was the country's oldest broadsheet. A year previously, most of that paper's editors had resigned when the Board of Directors issued instructions that they should not write editorials or news stories about the relationship between Prime Minister Ramesh Beta Dholak, Attorney General Basdeo Lyall Singh and a man named AlBu Cracker who was reputed to be the richest pimp in Trinidad and Tobago. The paper had since become a money-losing venture.

The Queres-McBuddy Group, which owned it, continued to produce the broadsheet since to close it down or sell it would have been to admit defeat. But the Group had financed a new tabloid newspaper named *The National Press* five months ago, deciding to upgrade the technology to the highest standard while the *Colony News* limped along with skeletal staff and outdated equipment. Sitting at her desk, Giselle thought, 'At least, I got a big career boost out of that ill wind.'

No one was in yet, except for Krishna Budhu who sat at the far end of the newsroom. He was one of the few editors who had not resigned when the controversy at the *Colony News* had erupted, and he might as well have been nobody as far as Giselle was concerned. But then she saw he had got up and was coming across to talk to her. Giselle sighed.

'You here early, Ms Karan,' said Budhu, who always spoke as though saying something clever. It was just one of several habits Budhu had that Giselle found irritating.

'That's right, Mr Budhu,' she answered.

'How you going?'

'Fine.'

Budhu smiled down at her. Giselle wondered why God had chosen to make Budhu such a poor human being when he could have been such a perfect rabbit. His teeth were just protuberant enough to give his smile a sly, rodent-like quality, his ears were set as nearly at right angles to his head as is possible for human ears and, though he was only in his mid-forties, his hair was like white fur on his skull.

'So you okay?' said Budhu.

'Yes,' said Giselle.

'You really here early.'

'Yes.'

Budhu smiled again. *I was wrong*, thought Giselle, *if he was a rabbit, he'd be one with both a nervous disorder and a bad memory. He'd also be rabbit pie within a week, I bet.*

She smiled back sweetly at Budhu, as she always did when having unkind thoughts about someone. Unfortunately this encouraged him to continue talking.

'I have to come in early, because I drop the kids off to school,' he said. 'But I kind of like it, eh, because I get chance to get organized early.'

'I see.'

'I get to read the papers, see what stories we have to follow and so on . . . so how the work going?' he asked, after a pause.

Giselle looked down. 'Well, it isn't,' she said. 'So I better get started.'

'Yes, yes. I didn't mean to keep you back. Just wanted to see how you going. So you okay?'

'Yes,' she answered, her head staying resolutely down.

'So you hear the government giving us pressure again?'

'Oh?'

'Yeah, man,' said Budhu, clearly glad to be giving news. 'Remember why the *Colony News* went through?'

'Yes, I read the papers.'

'Was because the Prime Minister put pressure on the Board because he say the editor's racist.'

'I know the story.'

'Right, you know the story,' said Budhu and, as if Giselle had not spoken, continued: 'We write a headline "PM – I Like Chutney Music". He say the headline racist because, in the same speech, he also say he like calypso. Then it had the AlBu Cracker issue. So Dholak tell the Board to fire the chief editor, or the government would stop granting import licences for cloth and remove duty on rum. And you know why he say that?'

'Yes,' said Giselle, a little impatiently now. 'I know the whole story.'

'Is it because the Queres-McBuddy Group does make rum and import cloth?' Budhu asked, with a toothy smile.

'You ever wanted to be a contestant on *Jeopardy*?' asked Giselle.

'Why? You think I'd be good?'

'Maybe. Look, I really have a lot of work to do, Mr Budhu.'

'Yes, yes. Don't let me keep you back. But the Chairman of the Group coming in at ten to give a speech to the staff.'

'Well, I'd better get to work then.'

'Yes, yes. You do that. It nice to see somebody else in here so early.'

'Right. See you later.'

'Right.'

He walked away and Giselle sighed again, this time with relief. She took out her diskettes and went to one of the large-screened computers. Basic writing instructions for the reporters and editors were already programmed into the system. Giselle had just needed to work out specific requirements. That had been relatively simple. She was now on the second phase: programming the hard drive for page layout, including standard logos which she had designed herself, for the sub-editors. She had to be finished in four months, when the second building was scheduled for completion. Then she had to supervise training of the newsroom staff, troubleshoot the inevitable programming problems, and update video and print logos as required. But, with the unexpected problems she was encountering, she hoped there would be a delay. She had been wrestling for several days – and nights, since she rarely left before eight in the evening – with some complicated programming tangles. This was why she had come in early, to get a head start while it was still quiet and, with luck, leave while there was still daylight. Living on your own was all well and good, but that didn't mean she liked driving up the steep and lonely road to her apartment after dark.

Giselle shared an apartment in Fort St George, overlooking the Gulf of Paria. Her room-mate (and best friend) was a woman named Vera Chancellor, but Giselle was virtually on her own since Vera, who was a flight attendant, used the apartment mostly as a place to keep luggage. Giselle's mother had not wanted her to move out and Giselle had wondered at the time how her father might have reacted if he had still been alive.

Admittedly, there were times when she regretted her decision. She had never crossed the red line, but there had been long periods when she'd stood precariously balanced on it. For most of the last three years she'd lived entirely without frills or luxuries – except, of course, for books, which she considered a necessity – and there were many times when her refrigerator could have been in commercials touting breakfast as the most important meal of the day – shelves empty except for cereal, yogurt, bread, eggs and milk. Mother Hubbard in those days had nothing on Giselle Karan, Giselle often said.

She reached behind the monitor and turned it on. The Macintosh symbols came up and she took the mouse and clicked on her name to enter the files. She opened the systems window and went into Control Panels.

The computer screen printed: **Good morning, Giselle. How are you?**

Not too well, she typed back.

I'm sorry to hear that, the computer typed. **Can I do anything to cheer you up?**

Giselle typed: **Come up with the winning numbers for a million-**

dollar lottery so I can stop busting my brains every day, find me a handsome, smart and rich man who will love me forever, or program yourself for convenient and superb layout so I can go to the beach. Preferably the last.

The computer flashed a repeating line of period points for several seconds, then typed: **Sorry, unable to comply.**

'Story of my life,' Giselle muttered.

She inserted a diskette on which she had written some experimental programs and began running them through. She had already worked out the major concepts: the problems lay in the details. It was easy to create a functioning system, but Giselle also wanted an efficient one. She knew intuitively that there were short cuts she hadn't thought of. It was just a matter of finding them. But this morning the programs ran meaninglessly. She could not get her mind to focus. The incident with the workman still disturbed her and she didn't understand why. Even if her reaction had surprised her, it was still a trivial incident. But, trivial or not, Giselle did not like reactions in herself that she did not understand. She prided herself on her self-control and, certainly, where men were concerned, she was always in control – a fact that had frustrated quite a few of them. *I wonder if I'd make a good prostitute*, she thought and now the voice in her head became Rod Serling's: *Submitted for your approval, Giselle Karan, decent young virgin, who at twenty-six suddenly discovers a stranger living in the dark side of her heart, in that region of the human spirit we call . . . the Twilight Zone.*

Giselle sucked her teeth in a steups – that peculiar sound Trinidadians make to express annoyance, which sounds like an expiring balloon with spit. *I got to stop watching so much cable*, she thought.

The fact was, Giselle had always been too busy with her academic efforts to have time for love or even the games of love. Nor did she change her attitude when she went to university. And now, busy building her career, she still had no time for a serious relationship. Or so she told herself.

But sometimes she wondered if it was just that blanking men when they started getting too serious had become a habit. At times, when circumstances were such that she found herself meeting a lot of new people, blanking would-be lovers even became a sort of hobby, like knitting.

11

Her mother, Giselle knew, worried about her: hardly a week passed when she didn't ask Giselle if she'd 'met anyone'. In fact, in the last seven years Giselle had received five serious offers of marriage. She knew this wasn't bad going these days, when it's both cheaper and less potentially litigious to just move in together. She had refused each man as gently as she could. She had liked each of them quite a lot. Yet there was no doubt in her mind about her refusals.

She wondered at that sometimes, wondered if there was not truly some coldness or some deficiency in her that other women were free of. Her younger sister, Tabitha, was already married and expecting her first child. Their youngest sister, Miranda, was engaged, though this meant nothing since Miranda got engaged the way other women bought evening gowns – 'Miranda likes having a fiancé to wear to important occasions,' Giselle had once told her mother.

But Giselle herself simply could not see a man as a crucial or permanent feature of her life. That, in her view, was what good furniture was for. A husband was not part of Giselle's self-image. She didn't even like the word 'husband'. For some reason, it made her think of a man sitting in a living-room with a newspaper, smoking a pipe, while she sewed. And Giselle didn't like being ignored in her own living-room – which, in this scenario, she was sure she had laboured for hours to clean – and she hated both sewing and men who smoked.

So why bother? She had friends, good health, enough money, books, an attractive appearance and her work. She was more than happy, she told herself.

Are you? said a voice in her head.

Yes, she answered. *Why spoil a good life with emotional entanglements?*

Giselle got up, went to the window and stared out blankly at the morning traffic below her. She didn't know why she was thinking in this way when she had work to do.

'PMS must have arrived early this month,' she muttered to herself, grimacing.

'She's here before me and she's talking to herself,' said a man's voice behind her. 'Bring out the straitjacket, doctor.'

Giselle turned. Robert Cardinez, the managing editor, was walking across the newsroom, smiling at her.

'Good morning, Robert,' she said, linking her hands primly in front of her. 'I didn't hear you.'

'Obviously. Carpet is a wonderful invention, eh? It makes newspaper work so much easier when people don't know you're standing right behind them.'

Giselle smiled.

'Is that the secret of your investigative reporting?'

'Listen, we're a small company. We can't afford hidden cameras like ABC *20/20*.'

He grinned down at her. Robert Cardinez was an energetic man in his late thirties. He was quite young to be managing editor of a newspaper, but he had been in the media since he was sixteen and he owned a reasonable-sized block of shares in CMC. At the time of the *Colony News* controversy, he had been running his own small publishing house but had taken up the offer to spearhead the new paper. It had been a good move by the Queres-McBuddy Group to hire him since, Giselle knew, he was a well-respected journalist. She liked his looks, too. Cardinez had brown hair, so tightly curled it was almost kinky, and sharp, alert features. He was always dressed in stylish shirts, colourful ties and well-cut trousers. He also had nice shoes, and he was tall. Giselle found him attractive without being attracted to him. In the five weeks she had been working for CMC, she still wasn't sure what he thought about her.

He sat on the edge of a desk and looked at her.

'You don't know it's against company policy for anyone to come in here earlier than me?' he said severely. 'You might spoil my reputation.'

She said, 'It might spoil your reputation if someone came in early and found us having this cosy *tête-à-tête*.'

Robert laughed. 'There's hardly any danger of my reputation being spoiled,' he said. He looked at her with sudden curiosity. 'You not worried about your reputation?'

She smiled. 'A nice girl like me?'

He shrugged. 'Nice you may be, but you're also rather attractive. You know how people talk.'

'With their mouths?'

Robert grinned. 'And a good dose of imagination.'

'Tell you what,' Giselle said. 'I won't worry about it if you won't.'

He spread his arms in an expansive gesture. 'I worry about nothing except headlines and deadlines. Speaking of which, is your programming on schedule?'

She shook her head. 'Actually, I was just hoping for a minor earthquake or something to delay the building so I could have more time. I seem to have hit a block.'

'Well, schedule a meeting with me if you can't get on top of it.' He stood up. 'But I'm sure you will.'

'I hope so.'

'Okay,' he said. He turned and walked off quickly to his office. Robert always moved quickly. He spoke to everybody, even the cleaning ladies, but never at length. It made it difficult to assess his feelings about anyone. *I wonder why he appointed a toady like Budhu as news editor?* thought Giselle. Then she dismissed the question – she wasn't interested in what Robert Cardinez was like on the job. She wanted to know what he would be like outside the workplace. *I bet he has really good table manners*, she thought. Then, with a sigh, she returned to the computer. From outside, there was a deep thump-thump, like a giant's heart, as the piledriver began hitting the earth.

Chapter Two

After Robert Cardinez left, Giselle settled down in front of the computer and, breathing deeply for a few minutes, shoved all thoughts of men, marriage and life in general out of her head.

The programs began running and she entered cyberspace. Giselle liked this world within the computer. It made sense, especially if you weren't overly attached to real life. Here was purpose and recreation and even communication with other human beings. It was just like reality but, in Giselle's view, better constructed. *And I sure ain't no virgin here*, she thought as her fingers stabbed busily at the keyboard.

People began coming into the newsroom. Phones started ringing insistently. A few people greeted Giselle. By nine o'clock the place had started to resemble a ward for the violently – or at least noisily – insane at the St Ann's Mental Hospital. The newsroom had begun another day.

Giselle, engrossed in her work, was not distracted by all the activity around her. She knew some programmers who would have ended up at that same Mental Hospital if they tried to work in this atmosphere. But Giselle thrived on it. It made her more aware of her goals. The foundation she was laying here, like the foundation of the very building itself, would have an impact on the world – or at least the society that made up her world. This was why she liked the phrase 'intellectual property'. Her thoughts – her knowledge and mental skills – were invisible yet had concrete effects. *Like a transparent bikini*, she thought, grinning, even as she continued writing her program. Knowledge was as much part of the world as land and buildings and machinery, but didn't take up so much space.

Sitting at her desk, these thoughts running through the back of her mind, Giselle smiled. After she was finished here, magazines and newspapers and videos would be produced. She knew the figures: the CMC was spending thirty-five million dollars to establish itself. But the newsprint and the magnetic tape and the cameras were only equipment. The essence of all those things was the thought, the creativity behind them. And she was helping to lay the mental foundation for that creativity to express itself more effectively. She liked hardware. She admired its cleverness; she appreciated the ease it brought to practical life; and she knew she looked impressive as well as attractive at a computer screen. But software was the most essential reality. Giselle thought of it as the difference between a person's outer self and the spirit within them.

But, she thought as she switched off her computer and pinched the skin on the bridge of her nose, *even the spirit has to obey the limitations of the body. That's why men aren't as capable as women in bed*, she decided, then frowned at herself. *What* was on her mind today?

Giselle got up and stretched. Her upper vertebrae crackled pleasurably as she arched her spine. Her bra pulled against the flesh just below her breasts: it was a little tight. She thought her period might indeed be near. Her breasts felt slightly swollen.

'Don't do that, Ms Karan. You're distracting my male reporters and making the female ones envious.' Robert Cardinez passed by, walking quickly, with a sheaf of papers in his hand. He flashed a grin at her. She smiled back, a little embarrassed, and sat down hastily, thinking it was becoming a habit for Robert to catch her unawares. He went past her – she almost imagined she heard a whoosh of air – and turned the corner before she could even reply.

Sharma Ramlogan came over. She was one of the sub-editors, an easy-going young woman with cool eyes, a wide mouth, and a direct manner Giselle liked. 'Well, Cardy certainly notices your every move,' Sharma said.

Giselle laughed. 'I think he notices everybody's every move. He moves so fast himself that everyone else probably looks like they're in slow motion.'

'I have the impression he likes your motion for sure,' said Sharma. She put her hands on her waist and began to sing: ' "There's a brown girl in the ring, tra-la-la-la-la, there's a brown girl in the ring, tra-la-la-la-la . . ." ' Her hips moved in wicked chutney rhythm in her green pleated skirt and Giselle snorted with laughter. Sharma was short, almost stocky, but she carried herself with a sensual, slack-bodied fluidity. She leaned down to Giselle, her black crow's wing eyebrows raised, a slow smile on her face. 'So, if he asked you, you would show him your motion?' Giselle hiccuped with laughter. Sharma grinned down at her.

'Please, Sharma,' Giselle said weakly. 'I didn't eat yet. I don't have the energy for you.'

'Okay, but remember – ' Sharma bent her mouth to Giselle's ear and whispered hoarsely: '"Every breath you take, he'll be watching you".'

Giselle sat up and wiped her eyes. 'Well,' she said, pulling at the thin material of her top and puffing out her chest, '"the little hills do rejoice on every side". Psalm 65, Verse 11.'

Sharma raised a hand. 'If you going to quote scripture at me, I shall retire. How a reprobate like you know chapter and verse so?'

'Just one of those things that stuck in my head. You should hear me on Shakespeare's sonnets.' She batted her eyes at Sharma and began declaiming: '"Shall I compare thee to a summer's day? Thou are *more* lovely and *more* temperate . . ."'

Sharma guffawed. Giselle grinned and opened her purse, checking to make sure her lipstick and eyeliner pencil were there. She did this whenever she had to freshen her make-up, even though she knew her make-up was always in her purse. 'Oh, that done me good,' she said.

'Yes, I see you were slaving over your true love all morning. You don't sometimes worry Mr Macintosh will begin to feel you too possessive and tell you he needs his cyberspace?'

'Of course not,' said Giselle. 'Mac would never desert me. Why do you think I love him so?'

Sharma shook her head. 'Poor Cardy. Edged out by a rival who doesn't even have a body.'

'Yeah, but you know it's brains I really like,' said Giselle. 'Especially fried.'

Sharma, frowning worriedly, put a hand on Giselle's forehead. 'Anybody ever tell you you a *weird* child, Karan?'

'Of course not,' Giselle answered. She got up and slung her purse over her shoulder. 'But then, I hardly ever speak to people I haven't programmed myself.' Sharma chuckled.

Giselle said, 'That meeting with the owner suppose to start now?'

'Of course. We have nothing better to do than hear old Bagasse tell us about our great purpose in life.'

'Don't sound so bitter. And why you calling him Bagasse?'

17

Sharma rolled her eyes upwards. 'God, Giselle, you are so out of it. You never see Spengler Payne?'

'Not in person, no.'

'But you know that his ancestors make their fortune from sugar cane back in the days when massa was master?'

'No.'

'Yes.'

'So that is why people call him "Bagasse"?'

Sharma grinned. 'Not exactly,' she said. 'The thing is, even though he's old and white, he has this really huge butt. Everybody says somebody pull a horn in the family closet with one of the slaves. So bagasse, big ass, get it?'

Giselle shook her head. 'Crude humour.'

'Best kind,' said Sharma.

People from other departments had drifted in by this time. Robert Cardinez came out of his office, followed by a short, thickset man whom Giselle figured was Spengler Payne, popularly called – though, she was sure, not to his face – 'Bagasse'. Payne wore a dark, well-cut suit and gold-framed spectacles; his hair was too black and well-coiffured not to have come out of a bottle. He was short, round and had a face like a roti. Although he reminded Giselle of the Pillsbury Doughboy, she found Spengler Payne had a curiously impressive presence.

'Ladies and gentlemen,' said Robert, 'this is Mr Payne and he wants to say a few words.'

Spengler Payne, standing with his back to the wall, smiled broadly and gestured for people to come closer. Most drifted forward a few steps. Sharma stayed where she was, so Giselle didn't move.

'Welcome,' Spengler Payne began. 'I am sorry I could not talk to you all before, but I were in Colombia settling a very important financial deal.' He paused. 'In fact, I will make the announcement here first: the Queres-McBuddy Group are now the fifth biggest producer of rum in conjunction with Colombia Alcoholia Company.' He smiled proudly. There was hesitant applause. 'I suppose you have a front-page story for tomorrow now,' he said, smiling at Robert Cardinez.

Sharma said to Giselle, 'Boy, I bet if he planted a garden his verbs would grow really well.'

'Shh,' said Giselle, hitting Sharma on the shoulder.

Spengler Payne turned back to the staff. 'Ladies and gentlemen. We involve in a great venture. It is up to us to make it succeed. One year ago, as you all know, several people attacked the *Colony News* newspaper, thus damaging the reputation of one of the great institutions of our country. But they failed to destroy the paper, as were their agenda. I said it then and I say it again.' Spengler Payne's voice rose and he pounded his fist with every other word. 'These so-called journalists was no better than the persons who loot and burn business places in the 1990 riots in Trinidad or, indeed, in Los Angeles.

'Unfortunately these people manage to deceive a badly informed public. But out of ashes cometh good, like the Good Book says. We have a new media company with the latest technology. The Caribbean Media Company is equal to any company in the most developed countries. The conglamerate have a responsibility to make sure the CMC succeed. The Board decide the policy, we decide what should go in. We have on the Board some of the smartest people in the country. And we will not allow this new company to be destroyed by self-serving individuals with secret agendas. Jobs are not easy to come by these days. We have a good team here and a good manager and chief editor in Mr Robert Cardinez. I am sure we will all put our best foot forward, in a competitive environment.

'Finally, let me say that, as a gesture of encouragement, Trinity Rum Inc, one of the base companies of the conglamerate, will be giving free bottles of our special white rum to all members of staff, including the labourers out in the yard.'

Spengler Payne smiled proudly again, and again there was sporadic applause. Robert stepped forward.

'I want to thank Mr Payne for taking time out of his busy schedule to talk to us, and I think we better get back to work so he can see we're earning the salaries he is paying us.'

There was a ripple of laughter and people began to disperse. Spengler Payne and Robert went back into Robert's office.

'I guess there's a third reason for his nickname,' said Sharma. 'Obviously, literacy and basic intelligence isn't crucial to build up a successful "conglamerate", especially when you start with inherited millions.'

19

Giselle pursed her mouth. 'But I want to be rich one day.'

'Well, stop reading books and, if you *really* want to get ahead, begin saving now for a lobotomy.'

'I think you're being a bit hard on him.'

Sharma shook her head and smiled at Giselle. 'Karan, if you were any more innocent, you'd be a virgin.'

Giselle cleared her throat. 'Yes, well, I'd better get back to work.'

◆

At twelve o'clock, Giselle's eyes felt like table tennis balls. She got up and went over to Sharma.

'You coming to get some lunch with me?'

'Can't, chile,' Sharma answered. 'I still have to do the comics page and we don't have Calvin, Ernie or Trini yet.'

'Hm,' said Giselle, 'if you don't get them, you might as well not bring out a paper. All right, I'll eat alone.'

'Bring me back a roti? I'll pay you when you come back.'

'Okay. But I won't be back for twenty minutes. I intend to take a leisurely lunch.'

Sharma looked at her with one eyebrow raised. 'So what do you define as a rushed lunch, Giselle?'

'A roti at your desk,' Giselle answered and walked off.

In the ladies' room, she checked her eyes. They did look tired. The mirror showed red lines like tiny tree branches on the whites of her eyes. There were dark circles below her lower lids. Giselle took out a bar of facial soap and a tube of moisturising cream. She had naturally healthy skin and though she rarely got pimples or blackheads, when she did she could squeeze them without leaving a mark. Giselle admitted this to be a disgusting habit, but it was not as disgusting, she felt, as leaving a pimple decorating her face like a miniature Christmas ornament. Luckily, she had the kind of skin which healed perfectly and, if God had not intended her to burst her pimples, she reasoned, why would he have taken such trouble over her skin? Giselle felt it was her moral duty to continue God's good work so now, before going out to lunch, she performed her daily ritual: washing her face thoroughly with the soap, wiping off all trace of make-up, then rubbing in a little moisturiser. Giselle always felt renewed after this small obeisance.

This time, though, she looked in the mirror and hesitated. She normally didn't put make-up back on after her midday cleansing. She didn't even put on lipstick. But now she wanted to redo all her make-up, even if it was just eyeliner and lipstick. Why?

Because you need it, you haggard witch, she thought, grinning into the mirror.

But she knew she was missing something. She had this irrational impulse to look as good as she could today, even if she had to use the artifices she normally scorned. Today there seemed to be some part of herself functioning out of her control, out of the sight of her mind. Giselle frowned at her reflection in the mirror, then shrugged. She heard Sharma's voice in her head: *Forget Dr Freud for today, Karan. A Herculean effort, I know, but you can do it if you really try.*

With sudden decision, Giselle opened her purse and took out her lipstick and eyeliner. The lipstick was a nice shade of muted bronze. She hadn't thought it would go with her brown complexion, but it suited her very well. Her eyeliner pencil came out next – basic black. It was the colour eyeliner she wore nearly all the time.

When she was finished, she looked in the mirror for a few moments. Giselle enjoyed her beauty, but it always gave her a strange feeling to look at her made-up reflection. She felt as though she was looking at someone who was not herself, out of that person's eyes. Her face was a disguise. Just lipstick and eyeliner – but now her eyes seemed more slanted, more Chinese, more mysterious. Her mouth looked more pouted, more sensual. Giselle felt, in a way, invisible. She thought this was the real reason she took the trouble to wear make-up at all. She liked playing the part, drawing attention to an image which was not her real self, while behind that image the real Giselle looked at it all and laughed secretly. *Or maybe you just like fooling with men's minds*, she thought. Today, though, there seemed to be a greater gap between image and reality. Giselle thought this was because she hadn't really been feeling like herself. Her sense of who-she-was, normally quite clear, was today elusive. She had been plagued all morning by the diffused shadow of uncertainty; and she didn't even know what she was uncertain *about*. But, walking out of the ladies' room, knowing she looked good, Giselle wryly admitted to herself that forming the image out of make-up was a way of retaining control. Like the computer program, it was a structure you created. And, in any case, Carnival, that season of masks, *was* just around the corner.

When she came out of the building into the heat and bright light of midday, she remembered the labourer. She walked down the stairs, glancing round casually. He was not in the yard. Even the pile of rubble he had been breaking was cleared away. But music was still blasting from the snackette: now they were playing that Carnival's most popular party tune – Sonny Mann's chutney song 'Lotay La'. Even as half her mind was distracted by this fusion of calypso and East Indian rhythms, Giselle had a feeling of being thwarted. When she reached ground level, she decided not to follow her usual route across the yard and out through the back. It was a shorter distance to the nearest eating-place if she walked through the girdered skeleton of the building. Even as she changed direction, listening to the *tassa* drums beat in the song, Giselle told herself she was being immature, if not downright stupid. She saw her real motive all too clearly: she wanted the worker to see her so she could ignore him. She did not want him thinking she had been giving him the eye that morning.

But you were, a voice inside her pointed out. That voice, with its habit of being perfectly truthful, always irritated Giselle. *Well*, she answered herself, *I don't want him thinking I was coming on to him*. And a third voice piped up: *This is really infantile*. But her feet kept walking, as feet tend to do when they know they're carrying the rest of the syndicate into trouble. And when Giselle saw the man under the building leaning against a workbench eating with a spoon out of a thermos flask, her stomach gave a little lurch. *Stay cool. Keep walking. Keep your head high. Pretend you're looking to see your way. Pretend you haven't noticed him*. But out of the corner of her eye, she saw him watching her. He was wearing the same rough trousers, but he had put on a frayed grey T-shirt. He did not stop eating as he watched her cross in front of him. Giselle found that irritating and her mind was so concentrated on ignoring the labourer that, when the shout came from above, she did not think it had anything to do with her. She continued walking superbly, but then, in slow, stupid shock, she saw thermos and spoon flung aside and she even noticed little grains of brown rice flying and then he had thrown

22

himself towards her. *I didn't think I was looking THAT attractive*, Giselle thought surprisedly before one muscular brown arm caught her like a solid whip around the waist and carried her backwards as a blurred object passed in front of her eyes, cutting the air where she had been. Then she hit the ground with a bone-crunching jar, knocking the breath out of her body.

Giselle thought she must have blacked out for a few moments, because the next thing she remembered was his dark eyes looking concernedly down at her and other faces behind and above him. He was saying something and after a gap of a few seconds she got it.

'Yes, I'm all right,' she said. *Except for feeling like a total moron*, she thought.

She tried to get up and he helped pull her to her feet. Right in front of her was an iron bucket caked with hardened cement. The bucket was lying on its side with yellow stones spilling out of it. A trailing rope, like a frayed snake, was attached to the broken handle. Giselle's legs suddenly felt like well-boiled macaroni; luckily, the worker was still holding her arm firmly.

'Did – did *that* nearly hit me?' she stammered.

'Oh no,' said the man calmly. 'I wouldn't have let that happen.'

Giselle looked at him wonderingly, then looked around as Harry Chan, the building supervisor, came hurrying up with another man behind him. 'Giselle, you all right?'

The man behind said, 'Miss, I so sorry. The damn handle just break. Is a good thing Vishnu move so fast.'

Giselle turned to the worker again. She saw the strong jaw with stubble on it and the nice mouth and the calm, dark eyes still full of concern. She said, 'I guess you save my life. Thanks.' She laughed shakily. 'God, that sounds so stupid. I never had my life saved, so I don't know what to say.'

He grinned, showing strong white teeth. 'Yeah, somebody should write an etiquette book for these occasions. I should probably have asked permission before I knocked you out of the way.'

Giselle thought dazedly: *He said 'etiquette'. What a strange word for a construction worker to use.*

'You sure you all right?' he said. She was suddenly aware that his hand was still holding her arm.

'Yes,' she said. 'I guess Sonny Mann distracted me. I was listening to the music,' she explained.

The labourer smiled. 'You must really like chutney,' he said.

'Not so much,' Giselle said, distractedly. She brushed her hands over the back of her clothes, feeling the dirt on them. 'I have to go home and change.' She turned and glimpsed the iron bucket of spilled stones. Her knees became very weak again.

Harry Chan said, 'I don't think you should drive, Giselle.' He turned to the labourer. 'I have a meeting in ten minutes. You could drive her home, Vishnu? Right at Fort St George. You can borrow my car.' He said to Giselle: 'Vishnu's very reliable.'

'No, please,' Giselle began.

'No problem,' said Vishnu. Harry reached into his pocket, but Giselle stopped him. Harry said, 'Giselle . . .'

She said, 'All right. But we might as well use my car.' She grinned shakily at the labourer. 'Rule number three at a near-conking by an iron bucket.'

Somebody handed Giselle her purse and she and the labourer walked away from the small crowd of concerned people. He held her elbow lightly now, without pressure. 'My car's right in the next car park,' she said. He nodded. When they got there, she handed him her keys. He opened the door for her and she got in. 'Thank you,' she said.

'No problem,' he answered.

He wound down the window on her side, and she said 'Thanks' again. He just looked at her, half-smiling. Giselle knew she was being too polite, but she couldn't seem to help it. The worker – his name is Vishnu, she thought – went round to the driver's side. Giselle leaned across and pulled up the door lock. He got in and looked at her deliberately and said, 'Thanks.' She smiled uncertainly and he grinned back at her. He adjusted the seat and rearview mirror, then started the car. They pulled out of the car park and on to the road.

'You really doing too much,' she said, looking at his profile. He was squinting against the midday glare. Giselle found herself studying the creases which radiated outwards from the corner of his eye.

He said, 'Is no trouble. Besides, in some cultures, I'd be responsible for you for the rest of my life. Probably have to feed you, clothe you

24

and make sure you practise good dental hygiene.' He flashed a grin at her. 'Guess you have to be careful who you save, eh?'

'I really don't know how I should thank you,' said Giselle. 'It's a kind of big thing. I mean, I'd be dead or badly injured . . .' She trailed off lamely. She knew she was only talking because she felt so awkward. She looked at his thin T-shirt. 'Anyway, I wish I could save your life back or something.'

Now he spared her a glance. But she couldn't read his expression. It was strange: she couldn't tell what this man was thinking *at all*. She supposed it was because he was outside her experience. He was unshaven, and looked unrefined. All the men she knew were the kind who used Gillette sensor blades, liked creased trousers and agonized over buying the right kind of shades. If this man wore trousers, thought Giselle, they would be the baggy, punk kind.

'Well, maybe you could rescue me from a burning building,' he said. 'But the trouble would be finding a building that was burning.'

Giselle smiled. 'There's always something.'

'And the firemen might get to me first.'

'That's how firemen are,' she said. 'Never giving anyone else a chance to be a hero.'

'And so there'd be a whole building wasted,' he concluded.

Giselle grinned, feeling better, and there was silence for a while.

'I suppose, though, if there *was* an etiquette book, it would have some suggestions,' he said. 'You know, Chapter Five – Proper Methods of Thanking One's Rescuers According to One's Own Special Standing.'

Giselle glanced sideways at him. 'Oh?' she said cautiously.

'Yeah. I mean, if you were an heiress it's obvious that you'd have to thank me differently than if you were, say, a hooker.'

'Well, I'm not either,' she pointed out.

'Then we'll have to compromise.' He thought for a moment. 'Ah, I know what you can do for me.'

'What?' said Giselle.

He grinned. 'Don't look so worried. Nothing immoral.'

Giselle flushed. 'I wasn't thinking anything.'

'Really?' he said, still grinning. 'I must be losing my mind-reading abilities then.'

'*What* can I do for you?' Giselle asked.

'Well, if you so worried about repaying me in some way, you could answer me one question honestly.'

They stopped at a traffic light. Now Giselle became aware of the heat. The car was not air-conditioned. She saw the gleam of sweat on his face. He had an interesting complexion, she thought – light brown shaded into gold. But his arms were very brown.

'What?' she said. A wild thought flew into her mind: was he going to ask her if she was a virgin?

'If I *hadn't* got you out of the way of that bucket, and if sometime I had asked you to have lunch with me, would you have?'

The lights changed and they pulled off.

'That's your question?' Giselle asked.

'Yep. Not a request.'

'Why not a request?'

''Cause you'd have to say yes, wouldn't you?'

Giselle looked ahead. The question had been asked seriously and she considered it seriously. 'I don't think so,' she said finally. 'I don't have lunch with people I don't know.'

'Okay,' he said. His voice was very casual, but she saw a small tightening of his mouth. She felt bad suddenly.

'But since you did save my life and limb,' she continued, in a too-bright tone, 'I'd be glad to. Since I know you now, I mean.'

She expected him to say no, and she would have deserved it. *This is why people aren't honest about things like that*, she thought. But he turned with a grin. *He really has very good teeth*, Giselle thought irrelevantly, and wondered if shock had unhinged her mind a little. *Just for the afternoon*, she thought and laughed inwardly.

'Well, since I saved your life and limbs, I think *you* should buy *me*· lunch,' he said.

She took a few moments to absorb this. Then she said, 'Sure, of course. I'd be glad to.' She thought that maybe a free lunch was a luxury for him. Times were hard these days, and she had never met a Trinidadian man who didn't place his stomach first in the scheme of things. She also felt a bit ashamed: she could have offered in the first place. Giselle searched for something to say. 'So have you worked with Harry Chan long?' she asked.

His brows slanted sardonically. 'This is the first time I've worked for Chan.' She noticed the slight emphasis on the 'for'. She wondered if he was mocking her. He might be, but she couldn't be angry. She was under an obligation. She didn't want to ask him the question which followed naturally: what he did. He might turn out to be the man who broke rocks on the site, as she had seen him doing this morning, and, while it was true that he did it very well and looked very well doing it, she figured he mightn't be proud of the job. Certainly, it was something Giselle found hard to conceive – a person with no special skills, suited just for brute work. She looked at the man beside her. Even for a labourer, he didn't seem that type. But they were at the point where they had to swing off the main road. She was saved from further conversation as she gave him directions to her apartment building.

'Left here,' she said. He swung the car in and they proceeded up a short driveway. Her building was at the end. He parked in her space and they got out. She waited as he locked the car, and then they went up to her apartment. Giselle found that her legs were still unsteady and it took all her concentration to mount the steps to her door. She had just installed an electronic alarm. She took out her keys and that was all right. But, as she tried to punch in the code, she found her hand trembling so badly she couldn't hit the right buttons. She watched in complete astonishment as she kept miskeying the buttons. Her mind was quite clear, quite calm, yet her hand refused to stop shaking.

He reached across and held her wrist gently. 'Easy,' he said. Giselle looked at him embarrassedly.

'I'm sorry,' she said.

'Anybody ever tell you you apologize too much?' he said, smiling. She began to answer, and he held up a hand. 'Ah, ah. *Don't* tell me you're sorry for saying sorry.' Giselle smiled. 'What's the code?' he asked.

'Seventeen-oh-one.'

He raised an eyebrow. 'Trekkie, eh?' He punched in the code and took her keys and opened the door. They went inside with Giselle wondering how he knew the serial number of the starship *Enterprise*. But then she questioned her surprise: everyone watched TV. She realized her real wonder was that he recognized the number. Or that he watched science fiction. If he had ever watched a science fiction movie, she would have expected it to be something like *Predator*.

'Can I get you something to drink? A beer?' she asked.

'A glass of cold water'll be fine,' he said. He raised a hand. 'I'll get it myself.'

Giselle smiled ruefully. 'That might be best.' She watched as he went into the little kitchen, opened the refrigerator and took out the glass bottle of water. He took a glass from the draining rack to the sink. His movements were very sure. 'There's beer,' Giselle said.

'So you said,' he reminded her. He drank the glass of water without stopping. She looked at his Adam's apple bobbing as he drank. She was suddenly very aware of his scent, strange in her apartment. It was sweat and dust and an indefinable *male* smell.

'I'm sorry,' she said. 'I don't know why I'm so confused. I'm not usually this inane – stupid,' she added, thinking he might not know the meaning of 'inane'.

He put down the glass. 'You mean this lack of *je ne sais quoi* is just an act? Well! You certainly had *me* fooled.'

'You know,' said Giselle, suddenly irritated, 'you don't talk like a man who works on a construction site.'

He leaned against the counter and folded his arms. Giselle got even more irritated with herself when she realized she was watching how strong the muscles on his forearms looked. He said, 'You have a shower or a bathtub?'

'What?' she said. He repeated the question. 'A tub,' she said. 'What does that have to do – ?'

He cut across her smoothly. 'I think you should take a nice soak in a warm tub and get your nerves unwound. Take about an hour. Then finish with a cold shower. Then, if you feel up to it, you can go back to work. I will leave now. Is only a fifteen-minute walk back to the main road.'

'No, don't do that,' said Giselle, regretting the words as soon as they were out of her mouth. She hesitated for a moment, politeness warring with caution. 'I . . . won't be long.'

'All right,' he said, turning and going into the living-room where the bookshelf stood.

'What you will do in the meantime?' she asked.

'I'll read something from your library.'

'You will?'

He glanced at her. 'Uh-huh,' he said.

'Ah, I didn't mean . . . I meant . . . that is.' Giselle stopped. 'Bath,' she said.

'Bath,' he agreed, taking out a book. He didn't look at her.

Giselle paused. 'I'm sorry,' she said. He looked at her in exasperation. Now Giselle raised her hand. 'Look, it's my favourite phrase, okay? I *like* saying I'm sorry.'

He grinned.

'You must think I'm a real ungrateful bitch,' said Giselle.

He waved a non-committal hand. 'All the best women are.'

Giselle stood for a moment absorbing that, then giggled. He grinned. 'That's better. Look, listen to Dr Traboulay. Go and take your bath and unwind.'

'That's your last name, Traboulay? Vishnu Traboulay?'

'Oh, so you know my first name,' he said.

'Oh, come on, I not that bad. If I hadn't heard Harry Chan say it, I'd have asked.'

'And you're Giselle what?'

'Karan,' she said.

'Pleased to meet you.' He pointed. 'Go,' he said.

'Yes, Doctor,' she said meekly. She turned, then looked back. 'By the way,' she said. 'There *is* beer in the fridge.'

◆

When Giselle came out of the bathroom an hour later, Vishnu was sitting at the dining-table reading a novel from her bookshelf. She would have finished sooner except for two things: he had told her to take an hour and, ten minutes after sinking into the hot water, she found herself falling asleep. Lying in the bath, just before drowsiness overcame her, it occurred to Giselle that she had left a man she didn't know with free access to her apartment. But Harry Chan, who had treated her like a favourite daughter since she came to CMC, trusted him. That was good enough for her. And Vishnu seemed decent enough. And, truth to tell, she kind of liked the sense of risk – even if it was a small risk – in having a strange man in her apartment. Giselle had never in her life taken any real chances where men were concerned. So she dozed lightly and when she got up she stood under the cold shower as Vishnu had recommended. He was right: it invigorated her and seemed to remove all the trailing cobwebs of shock from her mind. When she came out, the clock on the wall said 1:37.

'Sorry I took so long,' she said, towelling her hair dry. She had put on jeans and a big white T-shirt.

He closed the book. It was V.S. Naipaul's *Miguel Street*. Once again Giselle felt surprised – this man didn't fit any of her categories. 'Better?' he asked.

'Much. But I don't think I'm going back to work.'

He nodded. 'It's probably best. You up to giving me a drop down the hill? If not, I can walk.'

'No, it's not a problem,' Giselle said. She thought of asking if he wanted to take a bath, but then decided not to. There were stockings, panties and other feminine items in the bathroom. Besides, that might give him ideas, and then the risk factor might go beyond what she wanted. Before they left, Giselle phoned the office to tell Robert Cardinez she wouldn't be returning. He wasn't there so she left the message with his secretary. Then she got her car keys. Vishnu put the book back on the shelf – in the correct place, Giselle noticed. When they went out and closed the door, he glanced at the alarm and asked her if she preferred the original *Star Trek* series or the second one.

'The first,' she said as they walked down the stairs. Walking next to him, Giselle realized with faint surprise that Vishnu was only a little taller than she. 'What about you?'

'Likewise,' he said. 'Can't beat Captain Kirk.'

They got in the car and Giselle told him, 'I always liked Spock. I used to have a crush on him.'

'It's the ears. Women go wild over his ears.'

They didn't speak again until they reached the bottom of the hill. Giselle, to her surprise, found it to be a comfortable silence.

When she stopped to drop him off, he said, holding the door open, 'So we on for tomorrow?'

She had to think a few moments before she remembered she had promised to buy him lunch. 'Sure,' she answered.

'I'll meet you at the Beijing Palace,' he said. This was the same place Giselle had been going to that day.

'Fine,' she said. 'Thanks again for everything.'

He got out of the car. 'No problem.'

As Giselle turned the car to go back up the hill, she found herself wondering whether Vishnu Traboulay wanted a free lunch or to be in her company or both. She couldn't tell. But she thought it might be the last.

Chapter Three

Vera, Giselle's room-mate, came in that evening. Giselle had just fixed herself her usual evening drink: a tall glass of freshly squeezed orange juice with a touch of Angostura bitters, crushed ice, and a straw. The straw was an essential touch: it was the kind with a joint shaped like a small accordion. Giselle always thought the straw had been designed by someone who, after having a few of those deceptively powerful drinks with small umbrellas, found that bending his head to the glass was just too great an effort. She didn't drink alcohol; she just liked the fancy straw. It rounded off her feeling of relaxed luxury. She, too, liked not having to bend her head at the end of a long day.

She was about to go out on the small balcony and watch the sunset when she heard keys rattle outside the door. The door opened and the alarm went off with an ear-splitting whooping sound. Vera stepped in with an exasperated expression on her face, dropped her suitcase, and hit the off-button with her fist. The sudden silence seemed to echo emptily in the apartment.

'Seventeen-oh-one, Vera, seventeen-oh-one,' said Giselle. 'Didn't I give you a *Star Trek* novel so you could check it if you forgot?'

Vera grimaced. 'Yes, I know. It's in London.'

'By Brad? Or is it Fareed? I can't remember which is the London one.'

'They both live in London. Different ends,' said Vera, stepping out of her shoes and coming into the living room. She gave Giselle a hug. 'How you going, girlfriend?'

'Fine.'

Vera suddenly looked behind her, her large and expressive black eyes wide. She sniffed the air. 'Giselle!' she exclaimed. 'You've had a man in here!'

Giselle laughed. 'I don't know what that nose of yours would be like if you *didn't* smoke,' she said. 'You could probably help track escaped prisoners.'

'Huh! The kind of men I had to deal with on that last flight, I wish I *were* a dog. And I can't even be a bitch since they pay me to smile and look pretty.' Sitting on the sofa, she ran her fingers through her cropped, kinky hair. She had a finely shaped, round skull – she was one of those rare women who, even if she shaved her head, would still look strangely attractive. 'Ah, it is so *good* to be off my feet,' she said, flexing her neck. She pulled Giselle down beside her. 'So who is he? And what were you doing? And don't lie because I wouldn't even be able to smell him still unless he was exerting himself pretty hard. There was definite hormonal activity here. C'mon, tell Auntie Vera every disgusting detail.'

Giselle laughed and pulled away her arm. She put down her glass of orange juice on its wooden coaster on the coffee table. 'Sorry, Vee, it wasn't like that. He was just sweating because he had been breaking rocks and saving my skull from getting broken by rocks before he carried me home.'

Vera put her hand on Giselle's head. *Everybody seems to be doing this today*, Giselle thought, remembering Sharma.

'What, in heaven's name, are you babbling about?' asked Vera.

Giselle described her near-accident.

'So the worker, Vishnu, brought me home and I'm buying him lunch tomorrow to thank him for saving my life,' she finished. She leaned across and punched Vera on the arm. 'What are you looking so stuffy about?'

'Was I?' said Vera absently.

'Yes, you was,' said Giselle.

'Well, it's hard to believe you actually nearly died.' She grinned, though it looked a little forced. 'But I'm even more amazed that you actually let a man stay alone with you in the apartment. Most people have out-of-body experiences when they nearly die. You had a near-body experience.' Vera looked sharply at Giselle. 'Or was it an actual bodily experience?'

'Of course not,' said Giselle. 'A nice child like me?'

'Hm. Maybe I should see this guy and thank him better for you,' Vera suggested. 'After all, what is lunch? A mere passing pleasure. An experience with me, on the other hand, is something to remember for life.'

'Not that you're boasting,' said Giselle.

'Just stating the facts, honey.' Vera looked at Giselle. 'But it's really romantic how he saved you, don't you think?'

Giselle shook her head. 'Getting saved from a sinking yacht is romantic. Getting saved from Mexican bandits is romantic. I just got saved from being conked by an iron bucket. Not that I'm complaining, eh. I don't think a dented skull would have matched my face. But I wouldn't classify it among the great romantic escapades.'

Vera pouted. 'Well, I would.'

'Yeah, but you think leather underwear, handcuffs and a man with a whip is romantic.'

'Of course, once the scene is lit by candlelight,' Vera grinned.

'I'll pass.'

'Anyway, I'm glad you're all right, chile.'

Giselle put her hand on Vera's cheek. Vera had skin even better than hers: as smooth as dark chocolate, velvet to the touch. 'It was a close call. But I'm fine.'

Vera took Giselle's hand and squeezed it. 'I know.' She stood up. 'I need a cigarette. Let's go out on the balcony.'

Giselle took up her drink and followed her. Vera never smoked when she was at the apartment, except in her bedroom or out on the balcony, since Giselle hated the smell of cigarette smoke.

It had turned dark outside. They sat on the beach chairs they had put on the balcony. There were only two chairs and two small side tables. The balcony wasn't big enough for anything else. St James glowed yellowly at the bottom of the black hill. Out on the sea, pricks of lights showed on ships and marker buoys. There was no moon in the sky.

'Life is such a bitch, eh,' said Vera. Half of her face was in shadow. The tip of her cigarette glowed as she pulled on it. She tapped ash into the tray on her lap. Her bare feet, crossed at the ankles, were propped on the balcony rail. Vera was one of those women who look entirely natural smoking cigarettes. Giselle thought this was because there was a bright and destructive quality in Vera. You saw it in the wide black eyes – their very expressiveness had the quality of a dark and broken mirror. She smoked like a person who was indifferent to the idea of death.

Vera continued speaking, in a slow and meditative voice. 'You ever notice how, just when things start to go really well, just when you think life is just fine, is then fate decides to throw you for a loop.'

34

'You should stop believing everything you read on T-shirts, Vee,' Giselle said.

Vera drew on her cigarette again and shook her head. 'It is true. Look at you, Gis'. You've started your company, you've landed a nice contract with CMC.' Giselle saw Vera's half-smile in the shadow of her face. 'You even meeting men. So what does fate do? Try to lick you down with an iron bucket? You know how often accidents like that happen? Not very damned often.'

Giselle shifted uncomfortably in her chair. 'Well, maybe that just means I've used up my bad luck for good now.'

'I hope so.' Vera's voice was very quiet, and neither of them said anything for a moment. Vera herself broke the ensuing silence before it could become too heavy. 'So! Tell me about this man. A construction worker, eh? Good body?' She sensualized her pronunciation of the last word – 'boh-dee'.

Giselle sipped at her juice. It was cold and sweet with just a hint of acidity. She said, 'Yes, he has a pretty good body.' She had not told Vera why she had been passing through the construction site in the first place. It seemed even more foolish now.

'So wait, let me understand this,' Vera said. 'This man, a red-blooded Trinidadian male saves you, at the very least, from a really serious bus'-head and drops you to your apartment. You're all a-quiver, dizzy, weak. The man is your hero. He has pecs. And you don't even given him a kiss of gratitude?'

'Vera!' said Giselle, laughing. 'I don't even know him.'

'Oh, I'm not really surprised at *you*,' Vera said. 'I know you're a prude from way back. But I am appalled he didn't at least try to *take* a kiss. What are men becoming in these degenerate times?'

'Gentlemen?' suggested Giselle.

Vera nodded. 'It seems so. And this disease is spreading even among the lower classes. A common labourer and he did not even try to take advantage of a vulnerable female alone in her apartment. Next thing they will be vacuuming the living-room. And, when it comes to men, that's *not* the kind of suction that interests me.'

Giselle laughed. 'Well, in any case, I wouldn't say he was a common labourer. And he probably wouldn't make a pass precisely *because* I was vulnerable. *And* he looks like he has hundreds of women all over the place.'

Vera raised expressive eyebrows. 'Sounds like you find him rather attractive yourself,' she commented. She lit a second cigarette from the butt of her first one.

'I said he was good-looking,' Giselle said, wondering why she felt so defensive. 'But you needn't talk as though you regret he didn't take advantage of the situation to rape me.'

'C'mon Gis', you know I was only joking,' Vera said, leaning across and giving Giselle a remonstrative slap on her leg.

Giselle's momentary annoyance passed. 'Sorry,' she said, grimacing. 'I've been on tenterhooks since the thing happened. Even before.'

'I understand.'

Giselle chuckled. 'Actually, after I dropped him off, I did wonder why he didn't make some kind of pass. Even to say something suggestive. I mean, there wasn't even a *hint*. I was wondering: aren't I attractive enough to take advantage of?'

Vera leaned back in her chair and laughed. Giselle took another sip of her drink, thinking how smoothly Vera always slipped into her satirically witty persona. But she wasn't fooled by the bright facade. She knew all that talk about fate went straight back to Vera's failed two-year marriage. Although it had ended five years ago, Giselle thought that in certain ways Vera wasn't yet over the trauma. Perhaps she never would be. They had been friends since high school and Giselle knew her intimately. And she could see the difference between Vera then and Vera now.

Thinking about it, it occurred to Giselle that she was Vera's only real friend. Oh, there were people Vera kept company with more frequently: her airline friends and the party-goers and the wealthy crowd who owned houses on the small islands off Trinidad. But they knew only the fun-time Vera, the motor-mouth, the party girl who never said anything *too* clever. Giselle found that side amusing, too. But she also knew that Vera was as hard and bright as a glass diamond, and just as false. It was something Giselle tolerated in her friend – the smoking, the shallow talk, the accent which, in company, shifted from British through black American – because she knew the inside Vera.

The night was very quiet. A low, cool breeze had sprung up, blowing away Vera's cigarette smoke. Sitting out here together, Giselle thought, was a ritual she and Vera had performed many times. Their talks were always different – giggling animation, serious conversations about life, trivial chat about fashion or people or films, pouring out of personal problems, intellectual discussions on books or art or music, or just contemplative silence. But there was always an underlying feeling of contentment.

Vera said, 'I guess you don't believe what I say about fate?'

Giselle shrugged. 'Fate, luck, coincidence. Circumstances. Everybody has circumstances. Sometimes they help, sometimes they don't. But I don't believe circumstances can overcome anybody who's determined to succeed. We make our own way, by and large. I think I'm in control of where my life goes, within reasonable parameters.'

Vera raised her finely pencilled eyebrows once more. 'You've been reading that dictionary again. Didn't I warn you about that? I know you think you're immune to its influence, but next thing you know you'll be using words like parameters and syllogism. I don't want to be around for that.'

Giselle smiled lazily. Vera said, 'I don't know, though. I've always found the best people have the hardest fates. Look at yourself. You're bright and beautiful and one of the nicest people I know.'

'Go on, go on,' said Giselle.

Vera stubbed out her cigarette. She didn't light another. 'Haven't you ever thought about how much easier your life would have been if your father hadn't died in some stupid car crash?' she asked.

Giselle nodded. 'Many times. Till I decided that was a useless way to think. And maybe I'm a stronger person now because of that. I learned to be self-reliant.'

'Remember that book we had in Form One. *Roman Myths and Tales*? You know what I think is the definitive story of all those Roman myths? The story of Icarus.'

'The guy with the wax wings?'

'Yes. He flew too close to the sun, the wax melted, and he fell to his death. If you ask me, those old Romans had a pretty accurate view of this existence. Don't fly too high, if that doesn't seem like a hell of a thing for an airline attendant to say . . .' Vera paused and looked at Giselle and Giselle saw that somehow her eyes were very bright in the shadow. 'That's why I worry about you,' she said.

Giselle reached across and put her hand on Vera's arm. 'Well, you needn't. You missed the point about Icarus.'

'Oh? What is the point about Icarus?'

'He should have used super-glue instead.'

'Ah. I was never very good at literary criticism.'

'Besides,' Giselle continued, 'even if what you say is true, fate probably wants me to stay alive to suffer.'

Vera grinned. 'I'll take comfort in that idea,' she said.

She got up, holding the ashtray while she gathered her cigarette pack and lighter. 'Bath and bed for me,' she said.

Giselle snapped her fingers. 'Oh, the guy – Vishnu – he did tell me to take a bath. Think he was turned on by me being naked in another room while he sat out here and read *Miguel Street*?'

'No,' said Vera. She paused. 'He read *Miguel Street*?'

'Yes. Strange, eh?'

'He was probably trying to impress you. Fellers with muscles always worry that women think they're stupid. Most of the time because they are. Coming in?'

'Not yet. I'll stay here and take the breeze for a while.'

'All right.'

Vera went inside, then came back out after a few moments carrying a small package.

'Oh, I nearly forgot in all the excitement. Happy belated birthday.' She leaned down and kissed Giselle.

'Thanks,' said Giselle.

She tore off the gift paper. Inside were three CDs: Sheryl Crow's *Tuesday Night* album; calypsonian Shadow's *Greatest Hits*; and comedienne Terri Cross's *Womanish* collection of monologues.

'Make sure you listen to track three on Terri's album,' Vera said.

'Thanks, Vee,' said Giselle, giving her a hug.

'Later,' said Vera and went back inside.

She glanced at the title of the third monologue on Terri's CD: it was called 'Virgin's Lament'. Giselle grinned.

She would play it later. Right now, she wondered if Vera's last comment was right. Had the man been trying to impress her? It didn't fit with his manner. He didn't seem like the type to try and impress anyone. Although the ponytail was a small conceit, a vanity, wasn't it? It occurred to Giselle that social status limited a man's choice of women. Even a man like him – good-looking, reasonably intelligent – could only get a spouse from within his social class. Money was a great divider. A woman in a similar position – that is, with an attractive appearance – had a better chance of marrying out of her class. But the same could hardly happen for a man, if he was any kind of man and refused to be a lap dog for some rich, probably older woman. Romance was a nice idea, but the fact was that, for the majority of women, status was part of a man's attractiveness. Looks, intelligence, sensitivity – all those things were conditioned by social position. Karl Marx, Giselle mused, would probably never have written *Das Kapital* if he could have found a really attractive woman who was impressed by his intelligence and large beard.

Giselle thought she understood now why Vishnu wanted to have lunch with her. Marx would probably have done the same thing in his position. Yes, it was because he found her attractive. She thought she could safely assume that. But Vishnu also wanted to have lunch with her because, in the normal run of things, he would hardly get to socialize with someone like her. It was, she thought, a feather in his cap, something he could boast about to his partners afterwards. Giselle grimaced to herself. It was a small enough price to pay for having your life saved. But she suddenly felt sorry for Vishnu. She thought he deserved a better hand than the one life had dealt him.

Giselle sat on the balcony for a few more minutes thinking of nothing in particular. She wasn't tired yet, but she didn't feel like doing anything special. Then she remembered that she had bought the latest issue of *Atlantic Monthly* a few days before and hadn't read it yet. There was a story in the magazine entitled 'The Midges of Bradison County'. Giselle had read Robert Waller's novel *The Bridges of Madison County* a few months ago and found it a moving, powerful love story. She had liked the movie even more. But that didn't prevent her being curious about a satire of the story – P.G. Wodehouse was one of her favourite writers.

She went back out on the balcony, turned on the wall lamp, and opened the magazine. The author's pseudonym immediately made her grin. The heading read: 'The Midges of Bradison County' by Richard Kinky. Giselle settled down and began to read:

At seven a.m. on a Saturday morning in May, Bob James Wailer, who had been called 'Crybaby' when he was a schoolboy, loaded his spraying equipment into his old but well-kept van and set off for Bradison County. The three spray tanks were bright yellow with black rubber hoses and nozzles of dull gold. The tanks had straps to sling around the torso. The van was green.

There was a hard, purposeful look about Wailer – no easy feat when you're short, fat and have a hairline which starts at the back of your head. But Wailer was that type of man. His inner spirit triumphed over his looks, with a bit of help from Oil of Olay and Dr Troy's Reliable Hair Dye. He had once considered wearing a toupée, but this was impractical since he was afraid of strong wind and fond of stewed beans. He told himself he looked tougher without hair, like Telly Savalas and Yul Brynner. In fact, Wailer thought he had mastered what he described, in the deeply literary way he habitually thought, as 'Napoleonic indomitability'. Though he also thought he could look cute when he needed to, like Lou Costello.

As Florence Nightingale, an ordinary housewife of Bradison County, was to discover later that fine day in May, Wailer cultivated versatility.

'You can describe most people in three words,' Wailer wrote in a note to Florence penned on the back of the first bill for fumigating her house. 'For myself, you would have to use at least five . . . maybe even seven.'

He was then forty-three. And, though he fumigated her house three times after that, he never charged her save for that first time. And those cynics who doubt the existence of love at first sight should note that, even on that first job, he gave her a ten per cent discount.

But Wailer was that type of man, a kind this world perhaps will not see again. And that is why I have decided to tell this story.

Giselle put down the magazine, grinning. She wanted to read this in one go – obviously, the writer had not been too impressed with Waller's portrayal of great passion. This was something Giselle could sympathize with: she had often wondered if true passion even existed. Certainly, she had never experienced it. She thought of Vera. There was a good example of passion gone wrong. Vera, thought Giselle, deserved better out of life. And, funnily enough, Vera, as she said tonight, had the same idea about Giselle. Giselle was a little surprised at this. She thought she was doing all right now and, if she deserved better, she was sure she would attain it in time. To hear her mother talk, Giselle was already over the hill at twenty-six. Of course, if she was married with children, Giselle thought, her mother would define her differently – she would be a *young* wife and mother then.

Funny, how her mother never applied these same attitudes to Vera. Giselle's mother quite liked Vera. But, although Vera was already twenty-seven years old, her mother never even asked her if she planned to settle down. Perhaps it was because Vera had already made a bad marriage. In fact, Giselle had once overheard her mother discussing with Vera the disadvantages of marrying young – ideas she never broached with her own daughters.

Vera had married when she was twenty. Her husband, Andrew, was a manager in the firm where Vera worked as an accounts clerk. The wedding took place just before Giselle left to go to the States. Giselle had liked Andrew. He was tall and charming and he seemed totally in love with Vera. Vera – warm, vivacious and happy – told Giselle that Andrew was the ideal man for her.

But there is a saying: what attracts us to someone rarely binds us to them. In her letters to Giselle, who was then studying in Miami, Vera soon recorded the cracks in her marriage. Andrew was very possessive. He didn't like Vera liming with her friends, even the female ones. 'I'm thinking about getting a dog,' Vera wrote Giselle, 'but he mightn't like me cooking for it.' Andrew also wanted her to have a child at once; Vera wanted to wait a few years. Vera liked fêteing; Andrew liked reading the newspapers. Once, Giselle recalled, Vera described how she and Andrew argued for an entire night about how she wasn't 'lady-like' enough. He said she embarrassed him in front of his friends. 'I told him God designed me to wiggle when I walk. He wasn't very amused,' Vera wrote.

Then the letters stopped. Giselle wrote to her a few times, but received no reply, although she got cards at Christmas and on her birthday. Giselle wrote to a mutual friend to find out what was going on. The friend wrote back to say that Vera's marriage wasn't going too well. But she didn't know much more than that. Giselle, busy with her own life, lost contact with Vera.

When Giselle came back to Trinidad, Vera was already divorced.

She had quit her first job and become an airline attendant. When Giselle met her for the first time, she was struck by her hard, false brightness. Vera still looked babyish: the large eyes, round cheeks and button nose. She still had her humour. But experience had closed like a shell around her. Giselle found out that Andrew had begun hitting her. Vera left him the night he twisted her arm during an argument and dislocated her shoulder.

'Why you didn't leave the first time he hit you?' Giselle asked her once.

'I put that down to a mistake.'

'And the second time?'

'I put that down to experience.'

'And the third?'

'I was brain-damaged by then.'

Vera was already living in the apartment in Fort St George and her room-mate was about to emigrate. So Giselle moved in and they resumed their friendship. It wasn't like before, though. Despite sharing an apartment, they hardly saw each other. Their jobs ensured that they hardly met at all for the first year. Then, when Giselle settled down a bit, Vera was still hardly around and, when she was, she was always going out: parties, pubs, beach, cinema – wherever there was a lime on. Sometimes between her coming home and going out again there would just be time to say hello and goodbye. In fact, the only reason Vera would be in Trinidad over the coming weeks would be to go to the major Carnival fêtes and to play mas on the Monday and Tuesday. She always played mas with the same band, Poison, which was mostly favoured by the fair-complexioned and the wannabe fair-complexioned and which charged the highest prices for the skimpiest costumes. Giselle disliked the band on principle: in a street festival where for decades everyone, costumed or not, took part, Poison was the first to hire bodyguards to – illegally – keep people out, and to beat them up if they persisted. But she had never discussed this issue with Vera.

Giselle thought there was something obsessive in the way Vera set out to 'enjoy' life. She had had for example, no serious relationships since her divorce. But she'd had many casual ones in many different countries. Giselle never asked, but she knew that Vera had consciously decided that she would not be seriously involved with a man ever again. She had experienced too much hurt. Now Vera did not merely dread the fire; she told herself she did not need the fire. Giselle thought it was a cold life Vera led, bright without warmth.

But she kept her opinions to herself. Their friendship was based on a lack of judgement. Yet there was still that ease and comfort and unspoken intimacy between them. Each just assumed the other would always be around. Giselle thought that Vera knew, whenever she needed someone to turn to, Giselle would be there, in the words of the song, 'like a rock'. And, although she never said so, Giselle thought Vera appreciated this. Their friendship was simple and accepted.

It was getting a little chilly on the balcony now. Giselle drew up her legs. She thought how the circumstances of women's lives were defined by men: hers by her father's death, Vera's by her abusive husband.

Giselle recalled what one of her cousins had done with her when she was nine years old. He had been fourteen, a boy with rheumy eyes and a long nose. She had never told anyone about that – not her mother, not even Vera. The boy had been one of the acolytes who collected the offerings in church. Giselle remembered how, seeing him in his long robe with the tray full of money, she had thought he was a very important person. So she had felt more shocked and more guilty about what he started doing to her. But she had kind of liked it, too, and that had made her feel even worse. It had never reached to sex, and she had stopped him after a few months. Afterwards, she put the experience out of her mind. She hadn't thought about it in years and it didn't bother her now. But Giselle supposed that was the first time she learned about male power.

Men's circumstances weren't defined by women. But she thought their inner lives were. All their outward activity was meaningless without that centre. But things were changing, the world was changing. No man, now, would define *her* circumstances. She looked out at the dark night and wondered if she would find some man whose inner life she would define because he wanted her to and because she wanted to. Giselle knew what she wanted: a man as independent as her. She didn't want her life defined by circumstances. But the man must also be intelligent and attractive and sensitive. Giselle grinned as she realized how limited her own choices were, perhaps more so than

Vishnu's. And perhaps Vera had the right idea. Her life, in a way, was more practical. But Giselle could not bring herself to be so casual. If she ever had a serious relationship, she wanted it to have meaning in the deepest part of herself. She didn't want it just to affect her outwardly. So many people, she thought, settled for that. For Giselle, it was all or nothing.

And you'll probably get nothing, she thought as she took up her glass and went inside. But maybe that wasn't so bad as long as you were true to yourself. You didn't *have* to live according to the world.

She locked the balcony doors and pulled the drapes against the dark night.

Chapter Four

Giselle went to work early the next day. She had a lot of catching up to do now that she had lost an entire afternoon.

She had slept surprisingly well. She supposed it was because of all the stress. Giselle never went to sleep before she started to yawn. If she did, she would toss and turn for a long time and wake up feeling ragged, like something from a salad bowl. But sleep had come quickly last night, as if some keeper in her mind had thrown an off-switch the moment her head touched the pillow. She slept very deeply and, if she had dreams, they were so placid she could not recall them.

Maybe I should have a bucket nearly fall on my head every day, she thought as she got ready for work the next morning.

She dressed with special care that day. Having figured out why Vishnu was so insistent – rather crudely, she now thought – that she have lunch with him, Giselle decided to give him his money's worth. Then, she thought, her debt would be expiated. She put on a shimmering green top, a marvellous creation of Chinese silk, with wide sleeves reaching to her elbows, a keyhole-shaped neck and two big gold buttons at the front. She was wearing matching dark-green trousers with flared legs and a double-belted waist which clung snugly to the contours of her hips. She had not worn this outfit for some time and, standing with her back to the full-length mirror in her bedroom and craning her head around, Giselle saw she still looked good in it. Her bottom was high and round. She smiled secretly to herself: there was a certain exultation in knowing the inevitability of men's reactions.

Giselle did not clip her hair as tightly as she usually did. Instead, she tied it at the back but left it loose enough to frame her face with dark, undisciplined curls. She knew this altered her entire appearance. Her hair, unbound, erased the reserved Giselle. Now her pouty, full-lipped mouth better fitted the lines of her face. The clear and direct gaze seemed to acquire a sensual boldness. She accentuated these qualities with her make-up. Her eyeliner was just a little more marked. She put on a red shade of lipstick. She even went so far as to put on eye-shadow and blusher, which she never wore except at Carnival time.

Finally, Giselle put on her favourite pair of earrings. These were pyramids of silver rods. Within each pyramid was a small Mobius strip – that peculiar creation which has only one edge – of flattened metal and three tiny silver spheres. The Mobius strips twisted ceaselessly in the way Mobius strips tend to do and, if Giselle moved suddenly, the spheres gave off small ringing sounds which she seemed to hear in her inner ear. Giselle, who was easily bored, sometimes found this sound more appealing than the conversations around her. And she thought that Vishnu, though he did indeed have nice teeth, might not have much else to recommend his mouth.

Vishnu was not in the yard when she went in. She was glad of that. She did not want him to see her until lunch. It would spoil the surprise. Nor was anyone in the newsroom – except Krishna Budhu who didn't notice her – but Robert Cardinez came in about fifteen minutes after she did.

He walked over to her desk immediately. 'Giselle! I heard what happened yesterday. You all right?'

Giselle looked up, smiling. She immediately observed the change in his face as he absorbed her finished appearance, like a man who goes on a blind date expecting to meet Lassie and ends up with a Halle Berry look-alike instead. Robert's eyes gathered her image while the rest of his expression held on to his concerned inquiry. It was almost as though his face had split in some subtle manner.

She said, 'It was just a near-miss. I'm fine.'

He said, as she had known he would, 'Well, you certainly *look* fine.' He sat down on a chair beside her.

'Thanks,' she said, very casually. 'I called to tell you I wouldn't be coming back, but you were out.'

'Yes, Doris told me.' His eyes were still taking her in. 'These damned workmen are so careless.'

'Nobody's fault,' she said. 'The handle of his bucket broke.'

'Well, he shouldn't have been lowering a bucket with somebody passing below.'

'Actually, I think he was pulling it up,' Giselle said, although she did not know. 'I shouldn't have been passing through there in the first place. And it was another workman who pushed me out of the way.'

Robert shrugged. 'All right. Anyway, I'm really glad you're okay. The newsroom would miss you if you were away.'

'Yes,' she said. 'Who would program their computers for them?'

He laughed. 'That too, I suppose. But, really, you've been a most pleasant – and attractive – addition to the staff. And I'm really pleased with your work.'

'Well,' said Giselle, a little embarrassed, 'That means you'll have to get three people to replace me when I leave. One who's pleasant, one's who's attractive and one whose work will please you.'

'That's right, isn't it?' Robert said slowly. 'You'll be ending your contract with us in about four months.' He looked at her with a sudden, speculative expression which she couldn't quite read.

'Well, hopefully I'll be around after that, once CMC gives me the maintenance contract.'

'Yes,' he said meditatively. Giselle, feeling a little awkward, flicked her earrings. Tiny bells tinkled. 'I'm glad you're all right,' Robert said again.

'I'm fine, really,' she said.

He stood up. She noticed he had on a green, silky shirt. It was not the same shade of green as her top, but it was similar. He wore black, baggy trousers and brown leather shoes. His tie, set with a gold pin, was red and green. He was freshly shaven and Giselle smelt the fragrance of some pleasantly expensive cologne. *He could step straight into a page of* GQ, she thought, *one with a scratch-and-sniff tab*.

'How about having lunch with me today?' he said, smiling. 'We can discuss those scheduling problems you told me about.'

Giselle shook her head regretfully. 'Sorry, I'm tied up for lunch.'

'Oh. All right.' He seemed a bit put out.

'Some other time maybe,' she said.

'Sure.' But he no longer seemed very interested, although his gaze lingered on her. Giselle felt awkward again. 'We will talk,' he said. He turned with characteristic suddenness and bustled off to his office.

Giselle turned back to her computer. It was funny, she thought, what a difference appearance made. Robert had never asked her to lunch before. In fact, he had not seemed to really notice her before. But in just the one day she had abandoned her usual simple style, had put on her sophisticated image, his idea of her had changed. She had seen that in his eyes. The power. And, even if she came dressed in a flour sack tomorrow, Giselle thought, he would still see her in his mind's eye as she looked today. The irony was that she had not made herself up this way for Robert; in fact she had not made herself up this way for anyone really, not even herself. It was just a debt; and she always paid her debts.

Giselle shook her head and began writing her program. The difference in her appearance was just paint and cloth. But it had concrete effects. *Yeah, it makes men hard*, she thought with a small, cynical grin. Sometimes in her career, Giselle knew she had been hired mostly because of her appearance, and what surprise there was when she was found to be competent, too! She wished the world were more logical. Yet, at the same time, part of her secretly exulted in the power of outward things. Giselle felt this was a small, somehow mean part of her. But it was the way things were, too. What was it Kafka had said? 'In a fight between you and the world, bet on the world.' Vera, she thought, would agree.

Giselle did not get much done that morning. Everybody in the newsoom, it seemed, had heard about the incident and passed by to make inquiries about her well-being. Sharma came in around eleven o'clock. 'Yes, I'm all right,' Giselle told her as soon as she walked across.

'I don't care about that,' said Sharma. 'Where my roti?'

Giselle burst out laughing, only now remembering she had promised to bring Sharma a roti back from lunch the previous day. 'You'll get it today,' she promised. 'If another bucket doesn't fall on me.'

Several staff members from other departments also came by. Giselle could not fob them off when they were expressing concern. But she was surprised to realize how many people she knew at CMC. Giselle had a habit of speaking to everybody and her natural curiosity had led her into every department just to see how things worked in a daily newspaper. Besides this, it was one of the characteristics of computer work that your job impacted on virtually everything, although that didn't explain how she also knew the cheerful cleaning lady, Gemma, who came across and said, 'That man in the yard, Headers, still apologizing about how he bucket nearly fall on you. He say to tell you he making a special curry crab and dumpling for you and how he from Tobago and nobody's make a better curry crab and dumpling than he. But you all right, *doux-doux*?' Giselle listened to this speech with a smile and told Gemma to tell Headers she loved curry crab and dumpling and yes, she was all right.

It was as she was speaking to Gemma that Giselle's phone rang. 'Well, take care, dear,' Gemma said, and left. Giselle picked up the receiver.

'Hello,' she said, still a little distracted.

'Hello,' said a voice. 'This is Payne.'

'Do you want some Ibuprofen?' Giselle asked automatically. She always carried a few pills when her period was due.

'Excuse me?'

'I'm sorry,' she said, catching herself. 'Who is this?'

'This is Mr Payne,' said the voice, sounding a little offended.

Giselle hesitated. 'Do you work here?'

'This is *Spengler* Payne,' said the voice, now sounding really offended. 'Head of the Queres-McBuddy Group which own the company you works for.'

'Oh,' said Giselle. '*Oh*! I'm sorry, Mr Payne. You must have gotten a wrong line. Did you want Mr Cardinez?'

'No. I was just speaking to Mr Cardinez and – '

'Oh?' said Giselle, beginning to babble. 'And how is he?'

There was a brief silence. 'He is fine,' said Payne. 'He was telling me about your near-accident. I did just want to ascertain that you are all right.'

'Uh, yes, fine.'

'Good. The Queres-McBuddy Group are concerned about its employees. Did you go to a doctor?'

'No, it wasn't necessary.'

'Well, you should. Get the name of the company doctor and we will foot any bills.'

'I'll see.'

'Good. Goodbye.'

'Goodbye.'

Giselle hung up the phone and clutched her head with clawed hands. *I'd better show him my looks 'cause I'm sure I didn't impress him with my brains*, she thought. But she wondered why Payne was calling her personally. It was nice of him, but it made her feel uneasy. But, before she could go back over the conversation in her mind to figure out why, Headers came upstairs to see her. He was a short, barrel-bodied man, and reassured her vehemently about the excellence of his crab and dumpling. Giselle told him she was waiting for it, dribbling. This may have been unlady-like, but Emily Post had probably never tasted curry crab and dumpling in her life, and just the thought of the spicy dish made Giselle's salivary glands active. Giselle didn't mind taking food from a complete stranger. She had worked in restaurants in the States and knew that, on the whole, Caribbean people were far more careful in preparing their food than Americans. And, when she asked around, it turned out that Headers' crab and dumpling did indeed enjoy minor fame in the company. Giselle wasn't surprised. In Trinidad, boasts about culinary skill are not idly made. Headers often brought crab and dumpling to sell on Fridays to the CMC staff. It occurred to Giselle that in five weeks she had already become part of that staff. She would regret leaving when the time came.

◆

At twelve o'clock, she went across to the eating-place where she was supposed to meet Vishnu. It was just across the road but Giselle took the longer route through the back entrance. *Get almost killed by a falling bucket and you're prejudiced against it for life*, she thought, trying as usual to ease her genuine nervousness with a joke. But she only felt reassured when she was past the site and out on the busy square under the midday sun where she became very conscious of her shimmering green elegance. Giselle was especially, pleasantly conscious of her bottom flexing in the snug trousers. There were many stares from passing men, but Giselle's very elegance and confidence in her beauty seemed to silence most comments. *'Nuff respect*, she thought.

She walked up the cool, dark stairs and into the dimly lit eating-place. The place was pretty full. Waitresses in fitted red skirts and white blouses moved around quickly with trays of food. There were round tables with red tablecloths in the centre of the floor and booths with high wooden backs and padded seats to the side. Vishnu wasn't there. Giselle sat down in one of the booths – the idea that Vishnu might not show up never crossed her mind. She had never been stood up and, besides, she didn't think Vishnu was the type to miss a free lunch. The waitress, a pretty, dark girl, came over.

'Ready to order?'

'I'm waiting on someone. Check back in a few minutes, okay?'

'All right, dear.'

Giselle took out *The Atlantic Monthly* and began reading the story of Robert 'Crybaby' Wailer and Florence Nightingale from the point she had stopped the previous night. This part was being told in the authorial voice, and she grinned again as she recalled the 'Richard Kinky' pseudonym:

It was in autumn of last year that Florence Nightingale's two children, Kildare and Julia, called me up. Both had read one of my essays and were, naturally, impressed. They said they had a story to tell me that they thought I would be interested in and could they come up to see me. Normally, I don't encourage such visits, because as a published writer one doesn't want to encourage familiarity from the *canaille*. (This is not a selfish urge, but a compassionate one: one doesn't want other people to become aware of their natural inferiority, as inevitably must happen in one's presence.) However, they seemed like nice enough folks and their willingness to come all the way from Utah to see me piqued my interest. I mean, I lived right in the next state, right on the border, so it was only a one-hour drive but, as you know, we middle Americans are really territorial.

So on a Tuesday morning at nine a.m. they came to my house in their battered blue-and-silver Chevrolet. I arrived at ten a.m., having gone to the grocery and forgotten the appointment. But they waited patiently, and when they told me their story, as we sat in my living-room over three beers and roast beef sandwiches which they had thoughtfully brought along, I understood why. I made them tell the story three times, because they were initially reluctant to get into the sexy parts. And I listened hard and asked hard questions. Especially about the sexy parts, which got me hard even as I listened.

The story of what happened between Bob Wailer and their mother Florence Nightingale in three short minutes in May of 1970 is an extraordinary one. In these days of pre-nuptial agreements, easy co-habitation and condom machines, it is not easy to distinguish between true passion, trite sentimentality and malarkey: and I will leave it to the reader to judge what occurred there. I make no attempt to get into the minds of Bob and Florence. Only they knew what they thought, what they felt, and maybe even they weren't too sure. Kildare and Julia have supplied me with their mother's diaries, judging her story too important to respect her wishes that they, and Bob Wailer's letters to her, be burnt. I may as well say now that we also have an iron-clad contract, in case any distant family wants to waste time trying to get in on the royalties.

But I truly hope that no such distasteful occurrences will mar this venture. What I have tried to do here is tell this powerful story just as it happened. I will, however, say this. Bob and Florence have transformed what I think is possible in the arena of human relationships. As you read this story, I hope you will come to the same understanding.

This will not be easy. Where true passion ends and mawkishness begins, I am not sure. But neither is anyone else in this world, especially literary critics. Read this book in the spirit in which I have written it: believing everything. If you're a genuinely sensitive and passionate person, a citizen in the rare realm of gentleness, I am sure you will appreciate this book and recommend it to your friends. If not, see a therapist.

Giselle paused in her reading and glanced up. Vishnu stood in the middle of the floor, looking around. He was dressed in a white T-shirt and jeans and Giselle noticed how at ease he looked. His eyes crossed her without recognition and then snapped back. He smiled and came across and slid into the seat opposite her.

'Hi,' he said. 'I didn't make you out for a moment there.'

Giselle closed her magazine. 'Forgot me already, eh?' she said, with the confidence of an attractive woman who knows that any red-blooded male, having met her once, would remember her for life.

Vishnu looked at her consideringly with those dark, smoky eyes. *Was there grey somewhere in them?* wondered Giselle. He said, 'No. But you don't normally wear so much make-up.'

'Oh,' said Giselle. This wasn't the kind of thing she expected a man to notice, and it meant he had noticed her even before yesterday. Even Robert, who had seen her more often than Vishnu, and a lot closer, just found she looked different without really observing why. Giselle said lightly, taking the bull by the horns, 'Well, I thought I'd pretty up since I was buying lunch for you.'

'Oh.' Vishnu picked up her magazine and looked at the cover briefly. Then he handed it back to her, smiling as if something amused him. 'Well, if it was specially for this lunch, you shouldn't have worn any make-up at all. You look a lot better without it.'

Giselle only just stopped herself from gasping. The effrontery of the man! She controlled her irritation with an effort. She supposed she couldn't really expect any better from an ill-mannered labourer.

'I'll bear that in mind,' she said coolly.

He shrugged. 'It's just my opinion. You have marvellous skin and nice eyes and a nice mouth. You don't need make-up. But you please yourself.'

'I always do,' she said, still coolly. But her irritation was blown away, as suddenly as it had arisen, in the easy breeze of his directness. Now she felt a flush climbing into her face. Giselle was always glad of her brown skin – she blushed so easily! And there was another feeling – confusion. This man, within a few minutes of his sitting down, had her off-balance in a manner to which she was *definitely* not accustomed.

'How you slept last night?' he asked.

'Quite well,' she answered. 'I was surprised.'

'Good,' he said. 'I was worried about that. But I figured you were okay when I left.'

'Yes. My room-mate came in and we talked and I read a little. Slept like a rock.'

He nodded. 'You want something to drink?' he asked.

'You forget. I'm buying,' she said.

'You're buying lunch. I will buy the drinks.' He smiled. 'Can't let you do everything. I *am* a man, you know.'

Giselle smiled back uncertainly. His humour, if it *was* humour, puzzled her.

'I'll have some orange juice, then,' she said.

'Okay. I will get it from the bar. It'll be quicker.' He glanced at her. 'Those are great earrings,' he commented.

He got up and went across to the other side of the room. Giselle, touching her left earring lightly with her fingertips, looked after him.

He looked freshly bathed, but he had not shaved the stubble on his face. Dressed, Giselle thought, he looked like an ordinary leanly built young man. He wasn't very tall. She wouldn't have noticed him on the street. She flicked the earring, listening to the little ringing sounds.

Vishnu came back in a few minutes with her orange juice. He had a glass of coconut water for himself. Giselle put down the menu she had been looking through.

'You don't drink?' she asked.

'Not really. I'll take a *beastly* cold beer on a really hot day. You know the kind of day that makes you feel like all your muscles are dish rags?'

She grinned. 'Yes. I drink gallons of club soda and take cold showers every hour.'

The waitress came and asked for their order. Giselle took pork fried rice, lemon chicken and Chinese vegetables.

'I'll have two burgers and two portions of fries,' said Vishnu.

The waitress, the same girl who had spoken to Giselle before, smiled down at him as she wrote his order. 'Like you hungry today,' she said.

'No, just greedy,' said Vishnu, smiling back. Giselle watched how he gave the waitress his full attention for a few moments. *He's a flirt*, she thought.

Vishnu turned back to Giselle. 'I eat here sometimes,' he said, as if apologizing. 'They make good burgers.'

'I see,' she said. She sipped at her juice. It was freshly squeezed and tasted wonderful.

'I like burgers,' he said, waving a hand in the air as if to emphasize his comment. He grinned. 'And since you're buying . . .'

Giselle nodded to herself: she had pegged him exactly right. She felt pleased with herself. She liked being right about people. And now she was able to categorize him.

Remembering Vera's comment about him just trying to impress her, she said, 'So how you find *Miguel Street*? The book you were reading at my place yesterday,' she added, in case he had not looked at the title.

'It was pretty good,' he said. 'I've read some other books by Naipaul, but not that one.'

'Which story in it did you like?' Giselle asked, very casually.

He took a swallow of coconut water from his glass and thought about it. Or seemed to think about it. Just when Giselle thought she should ease his pain by naming one of the stories and talking about it herself, he said, ' "B. Wordsworth" '.

She started a little. This was also her favourite story in the book.

'Something wrong?' Vishnu asked.

'What? Oh no.'

'That guy, the calypsonian, you really feel sorry for him.'

'Yes,' Giselle said. Finding that Vishnu had not only read the book, but actually had an opinion on a story, she was once again uncertain of her ground. It contradicted her concept of him. But she told herself that *Miguel Street* was very simply written. It was one of its strengths. 'What other books by Naipaul have you read?' she asked deliberately.

'Mostly the non-fiction,' he answered. '*Overcrowded Baracoon, El Dorado*, the book about the Abdul Malik murders. But I've read *A House for Mr Biswas*, of course.'

'Of course,' said Giselle. Her mind, strangely, seemed to go blank for a moment. 'I like Naipaul's style, especially in *Miguel Street*. It's very . . .' she hesitated . . . 'pellucid.'

He grinned at her. 'You don't know you could strain your eyes reading all those dictionaries?'

Giselle gave a surprised laugh. It was just the kind of comment Vera would make.

Vishnu looked at her with a subtle shifting of his features. He wasn't smiling, but he looked as if something was amusing him. But he didn't say anything and Giselle suddenly felt a hot embarrassment at the way she had tried to catch him out. She hoped fervently he did not realize why she had really asked the questions she had.

The waitress came back with their food.

'Thanks, Darla,' Vishnu told her.

'Enjoy,' she said. Vishnu looked at the waitress as she walked away. Giselle also gazed after her critically. *She's too thin*, she thought and then wondered why she should even bother to think that. Vishnu turned back to her with a smile. Perhaps because he had been looking at the waitress, Giselle realized Vishnu had very sensual features. It was the slight pout of the firm mouth, the darkness in the eyes. She wondered why she had not noticed this yesterday; if she had, she would have been far more hesitant about letting him into her apartment, though in all honesty she had to admit she might also have been *less* hesitant.

She said, 'You know all the waitresses by name?'

He grinned. 'No. But I know some. Would you believe Darla has a two-year-old son?'

'That young girl?' Giselle said, astonished. 'She can't be more than eighteen.' She added, 'And she's built like a stick.'

'She's eighteen,' Vishnu said. 'And she lives on her own.' He shrugged. 'Life's a bitch and few of us are dog-trainers.'

Giselle said, 'My room-mate says that. Well, not the part about dog-trainers. You feel sorry for Darla?'

'No. Everyone has to make his own way.'

'And what you could do, eh?'

'Guess so,' he said.

He opened both burgers and added ketchup, mustard and an appalling amount of pepper sauce. Giselle said, 'You sure you don't want some burger to go with your pepper?'

He looked up, grinning. 'They make their own pepper sauce here. It's really good. Try it.' He made as if to squeeze some from the plastic bottle on to her plate of food. Giselle stopped him and took the bottle from his hand.

'I'll do it myself, thanks,' she said. 'I prefer to add pepper to my food, not the other way around.'

He laughed and bit hugely into his burger. 'Oh, this is good,' he said in a muffled voice.

'Don't talk with your mouth full,' Giselle told him.

'Sorry, Mom,' he said, still chewing.

She carefully heaped rice, chicken and vegetables together in one forkful and ate it. The food was delicious.

'Do you think you have a hard life?' she asked curiously. She was thinking again about seeing him breaking rocks in the yard of CMC.

'God, no,' he said. 'At least not now.'

Giselle wondered if that meant his life had been hard in the past or might be hard in the future. But she didn't ask him, watching as he speared a large forkful of fries and conveyed it to his mouth. He chomped hugely.

'Well, you certainly enjoy your food,' she said in some amusement, continuing to eat her own.

'One of life's great pleasures, along with music and sex.' He paused and swallowed. 'Though not necessarily in that order.'

'What kind of music do you like?' she said, ignoring his addendum.

He wiped the corners of his mouth with his napkin and grinned mischievously at her.

'Well, thank God you didn't ask me what kind of sex I like,' he said.

Now Giselle did blush furiously. She was sure even her brown tan wasn't hiding the blood she felt burning in her cheeks. The sudden, strange leap of heat in her stomach only added to her confusion.

'Excuse me,' she said in her best pert manner. 'Could we keep this conversation on a decent level?'

'Of course,' said Vishnu immediately. 'Although I should tell you I don't find anything indecent about sex.'

'Oh, obviously,' she said, finally able to look him in the face. It was a lame reply; but it was better than no reply at all.

'Music,' he said. 'I like pieces in nearly everything. Pop, reggae, blues, that old rock-and-roll. Laid back soca, not the party kind. Some Indian and African music really gets me, too. Musically, I'm very – ' he paused and looked her straight in the eye – 'eclectic.'

'Ah,' she said. 'You've reached the section with the Es.'

He grinned at her and began demolishing the second burger.

'How old are you?' she asked. She had been studying his face trying to guess his age. But he had the kind of mobile features which are difficult to assess.

'Thirty,' he answered.

'Thirty!' she exclaimed. She had thought he was younger. 'Are you married?'

He shook his head. 'How come?' she asked.

He glanced up from his burger. 'You ask a lot of questions, don't you?'

'Sorry,' she said. 'I'll stop.'

'It's all right. I'm not married because I never met the right woman.' A shadow passed across his face, but it was gone so quickly Giselle thought she had imagined it. 'I thought I had once, but it didn't work out.'

Giselle thought, *He's broke up and Robert Cardinez is divorced. It must be something with attractive men.* She suddenly realized Vishnu seemed to be a very separate kind of person. Even when she had seen him eating his lunch yesterday, he had been eating alone. Giselle thought she knew why. She had formed an image which she thought framed him perfectly. Vishnu was only a manual labourer, but he was obviously more intelligent than his peers. She figured he was relatively well-read, but probably not educated. His intelligence thus cut him off from those of his own station. Nor could he communicate with those at a higher social level, since he normally had no access to such people. Vishnu, thought Giselle, was a socially placeless man. He had nowhere to fit in. Giselle suddenly felt very sorry for him.

'You have family?' she asked.

'Well, I wasn't made in a test tube.'

'You know what I mean.'

He paused a while before answering. 'My father lives in St Lucia. My mother died when I was seven. I have one brother who lives in Moruga and a sister in the States and no children that I know about.' He looked down at his fries. 'And that's enough personal history for one day,' he said. He spoke very diffidently – but it was a definite snub. This time Giselle did gasp. In her experience, men did not snub her. She looked down at her plate of food, afraid to raise her head in case he saw the anger she knew was blazing in her eyes. She was just curious about him! Most men were quite happy to talk about themselves for hours. Most men were happy to chat with her and, damn, wasn't that why he had insisted on this lunch which *she* was buying? *An ill-mannered pig*, she thought. *Why did I expect anything better*? She had assumed his singleness was that of a lonely person. Now she realized that, even if that was true, his distance from people was allied to an overweening arrogance. And what, thought Giselle in slow deep fury, gives him any basis for arrogance? Her sympathy of just a few moments ago was transmuted to a cold, cruel rage.

'Thirty years old,' she said, with deceptive softness. 'You don't wish you were doing more with your life?'

He looked up. His face changed, all expression vanishing. Now he looked very cold. It was like looking at another person entirely. But Giselle felt that vicious hardness set in her. She would *not* give in to his arrogance.

'I mean, you satisfied being a temporary worker on construction projects? You don't wish you had more in your life?' she said.

Now he dropped his eyes. And his voice was also very soft. 'Well, let me see. I have a strong body. I'm good with my hands. If I can't find work here, I go up the islands. I have been living like that for the past two years and is a good life. But people like you can't see beyond money, eh? Just because I not rich, I have to "do something with my life".' He looked back up at her. 'I know your type too well.'

Giselle's fury was like strong poison in her veins. She met his eyes, which were now like two orbs of black ice, without flinching. 'And what do you imagine is my type?' she said. She heard the hard, unfamiliar clang of rage in her voice.

'Grow up in a nice, upper-class household. Had everything handed to you on a platter. Studied overseas – I can hear that little freshwater Yankee twang. And now you have a nice white-collar job and you'll marry a nice professional man and have two children who you will train to be just as shallow and short-sighted as yourselves.'

Giselle laughed – a harsh sound. He was so wrong! 'Oh, really?' she said. 'Well, let me tell you, Mr all-knowing Vishnu Traboulay, I had to work damned hard for everything I have. My father died when I was seven and there were four children in the family and my mother had to see hell to get the best for us. And I went to the States on a scholarship which I got by staying up late every night studying my books and since then I've been catching my royal tail to make ends meet and I don't have time for marriage or any of those luxuries because I'm *still* working hard putting in ten-hour days at my white-collar job. So why you don't put that in your pipe and smoke it?'

His face did not change at all. He got up. 'Thank you so much for lunch,' he said coldly. Then he walked out. It did not improve Giselle's temper to notice that Vishnu carried the remaining burger with him. She might have forgiven him being a pig but, as she opened her purse to pay for lunch, she knew she could never forgive him for being a *greedy* pig.

Chapter Five

Giselle went back to work furious. She could not even remember the last time she had been so angry. If rage was fire, she thought heatedly, Vishnu Traboulay could have immediately embarked on a career as a blackened cinder without needing any references. It was not just what he had said which had totally enraged Giselle. She could handle criticism, she told herself, even unfair criticism. But his manner! She couldn't get over the blunt way he had stopped her questions, the coldness in his face, and the way he had looked at her as if she was nothing but a bug on his highly polished windscreen.

Giselle did not look for him as she marched through the yard and went up to the newsroom. She did not even know if he was working that day nor was she interested. She went to her desk without a word to anyone, sat down, and turned on the computer. The Macintosh, far more dependable than men, glowed into life.

Sharma came over. Giselle looked up at her, trying to ease the rigidity she felt in her face. Sharma's cool gaze flickered over Giselle and the desk.

'A bucket fall on you again?' she asked.

'What?' said Giselle, confused.

'Where my roti, chile?'

'Oh, Sharma, I'm so sorry. I forgot. I will go out and get it for you now.'

'No, it's okay,' Sharma said. 'I finished page fourteen early. I'll go out and get it myself.' She peered closely at Giselle. 'You looking kind of hot and bothered, Karan.'

Giselle shook her head. 'It's nothing.'

'Okay,' said Sharma. Her eyes were very cool and wise.

She went out. Giselle turned back to the computer screen with its meaningless jumble of letters and numbers and symbols. She sat for a few minutes just looking. But her mind remained blank, inert. The anger in her was like a smooth white wall, blocking her passage into the world where she understood the rules.

On a sudden impulse, Giselle went across to another desk where there was a telephone and called the apartment. After five rings, Vera answered. Her voice still sounded a little croaky from sleep.

'Hi, it's Giselle. What you doing?'

'Hi, Gis. I'm just having some coffee and watching one of the soaps on TV. How's it going with you?'

'Terrible.'

'What? What happen? Tell Auntie Vera.'

Giselle smiled a little. This was the other reason she and Vera were friends – just hearing her voice could cheer Giselle up. 'Why men so obnoxious, Vera?' she said.

'They can't help it. They have an obnoxious gene in their Y-chromosomes,' Vera said. Giselle grinned into the phone. 'Which man has been obnoxious to a be-yoo-tiful girl like you?' Vera asked.

'Vishnu,' said Giselle.

'What? The hero of yesteryear, I mean yesterday? What do he did?'

'Well, he had lunch with me today.'

'The fiend!'

Giselle laughed. Already things were coming back into focus. She felt the blank white rage inside her being replaced by her normal cheerful self-control. Vera, she felt, was as good as one of those tonics that can only be sold with a prescription.

'So what happened?' Vera asked.

Giselle described the conversation at lunch. Vera listened without speaking except for an occasional 'Mm-hm.'

'So, just as I was thinking what an interesting person he seemed to be, he showed his true colours,' Giselle finished. 'You could believe that man?'

Vera cleared her throat. 'Well, actually Gis, it sounds to me like you're in the wrong,' she said.

Giselle drew back and looked at the telephone receiver as though it had changed to a snake in her hand. After taking a few moments to ensure that this phenomenon had not occurred, she put the phone carefully back to her ear.

'Excuse me,' she said, very calmly. 'Did I hear you say that you think I'm in the wrong?'

61

'Now don't go getting vex with me, too,' Vera said. 'Apply a little of that logic you're always boasting about. For Heaven's sake, you have the *Enterprise*'s call sign on our burglar alarm.'

'Serial number!' snapped Giselle. 'How many times I have to tell you it's the damned serial number?'

'Whatever,' said Vera. 'Cool yourself.'

'I'm quite cool, thank you.'

'Lord, you don't even know when you getting hoity-toity. Is no wonder the man get vex with you.'

'Vera, I really don't see how you can take his side. Didn't I just tell you what he said to me? He told me I was shallow, materialistic and short-sighted.'

'Yes, and he was wrong about that. I mean, you don't even wear glasses – I'm kidding! But, look, didn't you also tell me that you found out that he really read *Miguel Street*?'

'Yeah. So?' asked Giselle.

'Hel-lo! There's no need to sound as though you're chewing a cigar out of the corner of your mouth and holding a Tommy-gun, you know,' said Vera.

'Sorry,' Giselle muttered, knowing it was true.

'Okay. Anyway, you don't think Vishnu might have realized why you were asking him about the book. The man is apparently not stupid. You said so yourself. He knows he's just a construction worker and you would be surprised he reads a writer like Naipaul. And maybe when you started asking about his family, he thought you might just be mocking his humble background or something. Or maybe he doesn't like talking about his dead mother. You ever thought of that, Giselle?'

This hit Giselle like a slap in the face. She had to swallow twice before she answered. 'No,' she said in a small voice.

'Hm,' observed Vera. 'Sounds like Al Capone is suddenly dead, buried and regretted by few.' Giselle said nothing. 'Anyway,' Vera continued, 'my point is that, after all that, you go in for spite like a Scud missile asking why he hasn't done more with his life. And you don't know how snooty you can sound when you ready. So now do you see why I think you *may* have been in the wrong?'

'Yes,' Giselle said, still in the same small voice.

'I'm not saying you were, eh. You have to decide that for yourself. But there's no need to sound like Tweety Bird in a blue funk.'

Giselle was silent for so long that Vera said, 'Hello? You there, Giselle?'

'Yes,' she said. 'I was just looking for a good fishing hook to put myself on. Thanks, Vera. A real friend is the person who shows us how obnoxious we are.'

'You vex with me?' said Vera. There was a note of worry in her voice.

'No, of course not. You've made me think.'

'Yes folks, miracles still happen in this day and age!' Vera said, like an American evangelist.

'Ah, why don't you change your lifestyle and have a bath,' Giselle returned. Vera laughed.

'I'll probably be working until six,' Giselle said. 'You'll be home?'

'I'm flying out tomorrow night, I think, so I want to do some hoppin' and boppin' before I go.'

'Especially the latter.'

'You got that right, sweetness. So I don't know if I will be in tonight at all.'

Giselle sighed. This was the other Vera. Vera knew Giselle would like to talk to her later, but the fast track beckoned. And that was one siren call Vera Chancellor could not resist.

'Well, talk to me before you fly out,' said Giselle.

'I'll try. But you know how it is.'

'Yes. And Vera?'

'Yeah?'

'You're a good friend.'

'Thanks. But don't ever call me good, goil.'

Giselle, chuckling, hung up. Vera *was* a good friend – until the party started. Then nothing else mattered. Giselle, thinking of the Vera of practical common sense and quick perception and the Vera of the giddy social whirl, sometimes wondered if her friend was not a little schizophrenic.

The phone rang. Giselle picked it up, seeing from the electronic readout that the call was internal. 'Hello, Giselle?' It was Doris, Robert Cardinez's secretary. 'Could you see Mr Cardinez in his office now?'

'Sure,' said Giselle.

She went back to her desk and picked up a memo pad. Robert's office was just off from the newsroom, at the end of a short, right-angled corridor. He was seated at his desk signing some forms when she went in. 'Just give me a minute,' he said.

The office had only been finished recently and this was the first time Giselle had been in it. The walls were painted electric blue with red edging. The carpet was royal blue, matching the two padded chairs opposite his desk. His own chair was red. There were several framed photos on the wall. Most were prints of newspaper photographs of significant events in the Caribbean over the past few years. One showed Robert receiving an award at a United Press International function. He was dressed in a black three-piece suit and he looked very thin beside the plump white man who was shaking his hand and smiling. Behind Robert, Spengler Payne stood with his hand in a congratulatory pat on Robert's shoulder.

Robert put down his pen and leaned back in his tilted chair. He clasped his hands behind his head. 'The last set of hard drives will be coming in from Miami tonight. We'll spend the weekend unpacking them and so on, so by Monday you'll be able to check them out. You'll let Harry know exactly where you want them in which departments and list the software packages we'll need.'

'Sure,' said Giselle. She made some notes on her pad.

'So how's the mental block coming? That incident yesterday must have thrown you off.' He looked at her with relaxed and smiling eyes. It occurred to Giselle that this was the first time she had seen Robert in a relaxed attitude. Even when he sat in a chair, he was always perched as if ready to spring to his feet.

'Oh, no,' she said. 'Getting nearly hit on the head was just a warning. Now my brain knows if it doesn't get on the job, I'll take really drastic measures.'

Robert chuckled. 'So you don't intend to sue us, then?'

'Why?' said Giselle. 'How much do you think I'd get?'

He laughed. 'You should go and see the company doctor, though. We'll foot the bill.'

'I'll think about it.'

'And you must talk to me sometime about the work you do. I find it fascinating but, although I use computers, I haven't the faintest idea how they work. When I started out in this business, we were still using typewriters. If I had some time, I'd like to learn basic programming.' He shook his head. 'But I probably won't find the time until I retire.'

Giselle smiled. 'Somehow I can't picture you retired.'

He laughed. 'No, I'll probably drop dead before that.'

Giselle laughed with him. He said, 'Are you free for lunch tomorrow or are you going to blank me again?'

'No, tomorrow's fine,' she said.

He leaned forward. 'Good. We'll go to Mallory's,' he said, naming a restaurant about ten minutes' drive out of the city.

'I've never eaten there,' she said.

'The decor is really marvellous and the food is excellent,' he reassured her. 'A nice, quiet place, as they say.' He looked at her questioningly. 'You aren't worried about going to a nice, quiet place with the boss, though?'

'If I were permanently on staff, I wouldn't,' Giselle said. 'But as a freelancer on contract, the same rules don't apply.'

'You're an ethical person?'

She nodded. 'Be warned,' she said lightly.

'Well, I find it admirable that you can be so open about your weaknesses,' said Robert.

'Yes. They say it's the first step in curing yourself,' grinned Giselle.

'I'll be willing to help you any way I can.'

'I'll bear it in mind.'

Robert stood up. He was smiling, but his gaze was very sharp. 'Lunch tomorrow, then?'

'Yes.'

She turned and left. She knew his eyes were on her, but she didn't mind. Robert was an attractive man. There was pleasure and excitement in Giselle at the thought of being out with him socially, at the thought that he might be interested in her as a woman. *Oh, don't get carried away now*, she thought. *It's just lunch and he's a sophisticated man. Don't get giddy*. But, remembering the way he had looked at her that morning, Giselle knew it was not just a simple lunch date. Sitting back at her desk, worried thoughts flitted suddenly through her mind. *What if he thinks I'm boring? Or uninformed? Or suppose I get a bad period so I can't eat. Suppose I spill my food?*

Giselle caught herself up sharply for being foolish. *In any case, I know one thing*, she thought. *However it goes, I won't have to pay for lunch.*

◆

At three o'clock, Giselle made a decision. She had spent the afternoon working more or less on automatic pilot. But at the back of her mind, the issue of her argument at lunch with Vishnu stirred uneasily. She had not changed her opinion of him. She still thought he was insufferably arrogant. Nor had she changed her opinion of his reaction – his judgement of her was so absurdly ill-founded it was laughable. More significant, though, that reaction showed the gap between them in social terms. It was part of being middle class to be able to deal with issues tactfully, logically. But Vishnu had just charged ahead like a battering ram and totally embarrassed her. No discussion, just gut reaction. *I'm not a snob*, thought Giselle, *but the space between us makes the Grand Canyon look like a ditch.*

All of which didn't change the fact that his reaction was justified. Giselle didn't deny this, now that Vera had pointed it out to her. It was just the *form* of Vishnu's reaction that she had objected to. But that still didn't change the fact that she owed him an apology.

Giselle sighed. She kept remembering his cold face and the way he had stalked out of the restaurant, like a Hindu rajah who had just been served roast beef. It was not going to be easy to apologize. But Giselle had her principles: she had wronged him and it was the least she could do. She recalled how considerate he had been yesterday when he had driven her to her apartment. Nor was it just his obvious concern; he had been considerate in subtle ways, too. He had been careful not to stand too near to her nor even watch her too closely. Seeing him today, the way he had looked at the waitress, the way he had smiled at Giselle herself, made her realize this.

He's quite a nice fella in certain ways, thought Giselle. *But that other side of him could make me cheerfully dip him in boiling oil, if oil wasn't so expensive and if I wasn't naturally kind to dumb animals.*

Giselle grinned at her own sally and, coming to the end of the program she was running, closed the file. She got up, went across to a phone and dialled Harry Chan's extension. Harry himself answered.

'Hello Harry, this is Giselle,' she said.

'Hello,' he said, sounding pleased to hear her voice. 'Sorry I haven't been up to see you today, dear. I been on the run for the entire morning. But Vishnu told me that you were all right.'

'When did he tell you that?' she said, surprised.

'This afternoon sometime,' Harry said. 'Why, anything wrong?'

'No, not at all.' She wanted to ask Harry if Vishnu had volunteered the information or if Harry had asked him about her. It would help her know how to go about her apology. Was Vishnu regretful about the incident, as she was, or was he blue vex still? But, of course, there was no tactful way she could put that question to Harry.

Instead, she asked, 'Is Vishnu there now?'

'No, he not working today. And I could have really used a troubleshooter today.'

'Troubleshooter?' Giselle asked. She didn't like Vishnu, of course, but she was still curious about him.

'Yeah, he could turn his hand to nearly anything, nah,' Harry explained. 'Carpentry, electrical, even the plumbing. You always try to get a few men like that on these jobs. Vishnu like that. He mightn't have the piece of paper, but he know a little bit of everything and he don't 'fraid hard work. If you have any little job you want him do, just let me know.'

Giselle smiled cynically at the thought of Vishnu doing any 'little job' for her. He would probably prefer to be roasted slowly over hot coals.

'I'll keep it in mind,' she said. 'You have a number I could reach him at?'

'I think so. Let me check.' The line hummed emptily for a few moments, then Harry came back. He gave her the number and she asked if he knew Vishnu's address. 'Just in case I have to pick him up,' she said. Vishnu had an apartment in Barataria, which is just ten minutes' drive out of Port of Spain. Harry gave her directions, which she wrote down. She thanked him, hung up, and sat looking at the piece of paper in her hand.

She could always phone and apologize. Or she could wait until tomorrow. After a few minutes' reflection, Giselle decided phoning was not an option. It was too easy, the coward's way out. And she had a feeling Vishnu would think so, too. Nor did she want to wait until the next day. For one thing, it would bother her for the entire night that she had not carried through her decision. Giselle had a one-track mind, allied to an impatient nature. Once she decided to do something, she liked to 'do it now'. It was one American characteristic she was entirely in tune with. But she thought, too, that actually going to Vishnu's apartment would show him how sincere she was in her apology. And besides – Giselle grinned a little at the thought – it would catch him entirely off-guard.

Giselle went back to her desk. She would work for about two more hours and then leave. Settling down to it, she got a lot more done than she had expected. She felt curiously energetic and her mind ran smoothly. She supposed it was the result of having made a definite decision.

At five o'clock, she dialled Vishnu's number. She didn't need to look at the slip of paper again – she remembered numbers easily. When he answered, she said pleasantly, 'Hello, could I speak to Mr Selwyn Goodman please?'

'I'm afraid you have a wrong number,' said the voice on the other end.

'Oh, I'm so sorry. Thank you,' she said and hung up.

Well, he was at home then. She got her purse and went down to the car park. As she got in her car and drove towards Barataria, she was thinking that she hadn't realized Vishnu had such a deep voice. There was confidence in it. You heard things when you spoke to people on the phone that you never picked up face to face. Vishnu also had a husky timbre to his voice, like an echo of pain. Giselle remembered his dead mother and winced inside. *Open-mouth-and-insert-foot-Giselle, you bet*, she thought. Until Vera had pointed it out to her, it had not occurred to Giselle that his mother's death might be a trauma for Vishnu. This was partly because he had said it so matter-of-factly. But it was also because she, too, had lost a parent when she was a child. She had long adjusted to the fact and found no difficulty in speaking about her father. But people were different and men, she thought, did not deal with their pain as well as women, except when they got severely injured trying to get some sort of ball away from other men. Then they were proud of it.

When she reached Barataria, Giselle pulled the paper out of her purse. She was not as good with directions as she was with numbers.

She found the correct street without too much difficulty and drove along slowly, looking at the house numbers. The apartment building, when she found it, had obviously been built as cheaply as possible. It was severely rectangular, with a pointed galvanized roof. There were no porches. The downstairs apartments just had white-painted wooden doors set into the front wall. The building was bounded by a low concrete wall. There was no lawn. Three cars were parked in the pitch yard. One was a Mitsubishi Magna. Giselle wondered what kind of person would buy such an expensive car but live in such a cheap apartment. *Probably the kind of man who believes wearing three gold chains and leaving his shirt unbuttoned drives women wild*, she thought.

She got out of her car, opened the iron-framed gate and knocked at the closest door which had a small B set above it. She heard music from inside: the haunting sound of David Rudder's 'Song for a Lonely Soul'. She knocked again. After a few moments, the door rattled and Vishnu appeared. He was bareback, wearing only a pair of black boxer shorts, rubber slippers, and an oven mitt on his right hand. He was also holding a pot spoon. His appearance struck Giselle as faintly ludicrous. It wasn't the oven mitt so much as the pot spoon, which he held in a faintly challenging manner. Giselle smelled the fragrant scent of stew wafting out of the apartment. Vishnu was looking at her expressionlessly, but Giselle had the strong impression he was trying to be expressionless. She waited for him to speak.

'What you doing here?' he said.

With an effort, Giselle controlled her instant flash of irritation. 'I got your address from Harry Chan,' she said evenly. She looked him directly in the eyes. 'I wanted to apologize if I said anything at lunch to offend you,' she said. Her gaze dropped. She saw that his legs were hairy, the calves well-shaped. She looked back up at his face.

'Excuse me for a second,' he said. He turned and went back inside, swinging the door nearly shut and leaving Giselle outside feeling like a fool. Anger rose in her again. She thought she should get in her car and drive away at once. She had given her apology and if he wanted to be *ignorant* – in the Trinidadian sense which meant pig-headed – then that was his choice. But the door opened once again. The spoon was gone and he had put on a dark-grey T-shirt. 'I had to turn the pot,' he said. He stood with his hand on the latch of the door. 'I accept your apology.'

'Thank you,' said Giselle ironically. She couldn't help the little flare of nastiness. Something about this man seemed to rub her wrong. But she instantly regretted her little stab, so she added, 'A friend of mine more or less told me I can be a real snooty bitch. If I am, I can't help it sometimes, but I can be sorry for it.'

'Your friend sounds very direct,' he said.

'Yes. You might like her, I think.'

He nodded, but did not smile. Giselle realized everything she said was sounding slightly wrong. And he was standing at the door like a watchful guard. She could see a little into the apartment. It seemed to be little more than a long corridor. She glimpsed a wooden living-room set with cheap cushions. Further back, she saw a stove and one of those dwarf fridges which always look like the misplaced child of some larger appliance. And something else which, even if she had wanted to linger in hope of being invited inside, made her change her mind.

'Well, I've got to be getting home,' she said.

'All right,' he said.

Giselle went back to her car. The peaceful strains of Rudder's 'Chaguanas Evening' drifted out on the air from behind her. She started her car and, when she glanced back, the white wooden door was already closed. Giselle drove home feeling very bad. It was not that her apology had been so coolly received. She had done what she had to do. But as she drove home she kept remembering what she had seen behind Vishnu: on a small writing table set against the wall between the living room and the kitchen area, several sheets of paper covered with what looked like poetry. The handwriting was small and untidy. And she thought that Vishnu was even stranger, and in a way sadder, than she had first imagined.

Chapter Six

Giselle was hard at work the next morning when Vishnu came into the newsroom. She turned to find him standing behind her, and her breath caught in her throat. She had not realized anyone was near her. He was ill at ease, slowly twisting heavy workman's gloves in his hands as though trying to make them into corkscrews. From the way he was going at it, Giselle thought he might even succeed. He was dressed in blue coveralls with short sleeves. Giselle saw that his hands were well-shaped but marked by many small scars.

'Could see you for a few minutes?' he said. He did not look directly at her, seeming to find the spot just past her left ear more interesting.

Giselle glanced back at her computer. She hated to pause in the middle of a task. Then she looked back at Vishnu, seeing how uneasy he appeared, and she was very aware of glances from people on the other side of the room.

'Give me a second,' she said. She saved her file and ordered up screen-saver #2. Big black letters floated across the screen: WARNING – THIS COMPUTER IS PROTECTED BY A SELECTIVE FORCE-FIELD. ONLY MORONS WILL BE ABLE TO TOUCH IT SAFELY.

Giselle saw the slight twitch of Vishnu's lips as she got up and went into the corridor. He followed her. She stood waiting, not saying anything.

'Listen,' he said, then stopped. Then, in a rush: 'I'm sorry for the way I behave when you pass by yesterday. I wasn't expecting you. But I really did appreciate all the trouble you took, coming out to apologize. It was really nice of you and then I just behave like . . . like the kind of person who'd be able to touch your computer safely. I didn't even invite you in. But I was cooking and the place was a mess . . .' He trailed off. Sticking his gloves in his pocket, Vishnu ran agitated fingers through his hair. Some loose black strands curved like small scimitars on his forehead. 'The truth is, I was also vex because my idea about you was wrong and I hate being wrong. I even thought you must be lying. Anyway, I am sorry,' he said.

Giselle felt somewhat overwhelmed by these sudden confessions. 'It's okay,' she said.

'No, it is not okay,' said Vishnu. He looked at her full in the face again. His dark eyes were intense. 'We seem to have got off on the wrong foot from the start and I don't know why that should be. And I want us to get along.'

He was standing close to her. There was something overpowering in his presence to Giselle. She could handle the cold, arrogant egotist. But now he was unsure, intense, almost pleading. There was something strangely appealing about him. Giselle found this quite irritating.

'Why do you want us to get along?' she said.

'Because you're smart and I like your mouth and I like that you only wear silver jewellery and I like the way you tilt your head when you're thinking . . . hell, does it matter why?' The tension in him as he stood over her was like a drawn bow. It flowed like electricity into Giselle's veins so she felt strangely powerful, even as his closeness seemed to threaten her.

Robert came by and, seeing them, paused. He had been walking in his usual quick fashion and Giselle had a curious illusion as he stopped that he had run into himself.

'Everything all right, Giselle?' he asked. His voice was measured, with a hard confident tone. His glance slid sideways on to Vishnu. Vishnu looked back at him neutrally.

'Yes,' Giselle said. She gestured to Vishnu. 'This is Vishnu. He saved me from that bucket the other day. Vishnu, Robert Cardinez. Robert is the managing editor.'

'Ah,' said Robert. 'I must thank you. We don't know what we would do without Giselle.' He took Vishnu's hand in a strong clasp, at the same time clapping him on the shoulder. Vishnu gave Robert's hand a token shake, like a man holding a dead fish, then dropped it. Giselle got irritated with Vishnu all over again, seeing his reserve. Robert was taller than him, more dynamic.

Robert looked at Giselle. His expression was bright, alert. 'We still on for lunch?'

'Sure,' she said.

'Okay. We'll leave at 11.45. I want to avoid the traffic out of town and get a good seat at the restaurant, too.' He looked back at Vishnu pleasantly. Giselle saw his gaze take in Vishnu's ponytail, like a botanist examining an interesting floral specimen. 'Nice meeting you,' he said.

Vishnu nodded. 'Right,' he said. Giselle wanted to kick him. Robert walked off energetically.

Giselle said, 'Why are you like that?'

'Like what?' he said. His eyes rested on her with curious gentleness. A change had come over him.

'So rude,' she said.

'Was I rude?' His tone was very gentle.

'Yes. You didn't even seem to want to shake Robert's hand.'

'Oh,' he said. There was a little laugh in his voice. Giselle suddenly realized that Vishnu was entirely indifferent to the Robert Cardinezes of this world. Robert was indifferent to the Vishnus of the world, too. But at least Robert felt impelled to seem to recognize them. But a doubt bloomed in Giselle's mind: why should Robert feel so impelled? Vishnu was not. Vishnu would not even return the standard pleased-to-meet-you, because he was not. But it was so rude!

'He has nice ties,' Vishnu said. There was the faintest thread of mockery in his voice. Robert had been wearing a rainbow-coloured tie with a green background. It went well with his cobalt-blue shirt and dark, moss-green trousers.

'I like them,' said Giselle, almost defiantly.

Vishnu leaned one shoulder against the wall and folded his arms. His feet were crossed at the ankles. There was a slack, relaxed humour in his posture. Giselle thought he changed moods like a chameleon, but all his moods were true to him. He did not force the one image as most people, including herself, did.

'So,' he said. 'Can we agree not to get vexed with each other? It is really too upsetting.'

Watching his slack-humoured posture, and his subtly smiling face, a zany gaiety suddenly arose in Giselle. She would match this man! she thought. She felt suddenly drunk with laughter. 'Well, we can agree to try,' she said, smiling dazzlingly. Vishnu grinned back and his grin was full of mischief and humour and cheer. But behind this silent laughter there was also a keen intent in his eyes, so Giselle

73

cleared her throat and said, 'I should be getting back to work.' But laughter still bubbled silently inside her.

He straightened up. 'Of course,' he said. He still smiled and his eyes were knowing.

'Well, I guess I'll see you,' Giselle said.

'I guess you will,' he said.

She went back into the office and when she saw her own message on the computer screen, that gaiety rose anew in her, like heady wine. Giselle found she was no longer in the mood to work. She felt too energetic. She wanted to go to the beach, or sing, or eat ice cream, or dance to music, or laugh out loud.

Ahh, but I can't do any of those things, she thought. Then she said to herself, *Why not?* And that little mocking voice, which Giselle thought everyone had in them, answered, *Because you're a GOOD girl*.

Still, she wasn't able to concentrate. So she took her purse and went out to a place she knew would be quiet at that hour of the morning and where they served very good ice cream. And she sat eating ice cream and reading a little bit of *The Midges of Bradison County*, not laughing out loud, but certainly chuckling audibly at least twice:

Bob James Wailer worked for himself. That was how he liked it. He didn't have to wake up early if he didn't want to, and that meant he could stay up late at night watching pornographic movies. Like many short, fat, balding men, Wailer was very sexual. He masturbated regularly, and had a neatly clipped moustache of aggressive blackness.

As a young man, he had worked for ten years for the Bradison County Health Department, in their Insect Vector Section. It was here that he received his training in spraying. But when budget cutbacks led to him being retrenched, he decided to quit first – taking a Voluntary Termination Package – and open his own business. He had never regretted this bold decision. In his heart, Wailer realized then what he had always known in his secret soul – that he was a man born to live on the edge.

The county hired him on a contract basis. Wailer supplied his own tanks and pesticides. He hired two assistants when he needed them. He didn't believe in paying people a regular salary, because he felt it encouraged dependence. He voted Republican and he mixed his own chemicals, which was both cheaper and more effective than the pesticide purchased by the county. At first, small children had a tendency to vomit after he sprayed their homes, but Wailer knew he had increased their tolerance for the pollution-filled world they must eventually face.

It was this which set Wailer apart from other exterminators: he understood, as few men do, the deeper meaning of his job. 'Even though the world ignores me, I bring an unknown but essential comfort to the lives of men and women,' he once wrote. 'They think they can do without me. They cannot.'

In understanding this, Bob James Wailer showed he was not just an exterminator: he was an artist. And as he pulled up in front of the small farmhouse to ask directions that May morning in 1970, Florence Nightingale saw this spirit in him at once, though she didn't know she saw it when she first saw him.

She was throwing corn to the chickens when the old but well-kept green van stopped by her gate. She saw the short man in brown leather boots, jeans and a plaid shirt step down from the cab. He closed the door and leaned against the fender with folded arms, waiting for her to come to him. He wore black shades and, written in large letters on his van door were the words 'The Exterminator'.

Florence Nightingale felt a curious flutter in her breast [she does not say which one – R.K.] as she approached this strange man. He wore a white Stetson and she did not know he was bald. Her husband and children were away on an out-of-state trip.

Perhaps, even in that first glance, Florence suspected fate had intended her to meet Bob James Wailer. She was then forty-six; but she had been Jamaican since birth. Wailer looked at her walking towards him, feeling a shyness which at first surprised, then uneased him. He had never been alone with a black woman, never even been so close to one. But not a trace of this showed on his face. He was that kind of man.

'Howdy, ma'am,' he said. He did not take off his hat.

'How do, mon?' Florence said.

He heard the strange vibrations of her husky voice, seeming to vibrate with the very tom-toms of Africa, the blood of the first earth, as he thought of it. He had the soul of a poet, and sometimes wished he didn't. He saw too quickly into people, especially the unusual ones, plucked the strings to the music of their souls like a master violinist.

But no trace of this showed in his face.

'I'm doing pretty well, ma'am,' he said, as if he were an ordinary person. Some impulse in him made him want her to think he spoke to women like her every day. 'Looking for a place called Whitman's Pond,' he said, instead of telling her he was looking into her heart. 'Hear y'all got a pretty bad outbreak of midges round here.'

Giselle did laugh out loud when she saw how the title was linked to the plot. And she was pleasantly surprised to find a Caribbean character in the story.

She finished her last scoop of ice cream and, still happy but calmer, she went back to the office humming some tune she didn't know the words to.

◆

Before she met Robert to go for lunch, Giselle went to the ladies' room. She had put on only her usual eyeliner and lipstick that morning. Now she washed off her make-up and renewed it. But she put on the only non-black eyeliner she possessed – a deep blue pencil. She had also brought her eyeshadow kit. She took great care over this – copper shaded into subtle bronze highlighted into the lightest gold. When she finished, she studied the final result in the mirror and said to herself, 'Eat your heart out, Monet.' Her lipstick was a very discreet russet which you had to look at twice to be sure her lips were truly painted. She thought Robert would be pleased.

She had taken some care with her outfit. Although she considered herself perfectly within her rights to go to lunch with him, she knew there were certain people who would immediately be convinced that she and Robert were having an affair. (Although, even if they were, Giselle did not see that that would be anybody's business, either.) So she had dressed conservatively. She wore a straight black skirt which reached just to the knees and a white silk shirt with buccaneer sleeves. She had on pumps with low heels. It was the kind of outfit which made a statement without getting worked up about it. Giselle wore no jewellery except her *bera*, three bangles, and small silver studs in her ears.

Robert met her at his parking space in the yard. He drove a metallic-blue Honda Accord. 'You look very nice,' he said, as he opened the door for her.

'Thank you,' she answered. She sat down and crossed her legs as he went around to the driver's side.

Within a few minutes, they were on Wrightson Road heading out of the city. The day was bright and hot, but Robert had turned on the air-conditioning and it was wonderfully cool inside the car. He had donned shades for the glare; Giselle decided they gave him a finished look.

Robert told her that the computer equipment had arrived in the country on schedule and he had made all the necessary arrangements. But they stopped speaking when the midday news came on the radio so he could listen. The first item was about the CMC newspaper.

'I knew they would lead with this,' Robert said.

'This is Brenda Gold,' said the radio presenter. 'Government is once again criticizing the media for biased reporting. The target is *The National Press* newspaper, recently formed after senior editors resigned from *The Colony News* and sales of that paper slumped. In a press conference this morning, the Information Minister, the Honourable Peter Luke Flood, said that in the few months it had been functioning *The National Press* had deliberately published mostly colour photos of Prime Minister Dholak with glasses of amber-coloured liquid in his hands. "It is a well-known fact that the Prime Minister drinks mostly white rum, vodka or gin," said Minister Flood. "For a newspaper to publish only photos of the rare occasions where he might be drinking a screwdriver or scotch-and-soda reflects a clear intention on the part of this newspaper to convey inaccurate reports where the Prime Minister is involved. In fact, the government's information is that the newspaper is trying to subtly suggest to the public that, like the former Prime Minister of India, Mr Desai, Prime Minister Dholak drinks his own urine for health reasons. The government wants to say that such an implication is entirely without foundation. The Prime Minister is in excellent health and has no need to drink urine. It is clear to us that *The National Press*'s policy is not only biased but also racist."'

'We carrying that story tomorrow?' asked Giselle.

'Of course,' answered Robert. 'It will probably be the lead.'

'*Does* Dholak drink his own urine for health reasons?'

'We have no idea, but there's certainly a lot of people who will think so now. In any case, Flood is wrong. I've already had the photo files checked. Out of thirty-three pictures, only seven show Dholak holding amber-coloured liquid. In all the rest, the glasses are filled with clear liquid.'

'So what's the CMC going to do about it?'

'Report the news.'

'You all not going to be more careful how you deal with the Prime Minister? I mean, he apparently *very* sensitive.'

'I am not going to let any paranoid politician dictate what photographs we should or should not print. Freedom of the press is one principle you can't compromise.'

'And here I always thought all principles, by definition, couldn't be compromised,' Giselle said mildly.

Robert laughed and continued speaking. Watching his intent face, and listening to his comments as he gave an opinion or filled her in on the background of some of the items, Giselle felt strangely domestic. One of her few memories of her father was him watching the news on the television at seven o'clock and conversing with her mother. She could remember her father's deep, slow voice and the way he and her mother had seemed so used to each other. Sitting together in the living-room in the house where Giselle's mother still lived had been a nightly ritual. Now, sitting in the car with Robert gave Giselle a sense of such habits. And Robert had been a husband once. She wondered if he had worn shades back then.

By the time the news was finished, they were at the restaurant. It was a dimly lit place, not very spacious, with a quiet atmosphere. Everyone lunching there looked affluent and spoke softly as though they were saying important things. Some of them nodded to Robert as he walked in. The waiter, quite pretty in his matador trousers and ruffled shirt, came to take their orders for drinks as soon as they were seated. He was terribly pleased to see Mr Cardinez again, and introduced himself to Giselle as though she should appreciate the privilege. Robert ordered the usual, which turned out to be a scotch-and-soda. Giselle, perhaps influenced by the waiter, had a fruit punch.

'They specialize in seafood here,' Robert told her. 'The shrimp is very good.'

She went along with his recommendation. When the waiter came back, anxious to know what they had chosen, they ordered two shrimp dishes. Giselle had pepper shrimp while Robert had shrimp in tomato sauce. Each dish came with saffron rice and green salad.

Robert did most of the talking. He already knew a lot of details about her from her personal file. But Giselle was surprised that he remembered so many of them. He asked how she had liked studying in Miami, about her career and what she hoped to accomplish with the company she had opened. He asked which she preferred of the many islands she had worked in. He, too, had worked all over the Caribbean and was even more familiar with the islands than she. He talked about the politics in Guyana, the economy in Jamaica, and the military situation in Haiti. He told her he wanted to establish a series of Caribbean reports on Cuba. Giselle was fascinated by Robert's energy. He was well-informed, ambitious, concerned with social issues, and he seemed to believe he made a difference. This in particular set him apart from the other men Giselle knew.

'You never thought of getting involved in politics?' Giselle asked him. She was thinking how articulate he was.

'I *am* involved in politics,' he answered. 'My job in the media is to serve as watchdog over the politicians and try as far as possible to ensure they don't abuse their power. Thomas Jefferson once said that, if he had a choice between government without newspaper or newspaper without government, he would choose the latter. Politicians come and go, but the function of the journalist remains constant.'

'You weren't worried about your reputation, coming in to head the CMC where other journalists had resigned?'

'No. It was an entirely new venture. And people respect me.'

'Did you start off wanting to be a writer? Seems to me a lot of journalists begin like that.'

He shook his head. 'Actually, I started off as an office boy in the *Jamaica Gleaner*. It was a choice between that and a clerical post in the civil service. But I wanted to be a journalist. My father was *not* pleased. He said there was more job security in the service, and a pension plan.' Robert laughed. 'He was right, of course. But I worked my way up and now I make a lot more money in a far more interesting profession.'

'I think that's very admirable,' Giselle said.

'Good,' he said, giving her a glance so searching that Giselle felt he had taken, not only her dress measurements, but her shoe size as well.

Giselle realized he had misunderstood her: she had meant she admired the way he had worked his way up; but she got the impression he thought she meant something else. They moved on to other topics. When he found out she played tennis, his face lit up.

'I play twice, three times a week, if I can,' he said. 'We must play a game one evening.'

'I'm not very good,' she demurred.

'No matter,' he said. 'We'll play doubles, if you want. Where do you play?'

'On the public courts,' she said.

'Oh, those courts are beat up. I play at the Park Club, usually,' he said. This was the most exclusive club on the island. 'We will arrange a date.'

'All right,' she smiled.

They finished lunch. He drank another scotch-and-soda, and ordered a cup of coffee without cream. Giselle had another fruit punch, though she found it rather thick and sweet. The waiter drifted away, simpering.

'How was your food?' he asked.

'Good,' she answered. 'But the pepper shrimp should have been hotter.'

'Well, they don't cater for Indian mouths here,' he said.

'Oh?' said Giselle vaguely, finding his comment a little offensive. But she said nothing further, reminding herself that, unlike Vishnu, she had breeding.

As they continued speaking about various things, Robert asked her, very casually, if she was seeing anyone. Giselle told him no. There was a queer feeling in her stomach which she first thought nervously might be the shrimps acting up, but then realized was excitement at this definite hint that Robert was interested. She asked him why he had got divorced. He shrugged and said irreconcilable differences. He had been married for five years. There were no children.

The bill came, brought on a salver by the gorgeous waiter who invested the ritual with the solemnity of some holy rite. 'I'm sorry, Mr Cardinez, but we have no cream. Will you take your coffee without milk instead?'

Giselle looked at the waiter intently, but Robert just said, 'That will be fine.' The waiter, in hushed tones appropriate to the occasion, expressed the fervent hope that they had enjoyed their meal. Robert said yes it was fine and Giselle, though she thought of telling the waiter that she bet he said that to all the customers, merely smiled prettily. The waiter smiled back, and she had to admit his smile was prettier than hers. Robert paid the bill, leaving a tip whose size Giselle suspected had more to do with impressing her than the quality of service, and they went out to the car. The glare of the sun hurt Giselle's eyes after the dimness of the restaurant. Robert had put on his shades.

As they drove back into Port of Spain, it occurred to Giselle that lunch today had been very different from yesterday's: calm, classy, and with neither person stalking off with food at the end.

'Do you know the waiter's name?' she asked Robert.

'No,' he answered.

'I bet it's Leroy,' she said contentedly.

Robert gave her a puzzled smile.

Back at CMC, when she got out of the car and stood waiting for Robert, she saw Vishnu under the shadow of the construction shed planing a plank, the curls of shaved wood falling at his feet. He was bent over, concentrating on his task, but one of the men said something to him and he looked up. Giselle waved to him. He stood still for a moment, then bowed as though he was Romeo and wearing hose. Giselle's gesture felt suddenly false to her. She turned and walked up the stairs with Robert. He was saying something about the elevators, but she barely attended to him. At the ladies' room she stopped, not wanting to walk into the office with him. Returning together from lunch would seem too intimate, she thought.

'I just have to powder my nose, so I can put it to the grindstone,' she said.

He laughed. 'Thanks for going to lunch with me. I enjoyed it.'

'Me too,' she said.

'Perhaps we can play some tennis soon,' he said, his eyes intent on her.

'Give me a call,' she said. 'Doris has my number.'

He nodded. 'I'll do that.'

He smiled and walked off. Giselle went into the restroom. There, she washed off all her make-up. After two days of paint, she intended to wear no make-up at all for the next few days. She imagined her skin needed to breathe.

When Giselle went back into the newsroom, she found a slightly soggy white cardboard box on a folded newspaper on her desk. She opened it to see the yellowed shell of curry crab and half-congealed dumplings lying in a thin, oily sauce.

'Headers brought that for you.'

Giselle turned to find Gemma, the cleaning woman, behind her. She was regarding Giselle with small, sharp eyes. Her hands were propped on her ample waist.

Giselle said, 'Oh dear, I completely forgot.'

'Yes, I see you went out with Mr Cardinez. But I tell Headers I will leave it for you, you could heat it up in the microwave.'

Giselle did not miss the sarcasm in this comment. 'I will heat it up in my iron pot when I go home, Gemma,' she said.

Gemma said something that sounded like 'Hmph' and moved off. She had a scarf tied around her head, coming to two points at the front. She was from Dominica. It was an even smaller island than Trinidad.

Sharma came over and sat in a chair beside Giselle. 'So I hear you went out to lunch with Cardy,' she said.

'I feel that might be the headline in the newspapers tomorrow,' Giselle said, a little exasperated.

Sharma grinned. 'Aiy, I must be interested. I think you and Cardy would make a good match.'

'We just had lunch, Sharma.'

Sharma shrugged. 'Aiy, a little lunch leads to a little dinner, a little dinner leads to breakfast, breakfast leads to dessert . . .'

Giselle laughed. 'He'll have to wait a long time for *that*.'

Sharma said, 'Well, I'll tell you. Cardy might be ready to get serious now. If you play your cards right, who knows? You get my *double entendre?*'

'Yes, I get your *double entendre*,' Giselle said.

'And you need a man, Karan.'

'Oh, I do, do I?' she said, grinning back despite herself.

'Yes. All this work and no play is not good. Women are not like fruit, you know. They do *not* ripen until somebody plucks them – if you get my *double entendre*.'

'Sharma! You are too bad!'

'Yes, but I am married. And the good thing about being married is that you can be as *baaad* as you want inside it. A marvellous institution, if you know how to use it.'

Giselle flapped her hand, laughing. 'Go, go.'

Sharma got up. 'Just think about my foolish advice, darling.'

Giselle turned to her computer, shaking her head. Sharma was sounding just like Giselle's mother. Which reminded Giselle that she should phone her mother. She had not seen her for some weeks, having been so busy at CMC, and she had called her only intermittently. Giselle decided she would go down and spend the weekend at home. After the stress of the past week, she could use the comfort of being among her family where you didn't have to wrestle with questions of feelings because you already knew what all your feelings were.

Falling in love should be like that, thought Giselle, but it was just a random thought, and it flew from her mind as quickly as a bird which flashes by the opened eye of a window.

Chapter Seven

The next day all the programmers had a short meeting with Robert and two other managers for a progress report. Afterwards, as everyone was filing out, he came to Giselle's side and said casually, 'I'll be playing at the Club this evening with some people. If you want, we can make it a foursome.'

She nodded. 'All right.'

He smiled. 'Just like that?'

'If you take long to make up your mind, it means you have an unmade mind.'

'Ah. Sounds like something your mother taught you.'

'No, I just thought of it. It probably doesn't make sense, but I like sounding clever.'

Robert laughed. Giselle noticed that his teeth were small and seemed pointed.

'But you still decided quickly,' he said as they walked back to the computer room.

'Well, I was thinking about taking in a game this evening, anyway.'

'Oh.' They came to the door. 'Would you like me to pick you up?'

'No, I'll meet you there.'

'Sevenish, then.'

'Fine.'

Giselle ended up finishing work a little later than she expected. Even so, she reached home in enough time to bath and change, but a little too early to go to the Club, which was only five minutes' drive away. Giselle liked being right on time. In fact, it was a bit of a fetish with her. So she started 'The Midges of Bradison County' again, picking up the story where Wailer and Florence had just met, and thinking that she didn't even have time to read properly these days:

> Florence looked at him. She liked the way he called her ma'am. There was a politeness about him, almost an abasement, which

was like a caress. She felt a strange, liquid, flowing feeling within her: and was glad that her husband, Jimmy, was away for three days with the kids.

'Yes, mon,' she said. 'Dey been gi'in me 'ell for days now, don't mind de wire netting. You come to get rid of dem or what?'

Wailer inclined his head slightly towards his old but well-kept truck. 'That's my job, ma'am,' he said. He took out a matchstick and inserted it between his lips, looking at her from behind his dark shades. 'Own my own business, keep the county pest-free.'

She was impressed. 'Lan' sakes, mon, you must be does go all over de place!'

In an easy, well-practised gesture, Wailer hitched up his jeans. 'I get about,' he said easily. But beneath his ease he noted how quickly she identified the great adventure of his profession. *She is an unusual woman*, he thought. But not a trace of this showed in his face.

'I does only get as far as de grocery,' she said, and there was a silence, like a small tragedy, between them both for a few moments in eternal time.

'You don't sound like you're from these here parts,' Wailer said. He didn't normally talk much. But he realized he was feeling quite easy with this woman. Perhaps it was because she was black. The normal social standards didn't apply. Thus easily had he moved into a different world with her. 'I felt with you a timeless eternity,' he wrote later.

Florence gazed at Wailer with bright eyes. As a farm wife with farming neighbours, she wasn't used to being around people whose minds worked as fast as his.

She said, 'No, I from Jamaica in the Caribbean originally. Been in America 'bout fifteen years now.'

He nodded, understanding. 'Well, welcome to the Promised Land.'

Florence laughed. He had humour, and he was a poet, too. Jimmy never said things like that.

'So you lookin' for Whitman's Pond?' she said.

'Yes'm. Is it close by heah?'

'Just dong de road. I go show you, if you want.'

Wailer smiled for the first time, then. Shyly, but pleased.

Florence didn't ever know why she had made the offer, though she did want to get out of the house. Feeding the chickens grew boring after a while, though Jimmy would have been shocked if she had even hinted this.

'I'd sure appreciate that, ma'am,' said Wailer.

She could tell by his tone, and his expression, that he meant it. He was sincere, and he clearly didn't even consider the chickens. And he seemed like a man who, for all his travels, could get easily lost. Something about him aroused her maternal instincts.

So she got into the van, leaving the chickens complaining in clucks, and he started the engine and drove off, working the clutch and gas easily. The engine revved loudly, but smoothly.

'Your van working good,' she said.

'She's old, but I keep her in good shape,' he said. 'I think it's a good philosophy in life.'

Florence nodded. She was already glad she had come with him, as on an adventure. And it was good to hear someone use a word like 'philosophy'. This man spoke in a gentlemanly way. Jimmy used a lot of obscenities, especially when he and she were making love. Florence sometimes wondered how a born-and-bred American like Jimmy could be so much like a Jamaican man.

They had met when she was working as a go-go dancer in Los Angeles to put herself through night school; he had come on a two-day visit to the city that he had won in a raffle, including accommodation and spending money. They had had a drink after she finished her shift, then gone back to his motel room. She had given him a blow job, and he had asked her to marry him.

'What people go say?' she had asked him.

'Aw, the folks in Bradison County are real nice, sugah,' he had told her. 'Besides, I don't know if I can get a girl who'll give me head as well as you.' He had blushed. 'I don't know if I'll get a girl who'll give me head at all.'

She had liked how he blushed – they were naked during this discussion and she noticed that even his bottom turned red – and she was getting tired of shaking her hips in order to study, so she had said yes. And what Jimmy said turned out to be true: the folks in Bradison County *were* real nice. They smiled all the time. In fact, they smiled so much that several times Florence had wanted to wipe the smiles off their round and reddened country faces with a sharp axe. Jimmy would have been shocked had he known her thoughts. They screwed every night of the week and twice on Sundays to praise the Lord, so Jimmy thought Florence must be happy. But, in seven years of marriage, he had never once offered to wash the dishes. And Florence had grown increasingly discontented.

Grinning, Giselle read over this section before she closed the magazine and put it into her tennis bag. Richard Kinky, whatever his real name was, had clearly been unimpressed by Waller's idea of romance. Giselle still liked *Bridges*, although she was also enjoying this satire of it.

That's rather contradictory, she thought as she drove down to the Park Club, *I should think I'd be irritated by one or the other*.

When she arrived at the club, she found Robert on the far court. He was playing against a man and a woman. She walked across, her carry-bag and tennis racquet in its case slung over her shoulder. Robert turned as she pushed open the fence gate and came to meet her.

'You made it,' he said. His face was clear and animated. He was breathing quickly and there was a trickle of sweat down the side of his temple.

'Yes, I did,' said Giselle. 'I guess that takes care of all the obvious statements.'

'Yes,' he said, but he wasn't really listening, being far too busy drinking in her appearance. Giselle, as an attractive young woman, understood and even sympathized. She was wearing grey, mid-thigh-length shorts and a blue, loose-fitting T-shirt with a black stretchy top beneath it. Her legs were smooth and brown and strong. Her unruly hair was tied back and she also wore a headband. Robert, obviously not belonging to the modern or André Agassi school of thought, was more properly dressed in tennis whites – the pocketed shorts and collared T-shirt. His T-shirt was tucked neatly into the shorts. His legs were slim and smooth.

However, judging from the glint of approval in his eyes as he summed her up, Giselle could assume that Robert had no set prejudices in the matter of tennis wear. A wayward thought crossed her mind: *We make a nice couple*.

He took her lightly by the arm and they went to the net where she was introduced to the other two people. They were a married couple, both in their early forties. The man, whose name was Mark Armstrong, had faded blue eyes and pleasant, weather-beaten features. In fact, he looked a bit like the skipper from *Gilligan's Isle*. His wife, Sharon, although attractive, looked like the kind of person who always suspects she has left the stove on and wants to go back and check. The high cheekbones and aquiline nose of her high-caste Indian ancestry added to, rather than relieved, her worried expression. But her smile was friendly.

Robert said to Giselle, 'We'll knock up and when you're warm we'll start a match.'

'All right,' Giselle answered.

They returned to the baseline. She flexed her legs a few times and Mark knocked the green tennis ball to her. She returned it with a smooth forehand. Out of the corner of her eye, she saw Robert watching her to estimate if she was competent at the game.

After they had knocked up for ten minutes, Giselle was ready. She was breathing lightly, and her legs felt springy and strong.

It was a lively match, all four of them being fairly good players. But Giselle was not as stretched as she could have been since Robert ran down everything in his typically energetic fashion. He even intercepted some balls which were rightfully hers. Giselle was mildly irritated by this, but held her peace. She was, after all, his guest. And, from the way he played, she could see Robert didn't like to lose, even in a friendly match. He was a good player, not very quick, but with fine anticipation and timing. He also had a powerful serve.

They played only two sets. Giselle and Robert won both, 6-4 and 6-2. Giselle would have liked to go on - she never felt really satisfied unless she played a full three sets, and she had not really had a chance to extend herself even in those two. But the others had had enough. They went to the bar for drinks. Robert's T-shirt was now sodden, pale brown flesh showing through the clinging cloth. Giselle noted that his stomach, though reasonably flat, was soft. She was surprised - he looked so trim in his working clothes. Robert and Mark had beers. Giselle settled for cold water, while Sharon had a shandy.

They commended Giselle on her game and the conversation centred around tennis for a while. Giselle didn't say much at first, but she and

Sharon eventually started their own conversation while the men talked. Sharon, who, it turned out was a nutritionist with the Health Ministry, was even more conscious of fitness than Giselle. Besides tennis, she also took aerobics classes, ran and hiked. *So much for exercise being relaxing*, Giselle thought. Mark was Sharon's second husband, she told Giselle. She had two children from her first marriage, both in their early twenties. The children lived with her ex-husband and his wife. She and Mark had no children.

'I don't think, at my age, it would be wise to have another child,' she told Giselle. 'Mark wants us to try, though. He has no kids.'

'But you seem to be in very good health. If your doctor says it's okay . . .'

'No. Having a baby can be really traumatic on the body. After my first husband and I split up, I went on an intense workout and diet course. It was very therapeutic. I used to be fat. I don't think I could let myself slip back now. And Mark isn't the one who has to carry the child for nine months.' This speech was delivered as though Sharon had it written down on a card and memorized. She leaned forward confidentially. 'Even now, I have a bit of a gut on my lower stomach.'

'You kidding,' said Giselle.

Sharon shook her head. 'I'll get rid of it soon. I've begun a new abdominal regimen.'

'Good for you.'

'But having a child would just make it impossible to get back my abdominals, wouldn't it?'

'I suppose so,' Giselle agreed. 'Unless you hired a surrogate.'

'Oh, I couldn't do that,' said Sharon.

'Why not?'

'Mark is Catholic.'

'But aren't both of you divorced?'

'We don't agree with the Church's position on divorce.'

'I see.'

'You think using a surrogate is all right?'

'No. I don't think any woman should become pregnant unless she's had sex.'

'Because it's the natural way?'

'No, because nine months of misery should at least begin with some pleasure.'

'Oh,' said Sharon, clearly not getting Giselle's humour.

Giselle glanced at Mark. He seemed a very fatherly sort of man. She felt sorry that he had no children. Robert and he were discussing something about cars. Giselle always found it peculiar that couples could sit at the same table and the men would not hear what the women were talking about, as though there was a glass wall between them. Even though Sharon had been speaking in a low voice, Giselle knew that, had the position been reversed, Sharon – in the midst of her own conversation – would still have followed Mark's every word on a topic like that.

'Can I get you anything?' Robert was going to the bar.

'Club soda,' she said, after a moment's hesitation. She preferred to drink nothing but cold water after tennis, but she thought she should be social. As a chaser, club soda was about the only non-alcoholic social drink there was. As an inveterate orange juice drinker, Giselle knew that people resented the implication that you were trying to be healthy. Giselle thought this had something to do with the idea that a person who drank orange juice would outlive those who didn't.

Music was piping through the PA system. Giselle heard the first strains of a calypso by The Mightier Pen, one of the funniest – and certainly the most literate – calypsonians around. The calypso, which Pen had sung only last year in the tent, was called 'Ball Games' and Giselle supposed there was a DJ playing for the Club. She listened, tapping her foot to the laid-back soca rhythm:

> The other night I went to play tennis with my wife
> At that romantic time when twilight falls,
> Only to find when I reach the courts
> That I had lost my balls, Ah wanna fall.
>
> My wife steups at me in frustration
> Because she had been so looking forward to the game;
> She say, 'Man, without balls
> It just eh the same.'

Giselle smiled at Mark, who was watching her listening to the song. He grinned back and, to her surprise, sang along with the chorus in a pleasant tenor:

It have very few ball games
You could play without balls;
Some you play in field, some in court,
And some you play anywhere at all.
Ever since I small, I like playing with balls,
And now I older with ah older mind and all
I like ball games even more than before,
But I does keep forgetting my balls behind,
    Ah wanna fall.

Giselle laughed with Mark.

'You a calypso fan?' asked Sharon.

'Well, only of the better ones,' said Giselle. 'I like good lyrics or a good beat or both.'

The song continued and they all listened, all smiling:

Well, I look all over for mih balls
But I couldn' find dem anywhere at all;
I look in the tennis bag, car, I even look in my pocket
Though I know for sure dey wasn' there,
    Ah wanna fall.

My wife start to tap she foot,
I get so nervous, Ah wanna fall;
She say, 'Man, if you cah find dem
I will have to play with somebody who have balls.'

When the chorus came, all three of them sang along.

'Pen is a partner of mine,' Mark said. 'He told me he got the idea for this calypso from me, 'cause I'm always talking about tennis, and *The Onion Eaters*.'

'I read that book,' said Giselle. 'His calypso is a lot better.' The song continued.

I tell she, 'Doux-doux, I doh have balls
But I have ah good racquet;
Why we doh just go on the court
And both ah we could fake it.'

She say, 'Nah, I like it real,
Faking is just too dread.'
Then, like a woman, she smile at me
And say, 'Oh, leh we just go and eat instead.'

So we went out to eat a good meal
And my wife was well fed,
And when we reach back home we found the balls
Where I left them on the bed.

Well, my wife still wanted to play,
You know woman, Ah didn' want to fall;
So she put up she hoop and I get my racquet
And we play a nice game of basketball.

They all burst out laughing spontaneously as the calypso ended with the chorus. Robert returned with the drinks.

'What's the joke?' he asked.

'You had to be there,' said Giselle.

'All right,' he said, putting the drinks down.

Mark's twinkling eyes remained on Giselle. They were the colour of a washed-out sky.

'This is quite a girl, Robert,' he said.

'Yes,' said Robert, sipping at his scotch-and-soda.

Mark said to Giselle, 'You don't drink?'

'An occasional glass of wine,' Giselle answered after a pause.

'I read an article the other day which said that two or three glasses of wine a day reduces the risk of heart disease,' he said, looking pleased at this scientific confirmation of what drinkers through the ages have always wanted to believe.

'Women generally have much less heart disease than men,' Giselle said. 'Maybe wine reduces men's testosterone levels so there's less strain on their hearts.'

Mark laughed. 'So what are you saying? Our choice is either to have a sex drive and heart attacks, or reduce our sex drive and live longer?'

'No,' said Giselle. 'Don't drink, don't smoke, and exercise regularly.' She grinned. 'Then you can have a long life *and* enjoy it thoroughly.'

Mark draped an arm across Sharon's shoulder. 'See, darling? I knew there was a good reason why I run about that court killing myself.'

Sharon laughed, a little embarrassedly. The ease of a few minutes before had vanished, and she seemed to be thinking that she had left the refrigerator open.

'A little alcohol is good for the system,' she told Giselle, as if reassuring her.

Robert sat down so his body was turned a little towards Giselle. Giselle got that same domestic feeling she had felt in his car. It was very strange, yet sort of comfortable too.

The conversation became general. Afterwards, Giselle could not remember anything they had talked about. But it was very pleasant. She liked being on the terrace of the Park Club, with its sprawling and well-kept grounds which even in the night looked elegant. She liked watching the tennis players out on the courts, hearing their grunts of exertion and the lashing pops of the balls. And, of course, it was nice to be in the company of a sophisticated man who found her attractive. There was a sense of establishment here, though she couldn't decide if that was a matter of tradition or money. One thing she *did* know: she would have liked to spend every weekend like this.

Over the intercom, a pleasant female voice read out the news headlines – the Club's DJ had switched over to radio. There had been three murders that day, unemployment had increased, and the government was trying to establish a statutory body to regulate the media.

'Gee, Robert,' said Giselle. 'Didn't anything *good* happen today?'

'The Housing Minister opened a new housing scheme,' Robert said. 'We have it on page one.'

Mark said, 'I suppose if they set up this statutory body, that kind of thing will be your lead story.'

Robert grimaced. 'They won't succeed. But last year, the Information Minister accused the media of deliberately reporting more crime in order to embarrass the government because fighting crime was one of the main issues in the last election.'

Mark shook his head. 'So you not supposed to report when three people get murdered in one day?'

'Oh, the Minister was very reasonable. We should report it, he said.

But why not put it on page twenty-seven, so the public won't be overwhelmed by all this negativity? Making it front-page news was just sensationalism and irresponsibility.'

'I wouldn't have thought a blowhard like Flood was competent enough to handle the media,' said Giselle. 'All sound and fury him, signifying nothing.'

'Oh, he's just a yes-man. It's embarrassing when he opens his mouth. But it's Attorney-General Singh who's really behind it. After all, he's the one who's supposed to be spearheading the anti-crime drive. When he arranged for the US General Tim Warren to visit the country, he was livid we didn't carry the General's speech in full.'

'I thought you did,' said Giselle.

'Oh, afterwards, because Mr Payne thought we should. But we certainly weren't going to because Mr Singh felt we must.'

'Oh,' said Giselle.

Listening to Robert talk, she realized again how much at the *centre* of things he was. He was aware of the movements in the country in politics and business and in social issues. He rarely called names but, in speaking of things highly placed people had told him, implied that he could. In rumour, gossip and innuendo, Robert Cardinez, like the writers of *The Young and the Restless*, managed to find sense. It was this instinct, Giselle realized, which had carried him to the top in his profession. And his small-talk was imbued with the fascination of listening to a private detective or CIA agent, who knows all sorts of secrets about all sorts of people.

Eventually, the Armstrongs got up. They invited Giselle to come again at the weekend. Giselle said she would try. They took up their bags and racquets and left. Robert walked Giselle back to the shadowed car park.

'Would you like me to follow you home, make sure you reach safely?' he asked.

'No, that's okay. It's right there,' she said. 'But thanks.'

She unlocked her car, opened the door and threw in her bag and racquet. She turned to Robert, smiling.

'Well, thanks for inviting me. I enjoyed the game. I guess I'll see you Monday.'

'I guess so.' His face was hidden in shadow. He seemed about to lean forward so Giselle, an old hand at reading that kind of body language, turned and got into her car. He leaned down, arms resting on the rim of the window. He was smiling.

'Sure you don't want me to follow you?'

'No, it's all right,' Giselle answered definitely.

'Okay.' He leaned in to kiss her, and she presented her cheek. She felt the smile of his lips as he kissed her there.

'I'll call you to make sure you reached home safe,' he said.

'All right.'

She started her car and pulled out. Robert stood watching, white-clothed in the darkness, face and limbs a pale blur. As she drove home, Giselle found the chorus to 'Ball games' playing in her head:

> It have very few ball games
> You could play without balls;
> Some you play in field, some in court,
> And some you play anywhere at all.

Chapter Eight

Saturday morning found Giselle speeding down the Churchill-Roosevelt highway, which connects the southern and northern parts of Trinidad. Built with US money just a few years after Trinidad declared independence, this highway had been named according to the excellent political principle of using one project to pay tribute to two countries from which the government wished to continue borrowing money. Giselle's mother had called the night before to find out if Giselle was coming to visit. Giselle had not planned to – she wanted to get some work done.

'But you haven't been here for weeks,' said her mother.

'I know, Ma,' Giselle said. 'But I have this programming problem I want to get over.'

'You like a dog with a bone when it comes to work, eh?'

'Well, is you train me so,' Giselle answered.

'Just yesterday Tammy was asking for you,' said her mother, trying a different tack. Tammy was Giselle's three-year-old niece.

Giselle sighed. 'You know Ma, I bet Genghis Khan could have taken your correspondence course.'

'So you'll come then?'

'Yeah, I'll be there in an hour.'

Having decided to go, however, Giselle was glad she wasn't in front of her computer. Driving along with Elton John singing how wonderful life is now you're in the world on the tape deck, and the wind whipping her curls around, it occurred to Giselle that her life had quickened, both literally and figuratively, and she needed this break. The wind whooshed by outside the car window and Giselle sang along. Most of her attention was on the music but, underneath, her mind clicked rapidly along its own paths. In fact, her mind never clicked any other way. Giselle knew she lived at an accelerated pace. She sometimes wondered whether this was a bit neurotic, though Vera assured her there was no doubt about it. Giselle studied assiduously, she worked long hours, she read voraciously, went out occasionally, played tennis, ran regularly, and dabbled in myriad other activities, ranging from crochet to pottery, so she wouldn't get in a rut. She was one of those people who always had to be doing something or feel they are missing out on life. Only at home, in Freeport, did she truly relax, even when her mother was pestering her about getting married.

But, for all her frenetic activity, Giselle knew there was a part of her which remained cold and unmoved. *Bet that's how Charles felt whenever Diana wanted sex*, she thought.

The joke was merely her habitual response when she began seeing too deeply into herself. For she knew that this unquickened part of herself had changed two days ago, when she had met Vishnu's eyes and smiled with him.

Giselle was aware now that something hard had loosened inside her at that moment. Some hard crust had broken and within was – what? She was not foolish enough to believe this was love at first sight. But the blood flowed warmly in her veins now, as though someone had laced her circulatory system with brandy when she wasn't looking. A change had undeniably come over her and Vishnu was the key, or the catalyst. But she did not see him as being the desired object of this change. How could he be? *He has a ponytail, for God's sake*, she thought. And her mind switched to Robert Cardinez who, though he had no tennis manners, had many of the qualities she wanted in a man.

Although she had met Robert several months ago, when the CMC contract was first offered to her, Giselle had not noticed him particularly. She thought he was pleasant, forceful, well-dressed. She had dealt with him on a professional basis.

But that, she thought, had to do with timing. With the CMC contract now hers, and a hefty bonus waiting at the end of it, as well as a likely retainer fee for maintenance, the pace of her working life had slowed for the first time in years. And now, like a person taking a break from a long and arduous task, she was sitting up and looking around.

She had reacted to Vishnu, thought Giselle, because she was ready to react. He was an instrument, but not a cause. And then there was Robert. It was always like that: you went along uneventfully, life as smooth as butter, and suddenly all sorts of things started to happen at the same time. No wonder people said it never rained, but it poured. The question she asked herself now was: did she want an umbrella?

She reached the Freeport flyover and turned off the highway. Paul Simon, with easy music and laid back lyrics, was singing that there must be fifty ways to leave your lover. *I've never needed advice in that area*, Giselle thought.

She looked around as if with new eyes at the familiar landscape as she drove. Freeport is a small, strung-out village in central Trinidad. Central Trinidad is mostly flat land and the bulk of the island's sugar-cane crop is grown there. When indentured labour was brought in from India after the abolition of slavery, the central part of the island and certain areas in the south became East Indian settlements. Now, a hundred and fifty years later, the Asian work ethic is evident in the many business places, often with homes above them, strung along the main roads in these districts. Giselle had grown up here. When her father had died, the mortgage on the house was already half paid. Her mother could have sold the land and house for a profit and moved to a smaller place. Giselle's father had inherited the land, an entire acre, from his father.

Instead, Giselle's mother sold a half-acre, keeping four lots, and settled down to the task of raising her four children. Giselle thought the children were the main reason her mother had decided not to ease matters by selling and moving. She had three girls and, although she wanted them married and living their lives of their own, she did not want them to be too dependent on anyone else. 'Women have it hard enough as it is,' Giselle remembered her mother telling her. This had been Giselle's central feminist credo until a few years ago, when her mother said the same thing to Vera, who responded, 'And a good thing, too.' Her mother's cackling delight had instantly laid to rest that truism in her daughter's mind. Anyway, Giselle's mother saved the land to give to her children later and, in case it ever became necessary, as collateral to the bank. (It had, when Giselle's sister, Miranda, had to go to the Mona campus.) But Giselle thought her mother had also kept the house for other, less practical reasons: except for Giselle's brother, she had had all her children here. She and her husband had together planned and supervised the building of the house. Her husband had died while they were living here and, when her time came, she wanted to die here too, in a place of their own. Giselle wondered if this was still true now that her mother had remarried.

Giselle nursed her car carefully along the narrow, uneven pitch road. The road had been laid badly in the first place – it was more winding than a female chutney dancer's waist – and the many patched-up pot-holes and cracks added to the unevenness of the surface.

When she pulled in at her mother's house, which lay at the end of a short track off the road, the three dogs came running out to greet her, barking enthusiastically. Bear, a short-bodied, fluffy Pompek/Collie/Alsatian – as Giselle always described him, a pothound with class – was 'her' dog. She had got him as a pup, but she had had to leave him behind when she moved out. That had been the hardest part. But Bear always remembered her when she visited, no matter how long she had been away, and he was jumping up now, barking madly, as she closed the gate. She was wearing jeans and a T-shirt so she let him plant his paws on her stomach and she leaned down and kissed him. At this he went into paroxysms of delight, leaping away from her and chasing his tail. Giselle grinned to see him. She patted the other two dogs, who were less demonstrative, and went up to the house. The morning light was very clear, the sky a deep shade of blue.

Her mother's husband had come out on the porch to see what the commotion was about. He was a tall, spare man in his late forties. His face was creased and mild-looking.

'Hi, Ronald,' she said, giving him a perfunctory peck on his cheek.

'Hello, Giselle, how are you?' he said.

'Fine.'

'Your mother's inside,' he said, with a little movement of his hand.

'All right.' Giselle went into the house.

Her mother was in the kitchen, cooking. Giselle knew she had probably started as soon as she knew her daughter was coming. An olive-complexioned woman who looked East Indian, the only sign of her mixed heritage was a certain coarseness of the shoulder-length hair – still with only a few white strands even though she was forty-six – and a round fullness of the calves. All her children looked different, too. Anthony, Giselle's brother, looked liked a *dougla* – a person of African and East Indian parentage. Miranda, who had straight hair and slanted eyes, was often taken for Chinese. Tabitha looked as Indian as her mother. Yet people always seemed to see a family resemblance between all of them.

She kissed her mother. 'Hi,' she said.

'Hi, how you going?' her mother answered. She held on to the handle of the iron pot with a pot-holder and stirred the mound of vegetables inside it. 'You hungry?' she asked. It was always the first question. She seemed to think, as mothers do, that Giselle deliberately starved herself when she wasn't at home.

'You know, I was reading this really tragic story about a mother and her daughter in a small town in Cactus Burr, Mississippi,' Giselle said, picking up a small bowl of diced onions from the kitchen table. She propped herself against the table and threw some of the small onion cubes into her mouth.

'Oh?' said her mother, taking the bowl from her.

'Yes. It seems the mother was a five-hundred-pound woman and her daughter a mere three sixty. Anyway, the daughter got a job in a nearby town, Locoweed, and decided to move out and get her own place. Do you know, within one month, she was weighing only three hundred pounds!'

'Really?'

'Really. Needless to say, her mother was appalled. She insisted her daughter – whose name, believe it or not, was Isis – move back home. So the daughter did and within two weeks, she was up to four hundred pounds.' Giselle reached over and took some more onion cubes. 'So you see, the story had a happy ending after all.'

Her mother turned and looked at her.

'You know, I just can't remember raising any mad children. I think you must be inherit your father's genes. He used to always talk the same kind of stupidness.'

'Whoa! A shit-talking gene. That should interest the scientists up at MIT.'

'You hungry or not?' her mother said, returning to the crucial issues of life.

'A little,' Giselle admitted.

'Well, food will be ready just now. I just finishing these vegetables. I have bake chicken in the oven. There's some macaroni pie in the fridge. You could heat it up.'

100

Giselle listened patiently to this military-style list of supplies, then opened the refrigerator and took out a rectangular glass container covered by tinfoil. 'I bet I gain ten pounds this weekend,' she said.

Her mother looked at her critically. 'Well, you looking a little thin, anyway.'

'You only say that 'cause I'm not three hundred and sixty pounds, like Isis.'

'So you staying the weekend?'

'Yes.'

'All right.' Her mother turned back to the stove. Giselle knew she was pleased. She cut off a square of the macaroni pie, put it on a plate, then put the plate in the microwave. She punched up the time, started it, then stole some more onions.

'I don't know how you could eat raw onions, you know.'

'I like them,' said Giselle. 'I think they purify my blood. And, you know, a corrupt person like me needs all the help she can get.'

Her mother sighed. 'I hope you don't talk like this in work.'

'Oh, no,' Giselle assured her. 'Everyone there thinks I'm quite normal. Though when I wore that black mini-dress with fishnet stockings the other day, the boss did speak to me. But I told him I charged extra for those services.'

'Why you so happy today?' her mother said, then looked at her sharply. 'You didn't really wear a mini to work, did you?'

Giselle laughed. 'Ma, of course not! What you think?'

'I never know what you might do or not do.'

Her mother turned off the stove, clanged the spoon on the rim of the pot to remove a few vegetable fragments and put a lid on.

'So how work really going?' she asked.

'Pretty good.'

The microwave timer beeped. Giselle took out the plate and got a fork from the drawer. She opened the oven, speared a drumstick from the cooking dish inside, and took some vegetables from the pot. Giselle wondered if, even when she had her own home and family, she would feel as accustomed as she did in this house.

Her mother had gone into the living-room. Giselle joined her. She started eating while her mother leafed through the newspaper. They didn't speak. Giselle already felt the hectic pace of her life outside becoming suspended like a dream. It wasn't just the familiar surroundings. It was also her mother's calm, constant nature. They rarely spoke of anything important. They did not even gossip much. But everything was important and unstated. Giselle liked her independence, she liked being on her own. But she missed this sometimes, too.

'Where's Tony?' she asked.

'He went out to do something with the car,' answered her mother. 'But Fariel there in the back with Tammy.'

Giselle's brother lived in an annex to the back of the house with his wife and daughter. He could have lived on his own, and had in fact bought two lots of land in Piarco. But he had not wanted to leave his mother, nor his sisters for that matter, on their own after he was married. Fortunately, his wife got on well with the entire family. And Tamara, of course, was spoiled and pampered and petted constantly. Giselle had thought Tony might move out when their mother remarried, but he had decided to stay. He had a good job and, with no rent or mortgage, his family had a fairly luxurious lifestyle. Fariel was a lab technician. She worked ten minutes' drive from home, at a medical laboratory in Chaguanas.

Ronald came in, carrying the other daily paper, the one published by CMC.

'Leila, I going up by Ramnath for a while,' he said.

'All right, dear.'

'I should be back around five.'

He leaned down and kissed her on the cheek. Giselle felt a fleeting twinge of jealousy watching the familiar action. Even after three years, she still considered Ronald a stranger.

'See you later, Giselle,' he said.

'Okay,' she answered.

Ronald glanced back at her mother, who gave a slight nod, and then he went out. There was a small smile on his face. Giselle observed the byplay, but pretended to be absorbed in the papers. A few moments later, the car started up. Giselle heard the patter of the dogs' paws along the side of the house as they ran to see who was leaving.

'So things cool with you and Ronald?' she asked, very casually. Giselle had been asking the same question, in different ways, for the last three years.

Her mother looked at her with a calm smile. 'Yes. He is a nice man, you know, Giselle.'

'I know he's nice,' said Giselle. There was a faint protest in her voice. Her mother always answered her with some variation of this.

'And it's nice not to be alone and to have some extra money,' her mother continued. Ronald, like her, was a teacher. His wife had died several years ago and, when he married Giselle's mother, he had rented out his house. They had bought a new car last year.

'I'm thinking of taking early retirement next two years,' her mother said.

'Really?' said Giselle, surprised. She knew why she was surprised. Full of quiet energy, her mother was the kind of person who just seems to keep going, without making much of a fuss about it. Nevertheless, thought Giselle, her mother deserved it. She looked younger than she was. But there was also a certain set to her mouth, and a hard glint in her eyes, which Giselle knew was the result of the burden of responsibility she had shouldered by herself for so many years.

Her children had not been spared the effects of that burden. In fact, it sometimes seemed to Giselle that she had spent most of her teenage years being angry with her mother. Studies always came first, even when there was a party which everyone, including that cute fella who always watched her at the taxi stand in the evenings, would be at. Money was always spent on books or extra lessons, even when there was this absolutely gorgeous dress which had been just made for her. Adolescence, for Giselle, was a prison where you were tortured by hormones. She had to study when she wanted to be necking with that guy who was a cousin of her best friend and who had the most delicious-looking lips and a great butt. Even now, Giselle regretted that she had never had a chance to squeeze his backside. As a teenager, she was able to go out with her friends only occasionally and certainly never near examination time. Even her extra-curricular activities – tennis, dance, drama – were scheduled. For the entire year of her fifth form examinations, Giselle did not go out at all.

But now she was an adult, she understood why her mother had pushed her so hard and, in some ways, she appreciated it. It had given her discipline and the strength and skills to face whatever the world hurled at her. Even so, Giselle knew her upbringing had limited her in certain ways and, with the experiences of the past week revolving uneasily in some wakened corner of her mind, she was beginning to see those limits all too clearly. Because she was a self-development addict, for whom striving to improve herself was as much a part of her as the skin on her body, it was all the more shocking to discover an aspect of herself which was, to all intents and purposes, retarded. It was even more shocking to realize that she had never even been really aware of that aspect of herself until a couple of days ago. For the first time in her life, Giselle felt inferior. *Damn it, at twenty-six I should be the kind of lover who makes men scream for mercy*, she thought. *Men LIKE women who make them scream for mercy.*

Her mother was explaining why she was retiring. 'There are several reasons. All of you except Miranda on your own. And she will be married just now. So I figure I could retire and just wait for some more grandchildren.' She glanced sideways at Giselle in a meaningful manner.

'Yes, how is Tabby going?' said Giselle, ignoring her mother's look.

'Fine. She over the morning sickness now.' Her mother, of course, refused to be ignored. 'None of my children worry me except you, Giselle.'

'Well, there's no need to worry, Ma,' Giselle said mildly. 'I don't always talk nonsense.'

'You haven't met anybody yet?'

'You like bulldogs, Ma?' said Giselle curiously. 'They supposed to be very tenacious. I could get you one to practise with when I'm not around.'

Her mother refused to be distracted. 'There aren't any nice men in that new place you working?'

'Two, actually,' Giselle said, before she could stop herself.

Her mother's eyes brightened. Giselle could almost see the 'Finally!' flashing like a neon light in her head.

'What is this? From none to two? This is an improvement.'

'I'm just joking, Ma.'

Her mother scanned her sharply, and her mother vision was not fooled by Giselle's nonchalance.

'Tell me about them,' she said, putting aside her newspaper.

'There isn't really anything to tell.' Giselle grinned ruefully to herself. That was certainly true. But she did want to talk to someone about Robert and Vishnu. And who better than her mother? Vera, as expected, had flown out without even seeing Giselle.

Her mother was looking at her expectantly. Giselle said, 'It's just that there are these two guys at the company. They both seem interested in me. I don't know *how* interested, but they're both serious kind of men. And they're both attractive, in different ways.'

'And you feel you could get serious with one of them?' her mother asked hopefully.

Giselle shrugged. 'They made me think about that part of life. Even if nothing happens with either one, I still have a new way of looking at myself. One, he makes me feel strange inside. It's hard to describe. He is very good-looking and interesting, too. But the other one's more suitable for me. And he's attractive enough. Any woman would say he's a good catch, although I don't give two hoots about that.'

'Maybe is time you started giving two hoots,' her mother suggested.

'How you felt about Daddy when you all met?' Giselle asked and, in asking, realized she had never talked to her mother about this aspect of the past, except in very general terms. She supposed it wasn't the kind of thing you really discussed with your mother, like how the honeymoon was.

'First time I saw him was at a cricket match in the village.' A wistful tone had crept into her mother's voice and Giselle saw the gentle, eager girl she had been before life had sharpened her. 'He was a bowler. I liked him from the start because of the way he moved. He had a smooth run and, Lord, he could pelt that ball hard! I didn't take my eyes off him at all, even when he was just standing fielding. He noticed me watching, though, because he got one of his friends who knew me to introduce us. We talked a little bit, or at least he talked because I was too nervous to say anything, and then he just started dropping by the house, supposedly to see your uncle. The funny thing was, I don't think even your grandmother was fooled, but they never said anything. They liked him, I suppose. When he got the job in the bank, he started taking me out and that went on for a year and then we got married.'

'You don't ever wish you hadn't gotten married so young?' Giselle asked.

Her mother shook her head. 'Why would I think about that? I had.'

There was a long silence. Then Giselle, hesitantly, asked, 'How do you feel about Ronald, as compared with Daddy?'

'Is not the same thing,' her mother said, as if this was a question she had also asked herself. 'When you're older, you have different needs. You make different choices. It can't be compared, really.'

'Oh,' said Giselle. She thought about it. She supposed her mother meant things like security and companionship. These things were not as crucial when you were young and hadn't yet realized the world belonged to older people who didn't want it. But, Giselle thought, most people, even when they were young, did get married for things like security and companionship and even money. And conservative people, like born-again Christians, Muslims and people with really strict parents, even got married so they could have sex without feeling guilty about it. But nearly all of these people fooled themselves into thinking they were marrying for love alone. So what did she want? She knew she didn't want to fool herself. *The only thing I know for sure in this life*, Giselle thought, *is that chocolate tastes really good. God, I'm pathetic.* But how could she believe in love when she had never experienced it?

'Why Ronald look at you like that before he left?' Giselle asked, remembering what had caused her to ask her initial question.

Her mother cleared her throat. 'Well, I have something to tell you about us.'

'What?'

'Well, is a bit difficult to explain.'

Giselle, now paying her mother full attention, saw that she was looking very uncomfortable – and even, Giselle realized with surprise, embarrassed.

'Difficult?'

'I don't think you're going to be pleased.'

'What happen, you had an affair?

'No, of course not!'

'Well, what then?'

Her mother cleared her throat again. Giselle grinned.

'C'mon, Ma, you're a forty-six-year-old woman with four children. There's nothing supposed to embarrass you anymore, except your unmarried oldest daughter.'

'Well, it seems I'm going to be a forty-six-year-old woman with five children.'

It took Giselle fully seventy-six seconds to absorb this. And when she finally spoke, it was to say, almost hopefully, 'You and Ronald are going to adopt?'

'No. I'm pregnant,' said Giselle's mother.

The silence this time lasted ninety-seven seconds.

'How did this happen, Mother?' said Giselle finally. She knew it was a stupid question, and she knew it sounded even more inane because of the pompous way she asked it. But Giselle felt angry, disappointed and shocked. She felt, in fact, as though she had brought up her mother better than this.

Her mother smiled a little smile. 'The usual way, I think. I know is a miracle, but it's not an immaculate conception.'

'But Jesus Christ, Ma!' Giselle exclaimed, though she was not intending to be appropriate. 'Didn't you take precautions? I mean, a twelve-year-old schoolgirl knows better!'

'At my age, you don't expect to get pregnant,' her mother said gently.

'But you know your family. Everybody breeds like flies in a sugar factory. Auntie Lottie had eight kids before she stopped, and that was only because her husband had a heart attack and died. And no wonder! The poor guy must have been worn out.'

'Giselle, you're being ridiculous.'

'Oh, *you're* going to have a child at forty-six and *I'm* being ridiculous? We really need to get our value systems sorted out here, Mother.'

'You're being ridiculous because what's done is done. I've seen the doctor and he says, with proper care, there's no reason why I shouldn't have a perfectly healthy child.'

'If you'd taken proper care, you wouldn't be having a child at all,' Giselle said.

'That is enough!' her mother snapped. Giselle looked at her sullenly for a moment, then subsided.

'I admit,' said her mother, 'that I would have preferred not to have a child. But now it happen, I am quite excited.' Giselle saw it was true. Her mother's eyes seemed actually to shine. 'I'm sorry you uncomfortable about it, but you will get used to it.'

'I guess I won't have a choice,' said Giselle glumly. 'Like the pro-life people.'

'No,' her mother answered.

'And what does Ronald think?'

'He is very happy.'

'Like Pappy?'

'Giselle,' said her mother warningly.

'I'm just joking, Ma.'

She leaned over and kissed her mother. 'If you okay with this, I'm okay.'

Her mother smiled. 'I'm glad to hear that.'

There was another, more comfortable silence, then Giselle said musingly, 'And Ronald looks so quiet.'

Her mother grinned wickedly, and in that moment looked startlingly like her oldest daughter.

'That's because he always has to save his energy for the night.'

'Ma!'

'I *was* single for seventeen years, eh.'

Luckily for Giselle's peace of mind, a small voice at that moment shrilled: 'Auntie Giselle!' Giselle put down her plate and swept her niece into her arms as she came running into the living-room. Fariel, Tammy's mother, followed at a more sedate pace.

'How you going, Tamsy?' said Giselle. 'Give Auntie Giselle a big hug!' The little girl chuckled and hugged Giselle's neck. 'A *bigger* hug!' Tammy giggled and squeezed more tightly.

Giselle got up, balancing Tammy on the crook of one arm and leaned over and gave Fariel a peck on the cheek. 'How things?'

'Good,' said Fariel. She was a baby-cheeked young woman, not conventionally good-looking, but very attractive because of her delicate gold colouring and wide sensual mouth. Even after bearing a child, she still had a small waist and well-shaped bottom. Everybody called her Ellie because 'Fariel' was the kind of name even Hamlet's players had trouble bringing trippingly off the tongue.

Giselle liked Fariel, but she had been a little wary of her until Tammy was born. For one thing, she knew her brother had been sleeping with other women while he and Fariel were going around. And, back then, Giselle had had the type of mind which, while not excusing Anthony, tended to blame Fariel for not being enthusiastic enough in bed. Giselle refused to believe a woman could have a small waist, a nice bottom, good legs and not keep a man entirely satisfied unless she didn't *want* to satisfy him. Of course, as a teenager Giselle read a lot of romance novels which, she now knew, was not the best way for a young girl to learn about the male psyche. Later, however, she found out that Fariel was also having an affair, and, quicker than Pontius Pilate, Giselle washed her hands of both of them. That had been a long time ago, though. Marriage had settled Anthony down, and the child seemed to stabilize Fariel's tempestuous personality. And, since Giselle had moved out, a curious closeness had grown up between her and Fariel. Giselle now considered Fariel like a sister, whom she didn't know very well but felt close to. And Fariel seemed to understand Giselle better since Giselle had decided to live on her own. Giselle thought that perhaps this was because of Fariel's own background.

'Auntie Giselle, I got a new watch!' Tammy said, holding out one small arm.

'Oh, it's very nice. What time is it?'

Tammy looked fixedly at the digital face of her watch, then blushed and hid her face. 'I dunno,' she said.

'It's twelve thirty-seven,' Giselle told her, pointing at the numbers. Tammy stared fascinatedly at the watch.

'Is it?' she said.

'Come, Tammy, let's get some food,' said Fariel, ending the formalities. She took Tammy's hand and led her into the kitchen.

Giselle finished eating her meal and, when Fariel and Tammy returned, she fed the little girl. It was an entirely absorbing task and, in the warmth of family, Giselle forgot for a while all the vexed questions of love, including her mother's unexpected pregnancy.

Later, when her mother had gone outside to tend to her garden and Fariel was trying to get Tammy to take her afternoon nap, Giselle called her apartment to see if there were any messages on her answering machine. She wanted to talk to her mother some more about the pregnancy, mostly because she still couldn't quite bring herself to believe it. She figured talking about it would make it real. *Next thing I'll be getting into politics*, she thought. But she didn't feel like going out into the garden, and she also didn't want her mother asking further questions about the two men Giselle had mentioned.

Of course the issue of her mother having a child had overshadowed the issue of when Giselle would at least start thinking about having some of her own. *I thought I was setting Ma up for a shock*, thought Giselle, *but she sure had a great comeback*. Giselle knew, of course, that this respite would only be temporary. Her mother would not remain satisfied for long, just because there was some action, no matter how minimal, on that front.

There were three messages on Giselle's machine. The first was from Vera, saying she had got tied up and would talk to Giselle when she came in next week. The second was from Robert, telling her to call him if she wanted to go to the beach tomorrow. And the third was from Vishnu, asking her to give him a call. He had left his number.

She called Vishnu and he answered the phone almost immediately.

'Hi, it's Giselle.'

'Giselle!' he said, and she felt warm hearing the obvious pleasure in his voice.

'I got your message,' she said, wondering why phone conversations always started with obvious comments.

'Yeah, I forgot to ask you for your number. Actually, I was frightened to ask you for it. So I got it out of the phone book.'

'Sherlock Holmes would be proud,' she said.

He chuckled – a deep-throated, happy sound.

'Why were you frightened?' Giselle asked. 'I don't think I'm that scary.'

'I dunno. I just saw you drawing yourself to your full height and saying, "Sir, you strangely forget yourself."'

'At five foot three, I don't think I could talk like that if I tried.'

'Anyway, I was wondering if we could meet round the Savannah this evening.'

'For?'

'Drink of coconut, eat some *pholourie*, sit on a bench. Savannah kind of lime, nah.'

She hesitated. 'Well, actually, I'm in Freeport. I'm not sure if I'll be coming back up that side today.'

'Oh. Well, I know they have coconut and *pholourie* in Freeport. But do they have good benches?'

Giselle smiled. 'Not that I know of.'

'Well, start a petition. Meanwhile, what's happening in Freeport?'

110

'Nothing. I'm just here by my mother's house.'

'Oh.'

There was silence on the line.

'Maybe if I come up early enough tomorrow,' she said.

'Yes,' he said. He sounded cheerful again. 'So what do you do when you go by your mother's house in Freeport?'

'Eat her food. Laze around. Explain to her why I'm not married.'

He laughed. 'Sounds like a typical mother, even if her daughter is not. Why you not married?'

The question caught Giselle off-guard. Her mind went blank for a few seconds.

'Never met anybody I wanted to marry,' she said finally.

'Good answer,' he said. 'I keep being amazed at the number of people who meet people they *want* to marry. Especially when you consider the number of people – '

'Who want to get divorced,' Giselle said simultaneously with Vishnu, laughing.

'Exactly. You have any sisters or brothers who're married?'

Giselle settled into the chair by the telephone and tucked one leg under her. 'One brother and one sister married. One about to be. My mother re-married recently, too.'

'Ah. You are the black sheep, pardon my racism. Do you miss your father?'

'Why you flinging all these questions at me?'

'Because I think you're interesting, because I want to know about you, because I don't think we have enough time on this planet to waste it on small talk.'

'Whew!' said Giselle, and heard Vishnu's breathy laugh on the phone. But she was flattered.

'No, I don't really miss my father,' she told him. 'I got used to the idea of him not being around a long time ago.'

'I see. I never got used to the idea of my mother not being there, though I don't remember her very clearly.' His voice was strong and impersonal, as though he was talking about somebody else. 'There's always an emptiness there, as though part of myself is missing.'

'I understand,' she said. And, even though Vishnu's voice clanged so strongly, there was a strange breathlessness in Giselle's throat for him. 'I think I am stronger for it, though.'

'Perhaps I am, too,' he told her. 'If you get hit often enough, you learn to roll with the punches. Fate can have a wicked left jab, though, as Mike Tyson found out.'

They spoke about Mike Tyson for a bit. Giselle felt he had indeed raped Desirée Washington, but Desirée was a featherbrain. Vishnu wasn't sure, but Tyson was black in America so it didn't matter, he said. 'They give a man millions for being violent, then act surprised when they find out he is. As if there's a gentlemanly way to knock somebody unconscious.'

'They could apologize every time they landed a punch,' Giselle suggested.

'Yeah, but how'd you know the guy meant it?'

The conversation flowed. Vishnu asked about Giselle's mother, her brother and sisters, what she did in her spare time, her opinion on drug addiction, her opinion on education, if she enjoyed her job, and a hundred other things. But his curiosity did not seem merely idle and she answered all his queries readily.

When the flow petered out (though she had the impression he had only decided to turn off the tap) Giselle asked, 'So you satisfied now?'

He said, 'Knowing *about* somebody only gives clues to knowing them. Although you can't ever really know anyone. But it's fun trying. Of course, you find that most people are the same or else not very genuine where it counts. Only a few are really interesting.'

'And which category do I fall into?' she asked. 'Strangely intriguing, with a light sprinkling of garlic?'

She could hear the grin in his voice. 'Well, if I had any doubt before, that answer would have put you solidly in the interesting category,' he said. 'How many people do you know who are really real?'

'You mean like Coke?'

'Realer than that.'

'I don't think of people that way,' she said. 'I just think some people are really weird, present company *not* excepted.'

'Oh, that's very true. Since the age of three, I have weared clothes every day of my life.'

'Oh God, you make puns. I can't believe you make puns.'

'Oh, I am very popular at Easter.'

'Easter?' she asked, unguardedly.

'Yeah, everybody likes my hot-cross puns.'

Giselle groaned.

'Anyway, on that note, I'd better go. I've kept you on the phone too long.'

She glanced at her watch – they had been speaking for over two hours.

He said, 'I enjoyed the talk.'

'So did I,' she answered. 'Except for your jokes. Goodbye.'

'Love me, love my jokes,' he said and, laughing, rang off.

Giselle hung up the phone, wondering for a moment about that parting comment. Then she steupsed at herself – it was just part of his nonsense. She rubbed her left ear tenderly. It was aching from being pressed against the receiver and she felt tired after the conversation. But it was a contented kind of tiredness. And, for a long while, she just sat there thinking. But she could not have said exactly what she was thinking about. When she was finished – although she did not know either exactly what she had finished, except that some process in her was completed – she went to look for Fariel.

◆

Giselle knocked softly on the open door of the annexe and called. Fariel came out of the bedroom and closed the door quietly behind her. Hunters in the jungle stalking a wounded man-eating tiger could not have been more carefully silent. For Tammy, when awakened from a nap, was crankier than even a man-eating tiger, already irritable from a bullet in its backside, who has been denied its customary human for lunch.

Fariel had a novel in her hand. 'I was just reading while she slept,' she said, speaking like the wind in the trees.

A sofa and three chairs were arranged in a square in the section they used as a living-room. Fariel sat on the sofa and Giselle sat in an armchair next to it. Remembering Vishnu's comment about real people, Giselle considered Fariel. Fariel was real, she decided, especially since her breasts were so small. But you mightn't realize her reality unless you spoke to Fariel one on one. In company, she was the opposite to Giselle: vivacious, extroverted, with an outrageous sense of humour – the centre of attention. But normally, Giselle thought, Fariel didn't smile much. She usually seemed serious, even unhappy – but strong. Yet she was morbidly sensitive. All these things made her real, but Giselle noted with interest that her reality didn't prevent Fariel from being a consummate liar. She had never told Anthony about that affair – in fact, even now, he still thought the guy had just been her friend. And this despite the fact that she had been horning her previous boyfriend with Anthony for several months before deciding to drop the previous boyfriend. *Men*, thought Giselle, as countless women have thought before her and as countless women will continue to think after her, *are such fools*.

'Tammy is growing very fast,' Giselle said.

'She going through clothes like nothing,' Fariel said.

'Well, I hear there's going to be somebody to wear them.'

'Uh-huh.'

'So what you think about that?'

'I think it's cute.'

'Cute!' said Giselle. 'For God's sake, Ellie, Ma's forty-six years old! And Ronald's two years older.'

Fariel giggled. 'Yeah. Mom doesn't surprise me, but I wouldn't have thought Ronald had it in him. And here I was thinking they were going to bed early every night because they were middle-aged and needed the sleep.'

'Every night?' said Giselle, aghast.

'You bet. Though I suppose they talk a lot, too.'

'Apparently the art of conversation died at some point.'

Fariel laid down her novel. 'You don't seem too thrilled.'

'Having a child at her age is so troublesome. In every way.'

'You don't know any middle-aged women who've had children?'

Giselle's mind flashed briefly on Sharon. 'No.'

'Well, I do. It can be done.'

'Just because something can be done doesn't mean you should do it. That's how we got the atomic bomb. And soya burgers, which is even more obscene.'

Fariel grinned. 'That's better.'

Giselle, despite herself, chuckled. 'I dunno. This is going to take some adjusting to. I feel kind of vexed with Ma, actually.'

'You think she should have had more sense?'

'Yes, exactly.'

'Maybe she's been sensible for so long, she needed to do something . . . not quite sensible.' Fariel looked at Giselle reflectively. Fariel had light-brown eyes and her gaze often seemed removed from its object even when she was looking at another person. She could be intimidating when she looked like that. 'Maybe you could learn something from your mother, Gis. God knows you sensible enough for three.'

'Hm, well not lately,' Giselle said.

'How come?'

Giselle didn't answer. Instead, she asked, 'Ellie, when was the first time you fell in love?'

'When I was twelve years old I saw Bruce Lee beat up an entire army of gangsters in *Enter the Dragon*. I got a poster of him the next day and stuck it over my bedhead. Watching him before I went to sleep, it didn't seem life could get any better. In fact,' she said thoughtfully, 'it didn't.'

'So are you saying you like Tony because he looks kind of Chinese and has a black belt?'

'Well, there are other reasons, of course. He has a gorgeous butt, for example. But, yes, I suppose my fascination with Bruce did influence me.'

'So how many times you been in love?'

Fariel hitched herself up on the chair. 'Well, I'm in love with Tony and I was in love with the guy I went around with before Tony.'

Giselle knew of this person. His name, coincidentally, was also Anthony and Fariel had lived with him for three years. When she was twenty, she had quarrelled with her mother and left home. Her parents had been divorced since she was twelve.

'Is being in love with Tony the same as being in love with your past boyfriend?'

Fariel gave Giselle more or less the same answer her mother had.

'You can't really compare it,' she said. 'I had much less self-control with Anton. You know how Tony and I quarrel. Anton and I were ten times worse. I hurt him a lot and he hurt me a lot. But in the end I think I came out better, because he was hurt more. And the disaster of that relationship – which by rights should have been a marvellous one – taught me that I had to control myself if I wanted to have any sort of life.' She shook her head. 'I haven't learned the lesson perfectly yet, but I'm trying hard with Tony.'

'But you were in love with Anton?' Giselle asked.

Fariel nodded. 'Oh yes. You don't go through that kind of hell *unless* you're in love. Or really in Hell, of course. Was it Shaw who said we're all already in Hell and just don't know it?'

'I don't know. Was it worth it, though?'

Fariel shrugged. 'I don't know. Is it worth living? That's one I used to have trouble with sometimes.'

Giselle looked at her, baffled. 'I think it's worth living.'

Fariel looked back at her with her impersonal eyes, saying nothing, and Giselle understood that, even though they were the same age in years, Fariel was far, far older than she.

'Like you thinking of falling in love or what?' Fariel asked.

'Well, if it's going to happen, I don't suppose I'll have much choice in the matter.'

'Of course you do,' Fariel said. 'If you're smart you choose to fall in love with a man with a gorgeous butt who'll do anything for you.'

'Oh?'

Inside the bedroom, Tammy woke and called for Mommy. Fariel sighed. 'The goddess is restless today.'

'I'll leave you to make the burnt offerings,' said Giselle, getting up.

But she left with a troubled mind.

◆

Giselle had brought a Stephen King novel with her and she went to the back of the house to sit and read. There was a kind of big, open garage there. The breeze blew strongly and the green land sloped away to secret corners. Giselle looked at the several trees which made up a small and varied orchard. She had a habit of counting them whenever she came, though she was never sure why – did she expect some extra ones to have sprouted or the old ones to have uprooted themselves and walked away? There were fig trees (three) and orange trees (two) and guava trees (two) and pomerac trees (actually, only one and another on the way) and breadfruit trees (strictly speaking, one and no others in sight) and coconut trees (two, one of which had never borne a coconut in its life). *I'm sure this is some kind of neurosis*, she thought. *I bet there's even a name for it.*

Giselle unfurled the colourful hammock slung between two of the iron poles which held up the pale-green galvanized roof. Bear had heard her in the back and come to be in her company. He lay quietly beside the hammock while she read. She kept one hand on his head. If she moved it away he brushed her arm with his snout until she put it back. 'Spoilt dog,' she told him, and he wagged his furry tail in agreement. It was very peaceful and the breeze was very soothing. She eventually put the novel down and drifted into sleep. When she awoke, the evening light was fading and she went back into the house to have dinner.

Chapter Nine

Giselle woke before eight the next morning, and lay sleepily confused for some minutes wondering why she had done such an ungodly thing on a Sunday. She had stayed up late last night watching TV and talking to her brother. At weekends, it was her habit to go to bed after midnight and not to get out of bed until twelve the next day. Then she remembered: Robert had suggested going to the beach. Giselle felt a twist of excitement in her stomach. And then she remembered that her mother was pregnant.

She got out of bed and went to the bathroom. After she had brushed her teeth, she stepped into the shower, thinking. On the one hand, she wanted to have a serious talk with her mother. On the other hand, she loved the beach; and the tease in her wanted Robert to see her in a swimsuit.

By the time she finished her shower, Giselle had decided what she would do: she would let her mother decide.

Her mother was, of course, already up.

'You want bacon or ham with your eggs?' she asked as Giselle came into the kitchen.

'Bacon.'

Her mother opened the refrigerator and took out a packet of bacon.

'You up early.'

'A friend invited me to the beach today.'

'Thought you were staying for the weekend.'

'Yeah, well I don't have to go.'

'Who's this friend?'

'The managing editor. The one I think is interested in me.'

'Ah,' said her mother. She lit the stove and put the frying-pan on it. 'Well, is a nice day for the beach.'

'Mm,' said Giselle.

She watched her mother throw three strips of bacon into the hot pan. A sizzling sound rose in the air.

'So you getting any morning sickness yet?' she asked, feeling obliged to say something about her mother's condition.

'Yes. I've already vomited twice this morning.'

'I read once that morning sickness is caused by the brain becoming hypersensitive to toxins when a woman's pregnant,' said Giselle. 'It's a kind of defence mechanism.'

'If you ever get pregnant, I hope that consoles you when you're spewing your breakfast into the sink.'

'Sorry. Guess I sounded like a man there. It's the price I pay for being a modern young woman.'

Her mother turned off the stove and put the bacon onto a plate already heaped with scrambled eggs.

'There's coffee in the thermos,' she said. 'I made extra as I knew you were here.'

Giselle got up and poured herself a cup. The thermos of coffee was really for Ronald.

'Where's the proud daddy?'

'Went to the market.'

'I also read that many people who are sexually active in their older years drink a cup of coffee a day,' Giselle said. 'Guess is true, eh?'

Her mother started washing the breakfast dishes. 'You don't think you should call this feller if you going to the beach?'

'You want me to go to the beach?'

'Yes, if you going to spend the day telling me about everything you've read.'

'I was just sharing some interesting facts,' said Giselle, pouting a little.

'Go to the beach. Maybe someday soon you'll have something really interesting to tell me.'

'Oh, all right.'

Giselle went to phone Robert, thinking she had handled that rather well.

He answered the phone after the first ring.

'Hi, it's Giselle,' she said.

'Hi. How are you?'

'I was just wondering if that offer to go to the beach was still on?'

'Sure.'

119

'Good. Let's do it, then.'

He chuckled. 'Very well.'

She gave him directions to her place, arranging to meet in two hours. Then she gathered her stuff up and gave her mother a hasty kiss.

'Tell everybody I gone.'

'Why the rush?'

'Legs to shave – men don't like thorns on the stems of their roses. And, God, pubic hair to clip too! Why didn't you give me a modest bikini line, Ma?'

Her mother shook her head in exasperation.

◆

Robert arrived right on time, and Giselle came out with legs both smooth and oiled. She wore a beach outfit which consisted of a short skirt and top made of pale blue towelling and she was carrying an enormous drawstring cloth bag.

'What do you have in that?' Robert asked.

Giselle slung the bag into the back seat.

'Don't worry. If we get marooned, we can survive for several weeks until help comes.' In fact, the bag was an all-purpose hold-all for any kind of lime. Whether she was going to the beach or by somebody's house or a party, the bag had everything she might need: clothes, shoes, cutlery, notepaper, P.G. Wodehouse novel, a Discman and CDs, dominoes, a mini-Pictionary set. It even had a first-aid kit and chocolate. But Giselle wasn't going to tell Robert all that. What she called well-prepared, other people sometimes called paranoid.

There weren't many people on the beach when they arrived. It would get crowded after noon. Robert chose a spot near the centre of the beach. Most of the people tended to congregate there. Giselle normally went further down, where the groups were more strung out. But Robert seemed to like the crowd and, judging from the way he watched her, he also liked showing her off. It was kind of flattering, Giselle thought. She had worn a simple, black one-piece swimsuit. Giselle was not shy about her body, but she hadn't wanted to wear anything *too* daring. However, the swimsuit did have X-strips cut all the way down both sides – she hadn't wanted to wear anything too modest, either.

Robert wore bright blue trunks. His body was well-proportioned, lean and muscular. But, as she had seen the day before, his stomach was slack. His skin was also unsunned and, except for his forearms and legs, he was pale.

I'll get him to work on that, thought Giselle, then grinned to herself. She was already assuming power over him. She thought he would be pleased if he knew, but she behaved perfectly normally for the entire day. When they went into the water, he held her hand. She stayed in longer than he did. The water was very rough, the waves high. Giselle liked that. She liked feeling the massive power of the sea. Robert, however, felt cold and went out.

After she had tired herself body-surfing, Giselle rejoined him on the beach. He had packed a cooler – beer for himself, club soda for her. Robert had bought Kentucky Fried Chicken and chips, but Giselle ate bake-and-shark. She told Robert, 'You don't come to Maracas just for the sea. You come for the shark and bake.' But he said shark meat made him feel ill. She laughed, eating one. 'Half of your life gone,' she said.

After she had eaten, she napped. Robert read. Giselle was aware through the thin wall of sleep that he always touched her. His body might press against hers or his hand rest on her arm. It was a persistent intimacy. Giselle liked it. But it was so persistent. On the drive back, he held her hand. They left early, around three, because Robert said he had some business that evening.

Giselle let him come up to her apartment and they kissed for a long time. His hands pressed firmly into the small of her back and, once, slid over the full curves of her bottom. But he did not attempt to go any further and she was not tense, knowing he wouldn't. Robert was too experienced, too self-controlled, for that. And she would have slapped him silly if he had tried.

They would have kissed longer, but she had sand in her swimsuit. Robert grinned when she told him this.

'What happen?' she said, a little defensively. He was looking at her as if she was a rather adorable child. As a modern young woman, Giselle wasn't about to let Robert get away with this.

'You're very open, aren't you?' he said.

121

'Yep. Once I have sand on my ass, I just can't keep it a secret. Can you?'

Robert looked surprised, then laughed uproariously. Giselle smiled.

'Giselle Karan,' he said, 'they surely broke the mould when they made you.'

'Yeah, well, who wants to be mouldy?'

Before Robert left, he said, 'One day you must show me exactly what you have in that bag.'

Giselle grinned. 'Maybe I will.'

She showered and shampooed her hair when he had gone. Her skin felt smooth and silky, and she was deeply tired and contented. Her life had taken a new turn. There was excitement in that. But there was also a shadow on the edges of her mind, and Giselle did not know why. After she showered, she slept.

◆

The phone woke her at around six.

'Hello,' she said groggily.

'Hi, it's Vishnu,' he said. 'I thought I'd get your answering machine. I wake you up?'

'Uh-huh,' she said.

'Sorry. You sound like one of Kermit's cousins.'

'Who?'

'Kermit. Green guy. Lives on Sesame Street.'

'Oh.'

'Never mind. I thought you were staying Freeport.'

'I came up this morning.'

'Oh,' he said. There was a silence. Giselle cautiously opened slitted eyes against the evening light which still slanted in through the bedroom window with a brightness she considered deliberately offensive. Vishnu, getting no reply, continued.

'Actually, I wanted to find out if there's any chance of us having that Savannah lime this evening.'

'Oh.' She looked at her bedside clock. 'I don't know. I went to the beach today. I'm kind of knocked out.'

'Oh,' said Vishnu. It occurred to Giselle through her sleepiness that this monosyllable was enjoying a record run.

The silence on the line became a little full. Giselle hesitated, then, opting for honesty instead of tact, as she usually did, said, 'Yes. I went with Robert Cardinez. I introduced you to him in the corridor at CMC. Remember? The managing editor.'

'Yes,' Vishnu said. 'I remember.'

'Gee, don't those ice cubes in the vocal cords make your throat ache?' she said, trying light humour.

'Goodbye,' he said, with no humour at all.

Against her will, Giselle's own throat caught a little.

'Yes, bye,' she said, in the horribly cheerful manner she always assumed when she felt uncomfortable. 'Thanks for calling.'

'You're very welcome,' he said. Giselle thought he sounded as sincere as a two-dollar bill if a two-dollar bill could talk. Before she could say anything further, she heard a click and then the empty humming of the line. Her face tightened for a moment, then she shrugged. It was best that Vishnu understood the situation up front and, in any case, Giselle made it a point to be as honest as possible with people, especially men who found her attractive. *Maybe that explains why I've been single for so long*, she thought. She threw off the sheets and went to the bathroom.

◆

Giselle did not see Vishnu at work the next day and she was glad. If they had met, there would have been a tension in her that she could not have controlled. Vishnu brought out that reaction in her and she did not like it. There was, after all, no reason for her to feel tense about him. She knew he had been attracted to her, but she had given him no reason to think the feeling might be returned. Nor had it been, she told herself. She had just found him interesting, and she had felt sorry for him. But, as she told herself this, Giselle seemed to hear Sharma's ironic voice in her head: *Many successful relationships are built on far less than that, Karan*. And another voice said: *I don't recall him asking for your sympathy*.

No, he hadn't. In fact, he was a tough-minded man. He was strong. And that was what caused her tension. There was something untamed and uncontrollable in Vishnu. It was something that, for all her own willpower and beauty – and beauty weakened even strong men – she had been able to gain no sway over. Giselle did not think Vishnu would make a scene in public or anything like that. Even when he was enraged, as he had been at lunch that day, there was a fierce pride about him. So he might not even talk to her. But she knew, if she saw him, how her stomach would lurch, how her nerves would jump, as though she had done him an injustice. And Giselle preferred her body parts sitting quietly, drinking tea. So she was just glad not to see him.

Coward, jeered the voice in her head. *Oh, shut up*! Giselle snapped.

She went out for lunch with Robert that day. They went to the same place. Leroy was still glad to see them.

That night she called her mother. Yes, the beach had been nice. Yes, they were dating, Giselle supposed.

Her mother was still pregnant.

◆

Vishnu was not at work the following day. Nor the two days after that. Giselle met Harry Chan in the yard. 'He called in sick,' he told her. 'Sounded bad.'

That night, after Robert left her apartment, she called Vishnu's number. Not that she cared for Vishnu or anything like that, Giselle told herself. She was just naturally concerned. She would find out how he was, listen to some of his jokes, cheer him up a little.

But the phone just rang and rang.

◆

She did not go out to lunch with Robert the next day. She told him she had some business to take care of. They had been out to lunch every day that week. That in itself told her that Robert was serious. It wasn't only that he was spending money at expensive restaurants every day. But, if he had just been after a torrid affair – not, of course, that he would have got one from her since her supply of torrid affairs was non-existent – he would have been more discreet. Giselle knew people were already talking, but they were talking less, or at least less viciously, because she and Robert were so open. Or so she told herself. Some, she knew, could equally well be saying that, floozy that she was, she wasn't even bothering to hide their affair. Well, you couldn't please any of the people all of the time. Sharma, at least, was pleased about it. 'Ooh, sleeping with the boss. Good technique, girl,' she said.

'Excuse me, Ms Ramlogan,' Giselle had said with dignity, 'Mr Cardinez's conversations have not made me doze off yet.'

Robert had also been at her apartment every night that week. She had not gone to his place, however. When they were on her territory, as it were, Giselle felt she could lay down the rules. And, for some reason, she shrank from telling Robert about her experience, or lack of it, so soon.

But, even as she focused on Robert, Giselle felt as though there was something unfinished between herself and Vishnu. Her honesty, which could become quite irritating at times, did not allow her to escape this uncomfortable truth. Even if they could have seen each other just to exchange a hard look, or to ignore each other completely, she thought she could have closed that chapter. But she had not even been granted that opportunity. She even wondered, briefly, if this sickness was just a ploy to get her goat.

Yet, she admitted to herself, her need to break off with Vishnu in some definite manner was not all of it. If it had been, she would not have found herself heading towards Barataria in her lunch hour on a Friday.

She knew Vishnu might have just quit the job – 'fired the work', as they said in local dialect – and even left the apartment. But she did not believe that for a second. Vishnu was too conscientious a worker to do that to Harry. And Giselle did not think she could have upset him that much, anyway. So when she had received no answer on the phone, she had begun to worry. And the worry had grown in her through the night. Giselle did not believe in psychic phenomena, but she had an almost psychic presentiment that Vishnu was sick and alone in his apartment. After all, he had no one to turn to. And, for such a strong person to be sick, she thought, he had to be *very* sick. She had reached a stage where she almost saw him helpless in bed, so weak he was unable to even answer the phone.

As she turned into the street where Vishnu lived, Giselle was swearing under her breath. Her imagination had been working overtime on the drive down. She knew men – they would be as sick as a dog and refuse to get help, refuse even to see a doctor, unless blood was actually flowing in copious quantities. And Vishnu was an extreme example of that type of man. Giselle pulled up at the gate.

She rapped on the door, wondering what she would do if there was no answer. She could not see inside because the panes of cheap glass were frosted. The windows on the side were closed like blind eyes. The Mitsubishi Magna was still parked in the narrow yard. Giselle rapped again. 'Vishnu!' she called. She tried the handle. The door was locked. Then she heard shuffling footsteps. After a few moments, a key turned and the door swung open loosely. Vishnu stood there, wrapped in a sheet. His eyes were dull. His hair was tied back in its ponytail, but it was spiky and unkempt. Stubble stood on his cheeks like many black thorns. He looked like a cactus which has seen better days. He stood watching her for several moments with a dull, blank face and Giselle could find nothing to say. Then a faint flicker stirred in his eyes and he tried to smile.

'Hello, Giselle,' he said, in a hoarse, painful whisper. 'What you doing here?'

'You're sick,' she said.

He made a sketchy gesture with one hand. 'That I am.' He turned. 'If you don't mind, I need to lie down. My head doesn't feel too right.'

He went back into the apartment, walking slowly, bowed over. Save for the lack of yellowed bandages, Giselle was reminded of a mummy risen to fulfil a 3,000-year-old curse, still a little stiff from being dead so many centuries. Rubber slippers, also not habitually worn by the Egyptian living dead, shuffled on his feet because he was barely lifting his legs. *God, he must really be ill*, Giselle thought. She followed him, closing the door behind her. Vishnu went through the living-room and through another doorway, which had no door but only a curtain of beads. Giselle passed through the living-room and the small kitchen. The sink was empty and gleaming, dishes neatly piled on the rack, but the counter was stained with some spilled liquid. There was an empty frying-pan on the stove.

When she came in through the bead curtain, Vishnu was lying on his side curled in a semi-foetal position on the high bed. He sat up a little when she entered, with the sheet still around him, but it was an effortful movement.

'They should make sitting up an Olympic event for people with this virus,' he said, speaking as though the words were produced by some ancient and rusty equipment inside him. 'I mightn't get gold, but I'm sure I could cop silver.'

The effort of this speech ended in several, painful-sounding coughs. Giselle moved forward in concern, but he raised a hand. The bed had two large pillows and, having uttered the last hack, Vishnu propped one up so he could lean against it. But his head remained bowed.

'What you doing here?' he asked again, still hoarsely.

'I came to see if you were all right,' she said.

He made the sketchy gesture. 'I'm fine. Is just a virus. I should be over it by tomorrow.'

'How long you been like this?' she asked, a little more sharply than she intended.

He winced. 'Please, Giselle,' he said. 'I have a headache, among my many other aches. I don't usually get headaches. It's a real pain.' He coughed a painful chuckle. 'Aiy, I made a joke. I'm going to live.'

She sat on the edge of the bed. Vishnu did not look up. His eyes were closed, as though the light was too bright for him.

'How you get sick?' Giselle asked.

He drew some careful breaths through his mouth before answering.

'Went playing football in the evening. It was wet. And I guess somebody else had the virus and gave it to me. Then I went for a run five o'clock the next morning. More dew. And my resistance was low, I suppose.'

'When?'

'Sunday.'

Now Giselle winced. She could guess why he had been out running at five after playing football the previous day and why his resistance had been low.

He peered briefly at her from beneath a waxen brow. His eyes had lost that smoky look of vitality. In sickness, they just looked black and flat and dead. 'I always throw off the virus in about three days. Don't usually get it at all.'

'It's Friday and you don't exactly seem to be on the road to recovery,' she told him.

'Friday?' he murmured, with faint surprise.

She leaned forward and put the back of her hand on his neck. He moved his head in protest, but he was too weak to pull away. His skin felt like fire under her hand.

'Jesus! You burning up.'

'Fever's good,' he murmured. 'Means the body is fighting – what's the word? Infection! That's the baby.' He sounded a little delirious. Giselle looked around the bedroom. She noticed for the first time on the side table a teacup and a small plate. The teacup had a used Lipton teabag inside it, the white thread with its red-and-yellow label trailing over the rim. The plate had several chocolate cream biscuits, and a metal fork, on it. She peered into the small, plastic-lined dustbin at the side of the bed. Inside were several empty Vienna sausage tins and two Fisherman's Friend lozenge wrappers. She looked back at Vishnu, seeing how gaunt his face was under the stubble.

'Is this what you've been living on?' she said.

He shrugged. Even that seemed to drain him. Giselle made an exasperated sound. Vishnu swallowed painfully.

Giselle got up. 'Wait here,' she said.

'Don't make jokes,' he sighed.

She went into the kitchen. The cupboards didn't have much, but she found two packets of Maggi noodle soup and some potatoes. There were carrots, garlic and onions in the refrigerator. As quickly as she could, she peeled three potatoes and cut them up along with carrots. Then she diced the onions and garlic cloves. She dropped the potatoes into the pot of water she had already put to boil. When she estimated the time was right, she added the carrots, onions and garlic and the two packets of noodles. She opened a tin of Vienna sausages – Vishnu seemed to be well-stocked with those small pull-tab tins – and cut up the sausages and added them to the soup. It wasn't the best soup she had ever made, but it was hot and nourishing.

While the soup boiled, she found a small stoneware bowl and a deep plastic spoon, the kind you get when you buy Chinese food.

Giselle half-filled the bowl with soup and carried it into the bedroom. Vishnu was sitting up, staring into space like a man who has begun to get out of bed only to forget why he ever wanted to do such a silly thing. The sheet had fallen to his waist. His body looked shrunken.

Giselle sat on the side of the bed next to him. 'I made you some soup,' she pointed out. She dipped the spoon in the bowl and held it close to his mouth with the bowl beneath to catch any spills. She thought she saw a flicker of humour in the sick, filmed eyes.

'I can feed myself,' he whispered.

'All right.' She handed him the bowl. But as he brought the spoon to his mouth, the hand holding the bowl began to tremble. The spoonful of soup spilled back into it. Giselle deftly took the bowl from him.

He looked at her unhappily, the spoon clutched in his right hand.

'I have never been so weak in my life,' he said bitterly. 'Well, when I was three months old, I suppose, but I enjoyed it then.'

'Eat the soup,' she said gently.

So she fed him, blowing on the spoonfuls to cool the soup, occasionally flicking a little spill from his chin with the spoon. When the bowl was empty she took a napkin from her purse and wiped his mouth. His eyes were perceptibly brighter, his voice a little stronger.

'You shouldn't have come,' he said.

'You're welcome,' Giselle said drily.

He sighed. 'There I go again.' He swallowed, grimacing with pain. 'I always seem to say things wrong around you. I meant two things.' He paused, breathing through his mouth. 'I wouldn't like you to catch this virus. It's a bitch. And I don't *ever* let anyone see me sick and I hate especially that you, of all people, should see me like this.'

'Don't worry about it,' Giselle said. 'I never thought you were all that macho.'

He laughed tiredly.

'Besides,' she said, her head cocked thoughtfully. 'I kind of like seeing you like this.'

He whispered, 'You must have a fascination for the horrible.'

She said, 'You're not as intimidating.'

He said, 'Giselle,' and paused to swallow. Giselle liked the way Vishnu said her name. Even sick, there was an intimate tone to it. He took up a pack of Fisherman's Friends from the side table and put one white lozenge into his mouth. He wasn't looking at her and it was as if he was speaking to himself. 'Giselle, nobody is more intimidating than you. Those cheekbones and you look at people straight in their eyes and your voice is so confident.' He laughed, but it was a feverish sound. His head sank down to his chest. 'If it wasn't for that mouth, the smile . . .' He began mumbling and she heard 'kissable' and then he was asleep, sitting up, his head bowed.

Giselle pushed him back gently, arranging the pillows to support his head as best she could without disturbing him. It was probably better for him to sit up, the way his nasal passages were clogged. He might get a crick in his neck, but the more he slept the sooner he would recover.

She went out of the bedroom quietly. She wouldn't leave until he woke up. Maybe not even then, she thought, with some surprise. She realized she did not want to leave Vishnu until she was sure he was all right. She thought this was perhaps because she felt partly responsible for his condition.

She looked around for the telephone. It was on the table next to a typewriter case. She called Robert on his direct line. He answered immediately.

'Hi,' she said. 'Listen, I won't be able to come back to the office this afternoon. I'm taking care of a sick friend.'

'All right,' he said. 'Nothing serious, I hope.'

'No, just a virus. But it's pretty debilitating. I just want to make sure he's all right before I leave. He's sleeping now.'

Robert's voice changed. 'He?' he said, making it sound like a quotation from *Othello*.

Giselle held down her irritation. 'Yes,' she said.

'I'm not sure I like the sound of that, eh,' Robert said, like Othello with a Trinidadian accent.

'Oh really?' Giselle said coldly. She had never liked Othello much, anyway. She belonged to the feminist school of criticism, and, as a schoolgirl, had once written an essay which argued that Desdemona would have done well to give Othello a swift kick.

'Who's this friend?' asked Robert, foolishly continuing, in Giselle's opinion, to play the part.

'Just someone I know. I *do* know people,' said Giselle, like Desdemona with attitude.

There was silence on the phone.

'Well, call me when you get home,' he said finally.

'All right.'

'Listen.'

130

'Yes?'

'Sorry. A little jealousy there. I'm only human.'

Giselle let a little amiability creep back into her voice.

'That's okay.'

'I'll see you later, then,' he said.

'Okay.'

Giselle hung up. But she was still coldly angry. There was something in Robert's tone . . .

She looked around Vishnu's living-room. The writing table was still covered with the sheets of poetry. Giselle was tempted to pick up a sheet, but resisted. A guitar leaned against the wall beside the table. There was no television, but there was a stereo system with turntable and double cassette player. A bookshelf of unvarnished wood stood against the wall. She wondered if Vishnu had made it himself. There weren't many books, but what there were covered a wide range of authors, from Jean Rhys to Stephen King to V.S. Naipaul to Ian Fleming to Derek Walcott to Isaac Asimov to P.G. Wodehouse to C.L.R. James.

I won't be bored in this apartment, she thought. She pulled out *Something Fresh* by P.G. Wodehouse, kicked off her shoes, arranged the cushions on the narrow sofa, and settled back to read. Only then did she notice a type-written sheet of paper on the coffee table. It was titled 'Phone Sex' and it would have taken a stronger woman than Giselle to leave the sheet lying where it was. She thought it was a poem, but after reading the first verse she realized it was a calypso.

Vishnu must have written this, she thought in surprise. She began reading it, not even wondering if he would mind – it wasn't as though it was romantic poetry:

> I is not a violent man,
> I like a peaceful life,
> But I feel I go have to blow up TSTT
> For what they doing to my wife.
>
> My wife is a lovely woman,
> Who has given me a loving home,
> But now technology causing trouble
> 'Cause the woman always on the phone.

CHORUS:
My wife always taking calls in the living-room
And spending hours on the phone,
While I waiting in the bedroom
Watching cable TV alone.
And when I call she
She does say she comin' now, she nearly done,
But time does pass and she eh reach
And I already come.

Is when TSTT put call-waiting
That the trouble really start
'Cause she going like a chain-smoker
Talkin' with all she friends heart to heart.
My wife is a popular lady
And everybody does call she,
While I waiting in the bedroom
By myself watching cable TV.
Is one Friday night I get real frustrated
When I see a movie with a X-rating;
I gone out one time to the living-room
And say, 'Doux-doux, I have my own call waiting.'
My wife watch me standing dey and say, 'I comin' now
    for now.'
And she smile at me rude gyul rude.
I gone back in the room, but by the time she come
The movie done, and I wasn' in the mood.

CHORUS

Then TSTT bring three-way call
And we sex life really get put on hold;
The woman talking morning, noon and night
While I in the bedroom playing with my telephone pole.
    I tell she, 'Doux-doux, give me a chance,
Come get off the phone;
I know you like to use your mouth –
Why you doh come and talk on *my* microphone?'
So she take pity on me

And do as I ask – Hallelujah!
But just when I thought things was looking up
TSTT introduce the cellular!

CHORUS

I know the cellular is a great invention
But it just getting me vex,
'Cause now my wife talking *all* the time,
Even when we having sex!
The only advantage with the cellular
Is that you could try all kinda position;
So at least I getting some action
And I could still watch the television.
So we there doing it
And she would say, 'Faster – no, not you, Vashti.'
And I would say, 'Yes, yes,
Change – oh God – to Channel Three.'

CHORUS

But we know things couldn' continue so,
We had to find a solution;
Then my wife had a brilliant idea
And get me my own phone extension.
So now when I want some love up
I does call she on the phone
And give she some rude boy talk
And with call-waiting I does never get a busy tone.
So now I don' have to blow up TSTT,
Now I really like the technology,
The only thing I doh like
Is when my wife ask me to turn off the TV.

CHORUS:
My wife taking calls in any room,
We spending hours on the phone,
I doh mind this telephone lime,
Is just the wife, me and the twenty-five channels alone.

Giselle was smiling broadly as she finished reading. The calypso sounded like just the kind of nonsense she would have expected Vishnu to write.

The man is totally obscene, she thought. *I like that.*

She wondered if he was planning to perform it himself or if he had written it for someone else. She read the calypso over twice, and then opened the novel.

Later, she heard soft grunts coming from the bedroom. When she checked, Vishnu had kicked the sheets completely off his body. He was wearing only a pair of black nylon jockey shorts. His body was sheened with sick sweat. There was a fleshy smell in the room. His hand was clutching the bedcover as he writhed in the grip of a nightmare. Giselle sat down on the bed and put her hand on his cheek, hoping her touch would calm him.

'Shh, shh,' she said.

Her touch, and the sound of her voice, seemed to work, because in a few moments he stopped writhing and his hand relaxed its grip on the sheet. Then his eyes flew open, black and bright with fever, and he said in a very clear voice: 'That's the next thing I hate about being sick, the bad dreams.' Then his eyelids closed slowly, like trembling shutters, and he was asleep again.

Giselle went back outside.

When the light had changed in the apartment so she knew the evening sun was on its way down, she heard a small sound from the bedroom. She had napped a little. She got up and padded barefoot to the bedroom. Vishnu was sitting up, staring, with tears trickling down his cheeks. As she came through the bead curtain, his head snapped around and his hands flew up like birds to dash away the trickles on his face.

'I thought you had left,' he said gruffly. His voice was stronger.

'How do you feel?' she asked.

'Better,' he said. 'Eyes burning a little bit,' he explained.

Giselle sat down on the bed and studied his face.

'You still look like shit,' she said.

'Darling, you don't know how long I've waited to hear you say those words.'

She laughed. 'Well, you sound better.' But she noticed he had put his hands under the sheet covering his body and there was a slight trembling there.

'I really don't know how to thank you,' he said. His face was drawn, but there was some animation in it now.

'That's my line,' she said lightly.

He shook his head. 'You are so kind.' He bit his lip, and Giselle looked away, not wanting to meet his eyes.

He tried to smile, failed. 'So you heading back up the road now?'

She didn't answer. Eventually, she said, 'You want me to stay?'

He swallowed hard. 'I don't want to inconvenience you . . .'

'You're being polite, Vishnu. Now I know for sure you sick.'

He didn't laugh. There was a hidden appeal in his eyes. 'I'd like for you to stay,' he said.

'Okay,' she said. 'Would you like the rest of the soup?'

He nodded. But as Giselle was lighting the stove, she heard him retching in the bathroom which adjoined his bedroom. She hurried in to find him bowed like a cramped hand over the sink, racked with spasms. The sour smell of vomit filled the air. She rubbed his naked back, to ease the spasms, but he gestured her away violently. She went out.

After a while, there was silence from the bathroom. Giselle heard water running and then a small scrubbing sound. He was brushing his teeth, she supposed, getting the taste of vomit out.

She heated up the soup and carried it in. Vishnu was sitting on the bed, sheet clutched around him, looking miserable.

'Haven't been holding much down,' he said, apologetically.

'That's okay. You want to try and eat a little?'

'I suppose I should.'

He was able to feed himself, very slowly. Giselle sat with him until he was finished, watching.

◆

Later, she called Robert.

'I don't think we'll be able to lime tonight,' she said. 'My friend's still very weak. I don't feel comfortable leaving him just yet.'

'Well, what time you think you'll leave?'

135

'I don't know,' she said patiently, as if speaking to a backward child.

'Approximately,' Robert asked, behaving like one.

'Robert, I really don't know.'

'This must be a very good friend,' said Robert, clearly fishing for information.

'Yes,' said Giselle, even more clearly giving none.

'Where are you?'

'Does it matter?'

'No,' he said. 'I'd just like to know.'

'Barataria,' she said, a little tiredly.

There was a pause.

'I really not too happy with this you know, Giselle,' Robert said.

'I really don't care you know, Robert,' she replied.

The pause this time was full of surprise. A cartoon image came into Giselle's mind: a male spider looking shocked as the female black widow begins to make a light dinner off him. Giselle could even hear a cartoon voice: *Hey, hey! What d'you think you're doing? I just gave you sex and now you're eating me? Was it that bad? Listen, I can do better . . . oomph!* She had to stifle a sudden giggle.

'I see,' said Robert angrily, proving himself no spider, but not being very effective otherwise.

There was another silence. When Robert spoke again, his tone was surprisingly mild.

'I'm sorry. I'm only reacting like this because, well, my intentions, my feelings, to you are serious. Reach home safe. I'll talk to you tomorrow.'

'All right,' she said, a little mollified.

'Take care.'

'All right.'

Giselle hung up, frowning at the receiver. She was puzzled, much as a black widow spider might be if the male came offering one of its eight legs for a snack. She had heard the hardness in Robert's voice behind the apologetic words. He was still angry, still suspicious. So why try to placate her? Then her frown cleared. She knew why – just in case she was thinking of going with another man, and since she was already in that man's apartment, he didn't want to give her further cause. Giselle got up, shaking her head, and went into the bedroom. Men!

'Got through?' Vishnu asked. Giselle nodded. *No need to keep secrets from a naked man*, she thought, and almost giggled again.

She had made Vishnu a cup of tea. The hot liquid eased his sore throat. The light in the bedroom was dimming as the sun sank outside.

He said, 'I'd better take a bath before night comes and the pipes get cold.'

'You don't have hot water?'

'No,' he said. He finished the tea and tried to get up. She pushed him back easily. He said, 'Look, I've offended you in most possible ways already. I don't want to offend your sense of smell, too.'

She said, 'You're not going to bathe in cold water. Now you looking for your death in truth.'

'I've been bathing in cold water for the past few days.'

'I rest my case. Look, have you got a bathing sponge?'

'I don't know.'

'What you mean you don't know.'

'I don't know what a bathing sponge is. There's a new sponge under the sink, though.'

Giselle went and looked. It was a washing sponge, but she thought it would do. She warmed two pans of water. While she was doing that, she heard him trying to move inside. 'Vishnu! *Stay in bed*!' she yelled. He muttered something.

Eventually, she was ready. She had brought in a small coffee table from the living-room, on which she rested the two pans of water. She had the sponge and a clean dish cloth.

'I can do it myself,' he said.

'You'll just wet up the sheets. Relax, I'll only do your upper body. You can, uh, take care of the rest yourself.'

Vishnu lay down, tucking the sheet firmly around his waist. Giselle sponged him off with quick, expert movements.

'How you know about this?' he asked. His breath was a little short. His arms lay loosely at his sides.

'I did a basic nursing course once,' she said.

She was busy, intent, pretending not to notice what was happening below the sheet, but a wicked part of her wanting to say, *So THAT'S how you pitch a tent.* But, despite his calypso, Giselle thought that would embarrass Vishnu.

After she washed his back, she put the remaining clean warm water in the bathroom, where Vishnu finished for himself. He took a long while to do this.

When he joined her in the living-room, he had put on tracksuit pants and a black T-shirt. He sat on the sofa beside her.

'You don't want to lie down?' she asked.

'I'm tired of lying down.' He looked around the living-room. 'I think I'd have recovered a lot quicker if I wasn't so bored. I can't read 'cause it hurts my eyes. Can't listen to music for very long because I get a headache. And I can't even talk to you properly because my brain feels like it's filled with concrete.'

'So what shall we do?'

He looked at her hopefully. 'Play Chinese checkers?'

Giselle ended up spending the night by Vishnu. They played Chinese checkers, draughts, dominoes. They talked. They listened to a little music together. She had given him two Panadol tablets – he had no medicine of any description in the apartment, unless you counted Elastoplast – and his headache had eased. Vishnu's record collection included Billy Joel, Chuck Mangione, Bob Marley, Sting, Dire Straits, Neil Diamond, David Rudder, Shadow, Tracy Chapman and Ray Charles.

By the time Giselle was ready to leave, it was already eleven o'clock. She had changed into the spare clothes she always carried in her car – shorts, a T-shirt and tennis shoes – and brought her car into the yard. She wasn't comfortable about driving back home at that hour. There had been several incidents of motorists being held up on the stretch of highway between Barataria and Port of Spain. So she decided to stay.

'You can sleep on the bed,' Vishnu told her.

'I'll bet,' she said.

He shook his head tiredly. 'Sorry, I'm too sick for that.' She grinned, remembering his automatic response under the sheets while she had sponge-bathed him. 'But I meant you'll sleep on the bed while I sleep out here,' he continued.

'No, I'll sleep out here. You need to rest properly.'

He shrugged. They stayed up talking until one in the morning. But, having made the decision to throw some cushions on the floor and put a sheet on them, Giselle noticed fireflies, lizards and even a spider on the ceiling. Vishnu saw her worried glances.

'Sleep in the bedroom,' he urged her. 'There's a mosquito net,' he added persuasively.

Giselle looked at him. Perhaps it was the late hour, but she felt light-headed and careless. 'Tell you what,' she said. 'The bed's pretty big. We'll both sleep in the bedroom, once you promise not to try anything.'

Vishnu looked at her in surprise. Then he said, tiredly, 'Well, I think I can control myself if you can.'

Giselle started to laugh.

◆

When she turned off the light and crawled under the net on the far side of the bed, she said, 'I've never slept with a man before.'

He muttered, 'Kick them out afterwards, eh? Well, this'll be a new experience for you.'

Giselle realized he had taken her literally.

◆

In the morning, she woke to find her arm flung across Vishnu's chest. She moved away before he woke up.

◆

Giselle waited until Vishnu was awake before she left. His fever had broken and he had not thrown up again. But he was still weak. She made scrambled eggs for breakfast while he washed his face and brushed his teeth. She had bathed already.

When they finished eating, quietly and with little talk, he saw her to the door.

'You saved my life, or at least saved me a lot of pain. Thanks so much,' he said, then grinned. 'You right. Just saying thanks does seem inadequate.'

'Well, I'm glad I had the chance to sort of return the favour.'

He glanced at her. 'Is that the reason you stayed?'

She considered. 'Not the only reason,' she said.

'You always think so deeply before you answer questions?'

'I like to say exactly what I mean.'

He held out a folded sheet of paper to her.

'I wrote this the first time I saw you. You were in the yard at CMC. It's a *haiku*,' he said.

Giselle took the sheet and opened it:

> The sun beats
> like a tenor pan
> to the lovely music of her walk.

Giselle refolded the paper. There was a strange, breathless feeling in her. She searched her mind for something to say – something that would express her wonder, her appreciation, her sudden feeling of closeness to him.

'Exactly seventeen syllables,' she said.

He was standing very near to her, one hand on the door handle for support. 'You would mind if I kissed you?'

His gaze was very intent and serious. The smoky look had returned to his eyes. His face was still gaunt, cactus-like with stubble, and his hair was still unkempt. But his face was full of tenderness, and he watched her very closely. Giselle found she didn't mind at all.

'No,' she said, in a voice that seemed far away and not like her own.

His lips were very soft and gentle against hers, although the stubble pricked her skin. But he kissed her gently and insinuatingly and it was like a renewal, and she found her mind slipping, slipping. When they drew apart, it was as if they were, in some unknown way, two new people. But, lost in the moment, they were not yet entirely aware of this change.

Chapter Ten

Giselle's sense of bliss stayed with her as she drove to her apartment. When she arrived home, she made a cup of coffee, put on a Dire Straits CD, and sat down to think. And, in thinking, Giselle discovered something which rather surprised her: she didn't feel guilty at all.

Oh God, she thought.

She knew she *ought* to feel guilty: in fact, she rather wanted to. Guilt – or, better yet, terrible remorse – would confirm that she was basically a decent person. But, because she was honest with herself, Giselle had to admit that all she felt was a great sense of satisfaction. She was dating Robert; but she had thoroughly enjoyed being with Vishnu. And then Giselle realized that she did in fact feel guilty, but only for not feeling guilty at all.

Giselle sighed. Emotions were so complicated. She drew her legs up on the sofa, wishing Vera was there. Giselle knew no one better qualified to advise her on how to handle multiple relationships. Vera even had a written timetable.

Thinking of Vera reminded Giselle that she had not yet played the Terri Cross CD Vera had given her. 'Virgin's Lament' – that was the track Vera had wanted her to hear.

At the rate I'm going, I'd better listen to it quick before it no longer applies, she thought.

She ejected the Dire Straits album, put in the *Womanish* CD and skipped to the third track. Terri Cross, in a demure tone that was quite unlike her usual brash manner, began the monologue. Giselle grinned as she realized Cross was speaking in the character of a twenty-five-year-old virgin. No wonder Vera had bought her this CD. She settled down to listen to the monologue:

> I turn twenty-five yesterday. Twenty-five years old, and I still a
> virgin. I know what all-yuh wondering. How a nice girl like me

could be so old and still a virgin? Well, I don't quite understand it myself.

I think it was my parents' fault. My father was a lay preacher, you know. That is the main thing I remember from when I was small – my father every Saturday in the small church in we village, telling the congregation, FORNICATION is an ABOMINATION in the sight of the Lord! Hallelujah!' I remember that is the first word I learn to say – no, not Hallelujah. Fornication. I don't remember my father preaching about anything else.

I always like that word, you know. It does sound . . . interesting, yuh doh find? Fornication. It sound better than 'making love'. It does even sound better than the other F-word, because is not a cuss word. You would have to be real sophisticated to say 'Fornicate you!' But the way that word does sound does make me wonder if God really against fornication. I think, if He really didn't want people to fornicate, he woulda call it something else. something that doh sound so . . . titillivating. I eh know . . . something like 'cabbage'.

Think about it. If fornication was cabbage, I sure it would have a lot less people cabbaging or even wanting to cabbage. I mean, if a man trying to seduce a woman, he have to use lyrics. But if he ask she if she want to 'cabbage', the woman eh go fall for that! It sound too boring. And even if the man persist despite the woman not taking him on – 'cause yuh know why men have penises: so they could think – the woman could always say how she doh like cabbage without salad dressing. And you know how men does get confuse easy – he go want to know how anybody could dress for sex. But, let we say he go and get a bottle of salad dressing, you could still say that that only good for eating with cabbage – and you not hungry!

I will tell you this, though: even if he's one of those unusual men who know how to use the salad dressing, he still wouldn't be able to undress you. I mean, the bra over 200 years old, and these men ent learn how to unhook it yet. And if we have on a wraparound skirt, the kind with three belt and two zippers and twenty-five buttons, well, is then he totally confused.

That is the next reason I is still a virgin, you know. I doh understand how man could fix faucet, use drill, make bird cage, fix toilet tank, even take apart carburettor – and none of them could unhook a bra.

Anyway, like I was saying, I suppose hearing my father preach from so small must have had an effect on me. I remember once, after one of he sermons, I went in the back of the church and I see him on top one of the women from the congregation. I know they was praying, because both of them was saying 'Oh God, oh God' but I did never see anybody else, not even my parents, praying like that.

Later, I did ask my father what he was doing, and he tell me that because he was lay preacher he had to preach – and then lay on somebody. So that is how I find out the difference between a lay preacher and one who does stand up. I did ask my father to lay Theophilius Richards, who was always drunk and cussin' loud every night. But I don't think he ever do it, because Theophilius never change.

But I cyar say is because of my parents alone that I is a virgin. You see, after Common Entrance I went to a convent and did convert. I was about fourteen that time and I was starting to feel all kinds of strange feelings. I used to worry about it. But I couldn't talk to anybody about it except the priest. When I was ten years old, I ask my mother where babies come from. She tell me test tubes. I fail Biology because of my mother. I did pass Chemistry, though, because I real like using test tubes. I used to mix all kinds of chemicals and wait for a baby to drop out.

Anyway, as I was saying, I used to tell the priest about all these strange feelings. But he never give me any advice, just listen and tell me say one hundred Hail Marys. But the thing is, the lil boys who used to come to confess used to get plenty more time than me. Sometimes, they even get to be in the same booth with the priest. But you know how the Church sexist, eh. Is a real patriarchal institution. You know what patriarchal mean, right? Yes, they favour men.

But when yuh come right down to it, I have to blame myself, too. I mean, I cyar say I really *try* to lose my virginity when I was younger. All right, the truth is I was frighten to have sex. Not because I mighta get pregnant, because like I say I thought babies came from test tubes. But I was worried I might like it . . . a lot. Is

143

like with cigarettes, nah. You smoke one and you might cough and thing, but then you try a next one and then a next one and first thing you know you real enjoying this smoking thing – and yuh good at it, too! And, from the way people talk, it sound like sex even better than smoking . . . well, let me take that back, because men in prison does riot if they cyar get cigarettes but not if they cyar get sex . . . what you say? They getting sex? Well, that is like saying if you give dem seaweed to smoke instead of tobacco, that go satisfy them. I mean, is all right if you like seaweed or if you cyar get good tobacco. But you know Trinidad have real good tobacco – that is why being in prison is real punishment. But in any case, it have men outside prison who does smoke spend more on cigarettes than on seducing a woman – and the married ones does certainly spend more on cigarettes than on dey wife. Is dem kinda value systems which help make me a virgin today.

But, like I was sayin', I did fraid I woulda like the sex thing too much. You know, I mighta try one man, then another, then another, thinking I could take it or leave it alone. But pretty soon I mighta find men had become a habit. And, while smoking might be a bad habit, at least cigarettes only give you lung cancer. Hm! The world reach a nice stage, eh, where lung cancer is like a petty disease. I mean, if you dying from lung cancer these days, nobody taking you on. You not in *fashion*, you see. You have to be dying from AIDS or Ebola or else get shoot by a bandit or chop by some jealous man to get any attention.

Me, I prefer to die quiet and unfashionable. So it had a lot of things to make me hesitant.

When I turn eighteen, I start reading romance novels. I couldn't believe what used to go on in them books. The man always handsome, rich, strong, and faithful . . . is the last part I couldn't believe.

That is the next reason I'm still a virgin. With this AIDS thing why I should be doing thing with any man when he might be doing thing with other women? And doh forget gonorrhea, syphilis and herpes still around, eh. I mean, AIDS is the star, but them others still playing to large audiences. And my father was a lay preacher and I know the only faithful men are those who over sixty – and is not because they suddenly discover what a good wife they have. Is because by sixty they doh have enough energy even for she – unless you's Anthony Quinn. You know Anthony Quinn, the movie star with a big head and short legs? He seventy-eight years old and fathering child still. Just shows that you mustn't watch ugly men and think they slight.

Anyway, before I realize how hard it is for one man rat to live in one hole, so to speak, I used to think I woulda wait till I was married before I do it. But now I's wonder if it worth going through all the trouble of a marriage. You spend one set of money, have one set of stress planning wedding, invite one set of relatives you doh really like, and for what? What you does really have after you married? Housework and a man to mess up the house after you do your housework.

So I decide – it doh make sense waiting till I married. And, like I say, I always like the word fornicate. But you cyar fornicate if you married – at least, not with the person you married to. Is no wonder sex in marriage not as exciting – it doh have an exciting word. Even so, I want a man who untouched by another woman . . . or another man. But he have to be good in bed.

You don't think that possible? Of *course* it possible! Look how much do-it-yourself books they have out these days. Hear what I figure. If a man never do it, he go be all the more anxious to do it when the right woman come along, right? And I am the right woman. I ready, willing and able. I won' lie, though. I still frighten. Why not? Sex is a frightening thing. Yuh could know that from the amount of jokes people does make about it – you does only laugh to relieve tension. And I notice is mostly men who does crack sexy jokes . . . but is women who does laugh the hardest. But, say what, once we laughin' together, we could always work something out, right?

Unfortunately, Terri, thought Giselle, getting up to turn off the CD player, *cracking jokes not going to get me out of this situation. I really wish Vera was here.*

Keys rattled at the door and Vera stepped in with a suitcase in one hand and a *Star Trek* novel in the other.

'Vera!' Giselle exclaimed. 'I was just thinking about you.'

Vera put her suitcase down. 'I will live long then.'

Giselle stood up and hugged her.

'I am *so* glad to see you.'

'Of course you are,' said Vera, sitting down. 'Is it my natural charisma or do you just like my perfume?'

'I have a problem only you can help me with.'

'Me? I ain't exactly the most sensible person around.'

'Of course you have sense, Vee. You just choose not to use it.'

'Thanks.'

'Look, you remember the guy who save me from the falling bucket.'

'Yes. Vishnu. You went to lunch and got vexed and wrote him off despite his nice pecs.'

'I kissed him this morning.'

Vera's eyes opened wide, then she grinned. 'Well, congratulations! Is about time you got out of your shell.'

'But I'm dating Robert Cardinez.'

This time Vera's eyes just narrowed. 'Excuse me?'

Giselle repeated her story. Vera leaned forward, eyes still narrowed.

'Okay lady, what have you done with my friend Giselle?' she said.

Giselle punched Vera lightly on the arm. 'C'mon, girl, I need your advice.'

Vera threw up her hands.

'Advice on what?'

'On how to handle this situation.'

'Are you filled with regret and wracked with guilt? Knowing you, you must be.'

'No, I'm feeling very pleased with myself today.'

Vera's mouth dropped open. Giselle laughed.

'Well,' said Vera, 'now I know the real reason we're friends.'

'But,' said Giselle, 'I don't like feeling this way.'

Vera looked heavenwards.

'Let me get this straight. If I said that you're plagued with guilt and totally overcome with remorse at having kissed one man while you're involved with another, I'd be putting you in the most sympathetic and even moral light possible for an otherwise decent young woman who has committed such a serious breach in expected standards of decorum and good behaviour. I on track so far?'

'Yes,' said Giselle, 'and you put it so eloquently too.'

'Thank you, I owe it all to "Ophrah", the perfume that makes women eloquent. Now! Saying all this, however, would also be inaccurate?'

'Yes.'

'In fact, if your conscience is pricking you at all, the spot is clearly numbed with Novocaine?'

'Apparently.'

'Like Terri Cross's monologue really made you rethink your constipated value system.'

'No, I only just finished listening to it as you walked in. Ha! Her virgin thinks *she* has problems!'

Vera got up. 'Well, I don't see your problem. Enjoy your true nature for a while.'

'But maybe this isn't my true nature. Maybe is just my ego.'

'Tell me about the two of them,' said Vera. Giselle opened her mouth to answer and Vera, as if she still couldn't quite believe it, said, 'From none to two?'

'Yes, Vera, two. One is the manager of CMC – Robert Cardinez. I've told you about him. And the other is Vishnu, the guy who saved me from a broken skull.'

Vera shook her head with some violence. 'Wait, wait. Let me get this straight. You're not only going around with two men, but one is a company manager and one is a manual labourer. And both work on the same premises?' She looked at Giselle admiringly. 'You might be a slow starter, Karan, but you sure accelerate fast once you get going. Zero to sixty in ten seconds flat, you bet.'

'Yes. Well, I want to slow down and maybe settle down now. This situation will be too much of a strain.'

'Juggling will do that,' said Vera. 'Hell, Gis, even *I* keep them in separate countries. Well, most of the time.'

Giselle took a sip of coffee.

'So what do you think I should do?'

'Well, it's too early to tell. Really, Gis, all you can do now is go with the flow. Time will tell you what to do better than I can.'

'You sure?'

'No. But that's the best I can do after a five-hour flight.'

'Oh well, I suppose you're right.'

Vera put her hand to her breast and collapsed theatrically back on the sofa. 'My God, Giselle thinks I'm right and she's involved with two men. The endtimes are surely upon us.'

Giselle flung one of the sofa pillows at her. 'Shut up, fool,' she laughed.

'Okay.'

'Oh, speaking of endtimes, my mother is pregnant.'

Vera laughed. 'You'll make me think you're lying about having kissed the two men, too,' she said, and got up and went into the bedroom.

Giselle grinned. She would bring it up again later. She didn't want to give Vera too many shocks in so short a space of time.

◆

Having missed an afternoon, Giselle decided to go to work at least for a few hours. Besides, she knew Robert would be there, since he worked Saturdays, and she wanted to see how she reacted to him now. Vera was sleeping when she left, so Giselle left a note telling her where she was. As an afterthought, Giselle added: 'And call my mom!'

When she met Robert later at work, the first thing he asked was how her friend was. Giselle, feeling only a wicked tranquillity, said, 'Better. Poor fella, he was hardly able to stand yesterday.' And she was astonished at how smoothly she said this: there was absolutely nothing in her tone to suggest she had given her patient a little hands-on therapy and, indeed, helped him stand rather well. And she thought she should have felt terrible when, later in the morning, Robert stole from her a quick kiss in his office, and she responded with gratifying and even girlish enthusiasm. But, to Giselle's own wonder, her manner gave no hint that she had recently been kissing someone else with equal, if not greater, enthusiasm.

Well, it's always been my way, when I do a thing, to do it properly or not at all, she thought. But the Pope, she feared, would hardly have bought this argument. Neither, she suspected, would the Archbishop of Canterbury, the Ayatollah of Iran or even, were he still alive, Mahatma Gandhi.

But Gandhi lived with three women, Giselle thought, *so he might have been more understanding of the frailties of lesser mortals.*

'I hope you missed me a little last night,' Robert told Giselle. *I guess*

148

he believes the old-fashioned idea that only men are weak in the flesh, Giselle thought.

'Of course, darling,' she answered, thinking to herself that men, in fact, are more often weak in the head.

Giselle also knew that, for Robert to gain any inkling that his jealousy might have been justified, he would have expected to see signs of quietness, worry, even depression in her that day. But, had he been looking (and she figured he was) he would have looked in vain. Giselle went about her work with undiminished enthusiasm and great energy. And the thing was, it was all natural. She even whistled while she worked. *You are so low*, she thought to herself, *but it's kind of fun*.

Such gay spirits were not lost on Sharma, who was also working that day.

'See, Giselle, I told you what you needed was a man,' she said.

'Or two,' Giselle said.

'Eh?'

'And you were right, too,' she amended smoothly.

'Of course.'

'Of course,' Giselle agreed, laughing. Sharma grinned back at her.

'Tell me, Shams,' said Giselle, 'You ever slept with anyone before your husband?'

'Nope,' Sharma answered.

'And you've been married eight years now?'

'Uh-huh.'

'So you don't ever wonder what it might be like with someone else?'

'Well, yes. Especially when I meet a man with good teeth. I have a thing for good teeth.'

'Of course. Who doesn't?'

'But me and Kishan have a good sex life. So why take the chance? What happen? Cardy worried about your past experiences?'

'Not exactly,' said Giselle, and left it there.

◆

When Robert met her for lunch, she said, 'Let's eat in town today.'

'Where?'

'There's a place with pretty good food just across the road.'

Robert gazed doubtfully at the square. There were men with white caps selling corn soup, men with sharp cutlasses selling coconuts, large women with large bags walking everywhere, taxi drivers announcing their destinations to passers-by as though offering transport to the Promised Land, and beggars blessing everyone who looked as though they had spare change. Giselle wondered why she had never realized what an entertaining place the square was.

'You sure?' Robert asked.

'Oh, come on,' said Giselle and, looking like some explorer about to brave the wild jungle, he did.

However, the natives turned out to be friendly, and they arrived safely at the Beijing Palace after a two-minute trek. The place was crowded and noisy and the waitresses busier than ever. A faint pall of food-scented smoke drifted through the dining area. Robert ordered Foo Young Kai Nip soup and some spring rolls.

'I'm not very hungry today,' he explained.

'Well, I am,' said Giselle, and proceeded to prove it by ordering pork fried rice, chow veg and sweet-and-sour chicken.

The food came quickly, and Giselle attacked her heaped plate with knife and fork while Robert sipped sedately at his soup with a plastic spoon.

'This sweet-and-sour chicken is excellent,' she said.

'I'm glad you're enjoying it,' Robert smiled. He looked around. 'You come here often?'

'No, I've only been a few times. But the food's good, like I said.'

'Yes, this soup's not bad.'

'Pity you're not hungry.'

'Pity.'

Giselle cleared her plate quickly and looked at Robert with wide eyes. He gazed back at her.

'I hope you don't think I'm too terrible . . .' she began.

'No. I eat pretty fast, too,' he said.

'But I'd like a burger.'

Robert laughed astonishedly. 'You're kidding.'

'No. I just feel ravenous today. I think you've increased my metabolic rate.'

'Oh, well in that case I'll have to make amends.'

He signalled a waitress. As they waited for the burger, she said, 'Mind you, I kind of like having my metabolic rate increased.'

Robert chuckled and somewhere, no doubt, some mischievous imps were laughing heartily, too. Giselle, at least, was pretty sure she heard them giggling. She remembered an old quote: 'There is a pleasure sure in being mad, which none but madmen know.' *That is so true*, she thought, and giggled herself.

'What?' said Robert.

'Nothing.'

After work, Robert asked Giselle what time he should pass. But she told him that she was behind and would be working late that night then heading home. And she may even have meant it at the time she said it. But Vishnu called the office at around six.

'Hi, how you feeling?' she asked.

'Better. How you going?'

'Fine,' she said, laughing in spite of herself.

'You been sniffing glue or something?'

'Can't I laugh?'

'Incessantly, if it turns you on. Speaking of which, pass and keep me company when you're finished, nah.'

'I'll think about it.'

He chuckled, a little hackingly. 'Well, think on your feet because there are better things to do when you're on your back.'

'Oh?' said Giselle. 'Like what?'

There were several moments of blank silence at the other end of the phone. Giselle laughed again.

'Paint,' Vishnu said at last. 'They're still painting the office and the fumes are getting to you.'

'Maybe I'll see you later,' she said, and hung up.

Giselle finished at around seven and, having got into her car and started driving, found herself heading towards Barataria. Part of her said she should be going to see Robert if she was going to see anyone. What had happened with Vishnu could still be dismissed as a once-in-a-lifetime aberration. But if she went back by Vishnu and anything happened it would be a little more difficult to dismiss it as a twice-in-a-lifetime aberration. So Giselle argued but, for all the attention she paid to herself, she might have been lying on her back.

'You look a lot better,' she told Vishnu when she arrived.

He had shaved, washed his hair and tied it back, and his eyes, though still filmy, had a spark in them.

'There's a doctor called Deepak Chopra who says if you're in good spirits, you're going to be healthy. All you need is the right sort of stimulation.' Vishnu looked at her with his old, meaning humour. 'I'm starting to think he's absolutely right.'

'Down boy,' Giselle said, and immediately contradicted herself by coming into his ready arms.

'Woof!' said Vishnu.

◆

Giselle reached home about ten that night. Vera had gone out, but left a note. 'Your mom's really pregnant! Girl, enjoy life now because the end of the world is definitely nigh.'

There was a message from Robert on the answering machine. She would have to tell him she had been sleeping and had unplugged the bedroom extension. *Boy, you really have to be creative when you're having an affair*, she thought. She had spent most of the time by Vishnu necking – indeed, apart from those initial sentences, they had hardly spoken at all. Giselle loved the way Vishnu kissed. At times, he was gentle and exploring, then hard and rapacious. And he had marvellously soft and mobile lips. In fact, because of the way she reacted to him, Giselle had to cut her stay short. During their necking, he tried to cup her breast twice, and she stopped him firmly, the second time with a hard pinch.

'Ouch!' he exclaimed, then grinned at her. And it disturbed Giselle to realize that Vishnu was not in the least bit bothered by her resistance. It even – although she would never admit this – frightened her a little. He resumed kissing her with an enjoyment and passion and subtle desire, so Giselle left far sooner than she wanted. Vishnu seemed to make her stop thinking.

Now she had done this a second time, Giselle thought that, in a moral universe, she should have tossed and turned all night. But she again slept like a baby – rather better, in fact, since she didn't wake up in the middle of the night to be fed.

That weekend was also the first time she went to Robert's apartment. He took her out to dinner the next day and they went to a movie afterwards. Then they went back to his place. Robert's embraces were full of restrained passion. Giselle did not have to control his hands. He was a perfect gentleman. She told him this.

'You know, Robert, you're a perfect gentleman,' she said.

'That's because I'm serious,' he explained.

'Oh. And here I thought it was congenital.'

'I know we haven't been seeing each other long, Giselle,' he said. 'But I don't think you realize that I *am* very serious.'

'Yes. So you just said,' Giselle said thoughtfully. 'So, tell me. You think a man who isn't gentlemanly to a young lady like myself is therefore not serious?' she asked, smiling.

'Well,' he said, smiling back, 'A young lady with your figure would probably encourage a man to have most ungentlemanly thoughts. But if he took the trouble to truly know you, he would realize, as I have done, that you are in the most important ways, a true lady.'

'Please, Robert,' said Giselle. 'You'll make me blush.'

'I don't mean to embarrass you.'

'I'm not embarrassed. Your dialogue is just so corny.'

He smiled. 'But sincere.'

'But sincere,' she agreed.

As they resumed their embrace, Robert's hands moved a little more freely. They moved upon her now like those of a master pianist, and Giselle thought, if she *had* been a piano, she might have been right in tune with him. She realized Robert thought she had been encouraging him to be a little less gentlemanly and a little more of the demon lover. Actually, she had been thinking she didn't need to worry about Vishnu becoming too serious about her. *He's probably after only one thing*, she thought, relieved.

◆

Giselle thought that, given her conclusions after seeing Robert that night, she obviously had no excuse to continue seeing Vishnu. She devoted some serious thought to the matter. Yes, Vishnu had good pecs and nice teeth and he held her so firmly, so boldly, and he kissed like there was no tomorrow . . . By this point, she had lost the thread of her thoughts and had to start all over. Vishnu returned to work

153

that Monday, but he and she spoke only briefly in passing. He seemed to understand and accept, without her saying so, that Giselle didn't want people around knowing they were intimate. So that was one thing less on her mind.

But, even though she didn't feel guilty at all, Giselle knew that, merely from a practical point of view, things could not continue as they were for any length of time. And, knowing it must end, she decided it was better to end it sooner rather than later. The crucial thing, Giselle told herself, was that she had a man – Robert, that is – who was attractive, knowledgeable, sophisticated, well-off and who had a nice wardrobe. And, most important of all, according to Fariel, he was serious about her. Well, she had actually said the man should be willing to do anything for you, but it amounted to the same thing. And what were pecs, or even nice lips, in this crazy world? Of course, Vishnu did also have an interesting library and a really nice music collection.

But Giselle set her mind resolutely. She intended to stop this nonsense once and for all. She knew she was strong-willed and, now she had laid down the law for herself, there would be no gainsaying this decree. The next time she went by Vishnu's apartment, she told herself firmly, they would only talk about books and listen to music.

Having made this resolution, Giselle felt far more at ease and, with typical decisiveness, went by Vishnu that very night.

'I didn't come here to neck with you, eh,' she told him as soon as she came through the door.

'Okay,' Vishnu said.

Giselle turned to face him.

'Okay?' she said, suddenly and irrationally feeling like a tigress berating her mate for being out too late with the other tigers last Friday night. 'What do you mean "okay"?'

'We can just talk if you want. I *do* enjoy talking with you, you know. Or we could listen to music and not say a word, if you prefer.'

'Oh, hell,' said Giselle.

Vishnu smiled, puzzled.

'You all right, Giselle?' he asked.

'Would you mind,' Giselle said between clenched teeth, 'not saying my name so nicely?'

'Is not my fault you have a nice name,' Vishnu said, adding caressingly, 'Giselle.'

Giselle moved forward, and the resemblance to an angry tigress became even more marked. Vishnu looked suddenly nervous.

'Take-off-that-damned-T-shirt,' she said between clenched teeth.

'Take it off yourself,' said Vishnu, looking as if he was hoping she wouldn't disembowel him.

Without hesitation, Giselle grabbed his T-shirt, pulled it over his head with the sound of tearing cloth, and pushed him down on the sofa. She sat beside him, leaned down, and began to do things to his chest with her mouth. She felt quite savage. A visiting tiger, had one been present, might have thought she was making dinner off some tasty villager.

After about half an hour, they sat back while their breathing returned to more normal rates.

'I'm glad you didn't come to fool around,' said Vishnu, a little raggedly. 'If you had, I might be a dead man now.'

'I am so disappointed in myself,' Giselle said.

'I'm not.'

'I shouldn't even be here. I'm supposed to be going out with Robert Cardinez.'

'Oh? Then why are you here?'

'I don't know.'

'How can you go out with a guy who wears ties?'

'You have something against ties?'

'Yes. But I think that's because I was hanged in a previous life.'

Giselle smiled. She liked Vishnu's nonsense. 'That's an interesting theory.'

'Don't you get the impression, sometimes, that I was a great king in Mesopotamia and you were my favourite concubine?'

'No, I can't say that I have.'

'Funny, I could have sworn . . .'

He leaned forward. Giselle pulled back a little.

'If you were a king, how come you were hanged?' she said hurriedly.

'That was another life, when I was a pickpocket.'

He reached forward and ran strong fingers under her loosened blouse along her naked spine.

'How do you think I got such good hands?' he said.

'Oh, hell,' said Giselle.

Vishnu grinned. 'Here we go again.'

Though she felt a little foolish doing so, in the light of what had just happened, Giselle still told Vishnu before she left that she would not come by him again for the rest of the week.

'Aw, don't do that,' he said.

'I don't think it's wise.' She hesitated. 'And I don't want to lead you on.'

His face grew set. 'You can't lead me on. Even if you might think you doing so.'

'What you mean?'

'Figure it out.'

'We can talk on the phone instead.'

He watched her for a long moment, then suddenly grinned.

'Fraidy cat!'

Giselle was startled into laughter. 'What? Listen, buster, I am not afraid of anything.'

'Fraidy cat *liar*!' he crowed.

'Look, I'm gone.'

He continued grinning as he touched her hair, pulling at a stray curl. 'Call me when you reach home.'

'All right.'

So she did, and they spoke for two hours.

Well, at least I kept part of my resolution, Giselle said to herself before she dropped into restful sleep that night. She drew comfort from the thought that even those who might have judged her most harshly would not have been able to gainsay *that*.

◆

Giselle did not, in fact, go by Vishnu's apartment for the next three weeks. Instead, she went out to lunch every day with Robert and was with him every night. They talked or watched television or went out to dinner. They also spent time necking, in a restrained way. Giselle felt very comfortable with Robert. She was very attentive to him, and his talk grew increasingly serious. He seemed to be trying to push the relationship along. He talked about the mistakes he had made in his marriage and how he was determined not to make them again. He

156

talked about how well suited they were. He talked about the need for commitment. Giselle listened and thought about the things Robert said.

But she also spoke to Vishnu nearly every night on the phone. There was, she argued with herself, nothing wrong in just talking to someone. She talked to people all the time. It was wrong, Giselle told herself virtuously, to treat a man distantly just because he kissed really well.

The conversations she had with Vishnu were usually general. He told her about people he had met in the past two years while working through the Caribbean islands. (Strangely, he rarely spoke of his life before that period.) They talked about books and music. They discussed relationships and human attitudes and life in general. But he never inquired about her relationship with Robert or, indeed, spoke as if she had such a relationship. And Giselle noted another thing Vishnu never talked about: the calypsos and poetry he wrote.

'Are you happy?' she asked him one night.

'Just let me swallow these red tablets and call you back in an hour.'

'Come on, I'm serious.'

'With a face like that? Oh, all right. Yes, most of the time. Happiness, I think, is like your bladder.'

'Eh?'

'It's inside you and it ha' pee.'

'Oh God,' Giselle groaned.

'Please, don't get orgasmic while I'm philosophizing.'

'When should I get orgasmic then?'

'Oh, about ten minutes after we get naked.'

'I guess your idea of foreplay is "Hang on honey, here I come."'

'I was speaking about the first orgasm only.'

'Could we get back to the point?'

'Weren't we talking about happiness?'

'Yes.'

'Well, let me tell you, there are few things happier than a good orgasm.'

'Vishnu!'

'All right. I think happiness is inside you. Trying to find happiness in external things – money, fame, power – that's the great self-deception people practise. When you get happiness in yourself, the only thing you have to look for then is someone to share it with.'

'Why you need to share it at all?'

'Because by yourself, it not complete. It is just selfish. See how we get back to the orgasm metaphor?'

'And the times you aren't happy. Why is that?'

There was a pause.

'You not here, are you?' he said, and there was no laughter in his voice.

After a while, she said, 'Well, I'd like to be.'

'Then why aren't you?'

'I don't know.'

'Listen, I know you worry that we get too physical too fast. But I would promise not to touch you if that is what you want. Hell, we slept together already, and I didn't.'

'Yeah, you were sick.'

'Honey, I wasn't *that* sick. But you *can* trust me.'

'It's not you I'm worried about.'

He chuckled. 'I guess I should be flattered. But I'd prefer to be insulted and have you here.'

'That's because you have twisted values.'

'Nope. Just got my priorities right.'

'You know, as we on this topic of sex – '

'I love it when you start sentences like that.'

'Shut up, fool. My mom's pregnant.'

'At her age?'

'That's what I said when I found out.'

'Does she want to be?'

'Well, she didn't. But now it's happened, she's quite happy about it. She just wants the baby to be healthy.'

'How old is her husband?'

'Forty-eight.'

'Great.'

'Oh, you approve of this, do you?'

'Well, I certainly approve of people having sex past middle age. What do you think is my main reason for keeping fit? I think people should be able to do it until they ready to die.'

'I told you your values were twisted.'

'No, yours are. Listen, Giselle, if we ever have sex, I hope we continue until we're in our nineties.'

She laughed. 'Well, we'd have to take breaks to go to work.'

'I guess. And for meals.'

'No, we can always incorporate food into it. That might be fun.'

There was a bit of stunned silence. Giselle liked the way she could shock Vishnu. But he rallied gamely.

'And what about sleep?'

'Well, I suppose we'd return to the bedroom to finish off. After bathroom, living-room, kitchen. We'll be getting exercise and resting in the same place.'

'Sound ideal.'

'Yes, when you think about it. Heaven must be arranged along similar lines. Just with coconut trees close by.'

'So let's discuss recipes.'

'Recipes?'

'Yeah, you talking about using food . . .'

But, for all this spicy talk, Giselle still did not go by Vishnu. There was too much about herself she did not now understand. A new personality seemed to have emerged within her: someone who was careless and indifferent and exultant. The rational Giselle was not sure she liked this new person; but she could resist her no more than she could stop the wind from blowing.

Besides not understanding how she could have found herself in this situation, Giselle was no longer sure of the standards she had always lived by. She kept Robert and Vishnu separate in her mind. They meant different things to her. Robert represented the good life, the ideal, the things she had striven to achieve. As she saw it, he would be part of her achievements and he would help her attain her further goals.

But Vishnu. What was he? She felt a terrible physical attraction for him. This was the other part of herself that Giselle no longer understood. In the past weeks, her sensuality, which had formerly burnt with a steady but controlled flame, like a blowtorch, seemed to have flared into something more akin to the Great Fire of London. Her very veins seemed afire with sensuality, and all those veins seemed to lead to one place. She was more aware of colours, smells, sounds and, especially, touch. It was getting harder and harder to maintain her self-control.

For this reason, more than any other, she avoided seeing Vishnu. He seemed to spark off that fire in her too easily. It wasn't that he tried to. But Giselle sensed a spirit in him that revelled in its own sensuality. Sensed? She had seen it in his most casual movements, in the way he sometimes looked at her. That was why she had beat a hasty retreat. But, even on the phone, if their conversation turned to sex-related topics, or if he flirted with her, images and strange feelings would run through Giselle's mind. Vishnu was free, untrammelled, and that frightened Giselle. And what frightened her more was the discovery that such a spirit dwelt in her as well.

And then Robert began to get more persistent in that area as well.

At first, this had surprised Giselle. She had let his hands be reasonably free. But one night he went a little further, or tried to, and she moved back at once.

He was immediately apologetic. 'Sorry, I just thought . . . I mean, I expected . . . Well, anyway, I'm sorry.'

'It's all right,' she said, not looking at him. She was actually feeling more embarrassed by his apologies than his action.

'You know, we've been seeing so much of each other, and becoming more intimate. I felt we knew each other well enough . . .'

He trailed off again.

'Robert, I said it's all right.'

'You sure it's all right?'

'Yes.'

There was a silence.

'I've been wanting to get your view on something for some time now,' he said finally.

'What's that?'

'Well, what do you think of marriage? As an institution, I mean,' he added hastily.

Giselle grinned at him. 'I didn't think you were proposing, Robert,' she said.

He smiled. 'You never fail to surprise me, Giselle,' he said, returning to his usual sophisticated manner. In fact, thought Giselle, that was the first time she had ever seen him awkward.

'That's me,' she replied, 'a walking bran-tub.'

'Well, what do you think about marriage? I'm curious.'

'Oh, I have no moral objections to it,' she said.

'Ah, I see,' he said, clearly not seeing at all.

Giselle was content to leave him in the dark. That line of conversation was not one she wished to pursue just yet.

This took place near the end of the month; and the very next night Giselle was at Vishnu's apartment. She had not been there for over three weeks, and had seen him only in passing at work. In fact, it is also true that she had not intended to go there at all. But they had been speaking on the phone, he talking mostly nonsense, when he had asked what she was wearing.

'Just the T-shirt I sleep in,' she said. 'Why?'

'What colour is it?'

'Light purple. Why?'

'So I can imagine you in your bed. I miss seeing you, you know.'

'Well, it's a purple T-shirt with a large bunny rabbit on the front.'

'How long is it?'

'Oh, is just a one-foot bunny rabbit.'

'The T-shirt, not the blasted rabbit.'

'Why? And don't insult my rabbit.'

'I want to know if it's cute or sexy. The T-shirt, not the non-insultable bunny rabbit.'

'Just below the knees.'

'Oh.' He sounded disappointed.

'But,' said Giselle, 'I have on very sexy underwear.'

'Oh!' he said, a lot more enthusiastically. When she did not speak again, he said, 'What colour?'

'Should I tell you?' she said.

'Definitely,' he answered, and his voice had become very throaty.

Giselle ended up finishing her description at Vishnu's apartment very late that night. In fact, she let him judge for himself, and when he did the same thing Robert had tried – oh, but in such a different manner, not as if it was expected but because he wanted, he *desired* to, Giselle did not move away. Lady Chatterley, she thought, would have approved.

◆

After that night, Giselle realized she had to make a choice. She called Vera in London and told her she had to see her.

'I hadn't intended to pass in at all,' Vera said. 'Remember, I have to save my days so I could be there for the Carnival weekend and to play mas.'

'If you value our friendship at all, Vera Chancellor,' said Giselle, and it was the first time she had spoken to Vera like that, 'you will come and see me. I need you.'

There was a long, surprised silence on the line.

'Oh, all right,' Vera said, adding, 'There's something I want you to do for me anyway.'

◆

Vera was in front of the television when Giselle got home. She was sitting cross-legged on the sofa, eating ice cream from a tub, and looking like a contented child. She glanced around as Giselle walked into the room.

'I hope you know, Ms Karan,' said Vera, 'the great sacrifice I have made in order to hear your life story. My plans tonight, let me tell you, consisted mainly of sybaritic, uninhibited and extremely rude behaviour.'

Giselle threw her bag down on the carpet and collapsed onto the sofa.

'But you do that every night, Vee,' she said. 'You getting in a rut – if you get my meaning.'

'Don't be fresh, young lady,' Vera said. She grinned. 'Even if it is true.'

She took up the remote and switched off the television.

'What seems to be the trouble?' she said, turning to Giselle.

'I have to make a choice,' Giselle answered. 'I'm wondering if I should have sex with one of them.'

Vera's spoon dropped into her ice cream. After a moment, she retrieved it and slowly licked it clean.

'You know,' she said, 'I could have sworn I heard you say you were thinking about having sex with one of them.'

'That's because that's what I did say.'

Vera, grinning, held out her arms to Giselle.

'Girlfriend! I knew I would corrupt you eventually.'

'Vera! I'm serious! I need you to help me to decide what to do.'

'You seemed to be walking the tightrope pretty well.'

'Yes, well my circus career is about to end.'

Vera got up. 'I think we need to go out on the balcony for this one,' she said.

'All right,' said Giselle.

Dusk had not fallen long, but the moon already rode high and bright. A cold breeze blew. Giselle felt her flesh become pimpled under her thin blouse. Vera sat on the lounging chair and put her feet up on the iron railing.

'So why are you having trouble deciding?'

Giselle propped her denim-clad bottom against the banister and rubbed her bare arms.

'I don't know,' she pouted. 'I like both of them a lot. Robert is mature, sophisticated, ambitious. I feel very comfortable with him. More comfortable than I feel with Vishnu, actually.

'Why's that?' Vera asked.

Giselle hesitated.

'Well, uh, Robert doesn't push anything. If you know what I mean.'

Vera looked at Giselle with luminous, dark eyes. There was a calm, shattered knowledge in that gaze. Vera, thought Giselle, had the eyes of a person with nothing to lose.

'You haven't slept with either one yet?' said Vera.

'No. But I want to. It's time. That's partly why I have to choose.'

'I see.'

'Robert's very gentlemanly. But I know he's getting impatient. And I don't want him thinking I'm just a naive prude.'

'Yeah. There's just one problem with that.'

'What?'

'You *are* a naive prude.'

Giselle gave an irritated click of her tongue. 'No, I'm not.'

Vera waved a dismissive hand.

'Anyway,' Giselle continued, 'Vishnu is even less understanding. He just assumes we should sleep together and, God, does he want to! I feel really bad about frustrating him. He must think I'm a tease. If he only knew how much it's costing me to resist him. In fact, I don't think I can for much longer.'

'I see,' Vera said again.

Giselle slipped off her shoes and sat on the stool.

'What would you do in a situation like that, Vee?' she asked.

Vera shrugged. 'The question doesn't arise.'

'Are we so different?'

'Well, for one thing I wouldn't want to settle down. I'd probably take the easy way out.'

'Which is?'

'Sleep with both of them. But you want to make a serious choice. If you didn't, we wouldn't even be having this conversation and I'd be carrying on with wild abandon by now.'

'Yes, well you can thank me for saving you later,' said Giselle. 'C'mon, Vee, I need feedback here.'

Vera looked at Giselle thoughtfully.

'If you were married, who do you think would make the better husband?'

Giselle frowned thoughtfully.

'Robert, I suppose,' she answered.

Vera nodded. 'Who do you think would be better in bed?'

'Vera!' Giselle exclaimed, laughing. 'I dunno.'

'Oh, come on. Don't tell me you haven't thought about it.'

'Well . . .'

'*Well*?'

Giselle laughed. 'I have thought about it. Pretty often.'

Vera grinned. 'And the winner is?'

'Vishnu,' said Giselle. 'He's kind of wild, I think. I've been having some pretty lurid fantasies about him.'

'Is that why he makes you uncomfortable?'

'I don't know. Maybe.'

Vera raised an eyebrow. 'Interesting kind of discomfort.'

'You can't base a relationship on physical attraction, Vera,' Giselle said, almost angrily.

'No. You can't base it on a charming manner, either. I found that out in my marriage.'

Vera rubbed her shoulder as though a sudden chill had penetrated that spot.

'So whom do you think I should choose?' said Giselle.

'You really want me to answer that?'

'Of course.'

'Neither.'

There was a short silence. Giselle's eyes were clouded.

'Why?' she said finally.

'Because you're still not sure what you want out of life, Giselle. And I can't tell what you feel about either of these men to tell what the best decision would be. Maybe you should continue as you have been.'

'I can't. That's not me. Not anymore.'

Vera shrugged. Giselle, suddenly irritated, stood up.

'What you going to do?' Vera asked.

'I don't know. You haven't been much help.'

Vera said nothing, looking out at the dark sky.

'Sorry,' said Giselle.

'Mm-hm,' said Vera.

There was another silence.

'Listen,' said Giselle suddenly. 'Why don't we go and check them out?'

Vera looked up at her with arched eyebrows. Then she grinned wickedly.

'Both ah dem, as Sparrow puts it?'

'Sure. I want to know what you think. It'll help me decide.'

Vera got up. 'What fun!' she said, and went inside to change.

◆

They visited Robert first. Giselle had deliberately not called ahead, and when Robert answered the doorbell his hair was dishevelled and his eyes were puffy with sleep. He was wearing a maroon robe.

'Hi,' she said blandly. 'I caught you at a bad time?'

'Just taking a nap,' he said. His voice was rough with sleep. 'I was going to call you later.'

'This is my friend Vera,' said Giselle.

Vera peered brightly from behind Giselle.

'Hi,' she said.

'Hello. Please, come in.'

'We didn't intend to stay,' said Giselle. 'We were just liming by the mall and I thought I'd surprise you.'

'Of course you must stay for a while,' said Robert, taking her by the hand.

'Well, just for a while,' said Giselle, coming in.

Vera whistled. 'Nice pad, Roberto.'

He smiled. 'I'm comfortable.'

Giselle and Vera sat down in the living-room.

'Just let me freshen up,' said Robert.

He disappeared down the corridor. Vera immediately slapped Giselle on the shoulder. 'Karan, you are such a smooth liar. I didn't know you had it in you.'

'I didn't, either. I suppose I've had great practice these past couple of weeks.'

Vera looked around. 'This is really a nice apartment.'

Giselle nodded. The apartment was quite spacious, with two bedrooms, a kitchen, a dining-room, a washroom and the well-appointed living-room in which they now sat. The living-room was discreetly lit by wall lamps, the walls were painted lime-green. A blue pile carpet lay on the floor and there were hanging plants and paintings. To one side, sliding glass doors led to a small patio with moulded furniture of clear plastic. The living-room suite had crushed velvet covering and the dining-room furniture was made of polished oak. The television and compact disc system were imported. The air-conditioning unit hummed quietly. Everything was very neat, except for magazines and newspapers thrown carelessly onto a coffee table in front of the sofa.

'Seems a sin to actually live in a place like this,' Vera commented.

'You should be comfortable then,' grinned Giselle. Vera pulled a face at her.

Robert came back. He had changed into a T-shirt and trousers.

'Can I get you all anything to drink?'

'Nothing for me, thanks,' said Giselle.

'I'll have some white wine if you've got,' said Vera.

'Sure,' said Robert. He went across to a small cupboard of polished wood and opened it to reveal a small but perfectly equipped bar. He brought back a glass of golden-coloured wine for Vera and a small brandy for himself.

'So what were you all doing in the mall?' he said, sitting beside Giselle and taking her hand.

'Just window shopping,' Vera answered. 'Do you always sleep this early?'

'Well, I take a short nap when I come home. Then I go and play tennis or read. These days, with the company still setting up, I mostly end up working.'

'What were you going to do tonight?' Giselle asked.

'I have to check over some invoices, accounts, and read some reports and so on.'

'What a life,' Vera said.

'I enjoy it. How do you like being a flight attendant?'

'Oh, it keeps me in trouble,' said Vera.

'Keeps you in – ? Oh, I see.' Robert smiled.

'Don't mind her,' said Giselle. 'Insanity runs in the family.'

'Yes, I have a cousin who thinks he's Derek Walcott,' said Vera.

'Really?' said Giselle. 'I didn't know that.'

'Why does he think he's Walcott?' Robert asked.

'I don't know. But since he won the Nobel Prize for Literature, he's even more convinced about it.'

'Oh God,' said Giselle.

Vera, laughed, leaned across and poked her in the ribs, 'Psyche, Karan.'

Robert, smiling, sipped his brandy.

'So Walcott's really your cousin?' he asked.

'Yes, but I keep telling him to stop boasting about it.'

With a final gulp, Vera finished her wine and stood up.

'Well, Roberto, I hate to drink and run. But I got places to go and things to do and I need my riding partner with me.'

He saw them to the door.

'It was nice meeting you, Vera.'

'It was nice to be met,' Vera answered.

He turned to Giselle. 'See you tomorrow?'

'Sure,' said Giselle.

She leaned forward and gave him a quick peck on the lips.

In the car, Giselle said, 'God, I feeling bad now.'

'Why?' said Vera, who was freshening her lipstick.

'I've never seen both of them on the same night.'

'New experiences, chile, new experiences. Onward.'

Giselle started the engine.

'What you think of Robert?' she asked.

'He seems cool enough. And he's got the stuff.'

'What stuff?'

Vera looked heavenwards. 'Money, girl, moola, the big C.'

'Oh,' said Giselle.

◆

Vishnu, wearing only shorts and sandals, opened the door as soon as Giselle knocked and kissed her deeply.

'Vishnu!' she exclaimed.

'What wrong?' he said, then saw Vera grinning behind Giselle.

'Hi,' he said. 'You must be Vera.'

'My reputation precedes me,' Vera said.

'Yeah,' said Vishnu, taking her hand. 'Are you embarrassed about me kissing Giselle in front of you?'

'No.'

Vishnu turned to Giselle, who was still blushing.

'See? She isn't embarrassed.'

'Oh?' said Giselle.

Vishnu grinned at Vera. 'You can always depend on Giselle for a cutting reply,' he said.

Vera laughed. Vishnu bustled them inside the apartment and closed the door.

'So what you all doing in these parts?' he asked.

Vera glanced expectantly at Giselle.

'Well, we just went Curepe to get doubles from Sauce,' said Giselle, 'so we thought we'd pass in.'

'To check me out, eh?' said Vishnu, grinning again.

'Can't I come and see you unexpectedly?' said Giselle.

'Of course, darling. You know seeing you makes my night, my day and my twilight.'

'Please, please, I'm on a sugar-free diet,' said Vera.

Vishnu chuckled. He took Giselle's hand and pulled her down beside him on the cheap sofa. Vera sat in a chair. Giselle noticed how Vera's eyes slid over Vishnu's bare torso before he pulled on a sleeveless T-shirt hanging on the back of the sofa.

'We haven't interrupted you from anything?' Vera asked.

'No. I was just relaxing.'

'Oh. How do you relax?'

'I read, play football, listen to music, go to a movie and whatever else catches my fancy. How do you relax?'

'Sex.'

'Oh,' said Vishnu.

'You should approve of that,' said Giselle.

Vishnu smiled at her. 'A good boy like me?'

'Don't abuse your adjectives.'

Vera laughed. 'Can I get something to drink, Vish?'

'Sure. Coke, club soda, orange juice or boiled water?'

'Don't you have beer?'

'Nope. Only addictive beverages here are tea, coffee and me.'

'I'll pass,' said Vera.

She glanced around the apartment, and her gaze stopped at the writing desk which was covered with sheets. 'You write poetry?' she asked.

'Sometimes,' said Vishnu. 'But those are mostly calypsos.'

'You never told me you wrote calypsos,' said Giselle.

'You never asked,' he replied. 'Besides, you've been here often enough to have seen some.'

'You sing?'

'Just for myself. I sell these as a sideline, but only write tent calypsos, not party tunes, so I don't make much money. But is fun.'

'And you contributing to the culture,' Vera said.

'Exactly.'

Vera looked at Giselle. 'Can we go, kid? I got to fly tomorrow.'

'All right.'

At the door, Giselle tried to give Vishnu a light peck, but he grabbed her curled locks firmly and kissed her deeply again. She drew away, blushing, but said nothing. Vera stood waiting.

'I'm glad you passed,' he said, in a low voice.

'I'll see you tomorrow,' she said.

'Nice meeting you, Vishnu,' said Vera.

'Likewise,' he answered.

He stood in the lighted doorway until they drove away.

◆

Only when they were out on the highway, heading back to Port of Spain, did Giselle turn to Vera.

'Well?' she said.

'He seems cool, too. Nice pecs, also, although Robert is better-looking.'

'That doesn't help me very much, Ms Chancellor.'

'I know. But I can see why you're having trouble making up your mind. I mean, Robert has good wine but Vishnu can wire your house. But Robert could buy you a house with good wires in the first place, while Vishnu could write you a calypso.'

There was silence for a while. The car's headlights stabbed into the rushing night.

'Vishnu isn't very secure financially, is he?' said Vera.

Giselle shrugged. 'He seems to do all right. I'm not secure, either, if it comes to that. And we're both young and strong.'

Vera looked at her.

'You've been reading too many romance novels,' she said.

'So you think I should choose Robert?' Giselle asked.

'Well, let me put it this way: I don't see any reason why you should *not* choose Robert. You could always have an affair with Vishnu.'

Giselle shook her head, and there was another silence as they reached the turn-off to St James.

'Whom do you like best, Gis?' Vera said.

Giselle didn't answer at once. After a while, she said, 'I feel more excited with Vishnu. But, like I said, I feel . . . at ease with Robert.' She bit her lip and glanced at Vera. 'Excitement doesn't last, does it?'

'Most of the time, no,' said Vera.

'But Vishnu isn't like most men, either.'

'And Robert?'

'I suppose he's better than most men. He's very successful.'

They pulled up at the apartment.

'It's too close for me to call, Gis,' Vera said, regretfully.

Giselle nodded. 'Thanks, anyway.'

They got out of the car and walked up the stairs.

'Maybe you should write a computer program to help you figure this out,' Vera suggested.

Giselle punched in the alarm code and opened the door.

'I just admire Mr Spock, Vera. I don't want to be like him.'

They went inside. Giselle switched on the CD player and put in

Rudder's *Lyricsman* album. She was in the mood for satirical music. Vera went into the kitchen and filled the kettle.

'You want a cup of tea?' she asked.

'Yes,' said Giselle.

Vera plugged in the kettle and came and sat down beside Giselle.

'Well, a program mightn't help you. But I wish you could write one for me,' she said.

'What for?'

'You might be surprised.'

'Well, what is it?' asked Giselle, switching off the kettle and preparing two cups of tea.

'Some background first,' said Vera. She began pacing up and down while Giselle sat on the sofa, sipping her tea.

'You remember a flight attendant named Tsai-Ann Chang? I've spoken about her sometimes.'

'Actually, you've said she's a Chinese bitch who walks with a quick twitch.'

'Right. Shakespeare has nothing on me, you bet. Anyway, you know she and I joined the airline at the same time, but she entered the Mile-High-Club before me.'

Giselle nodded. She knew about the Mile-High-Club, which was made up of people who had sex above 30,000 feet.

'Well, she's always held that over me. But then I've been able to counter with being single while she's married. She can't top me on that.'

'This gives you status?' asked Giselle.

'Of course. A husband can place serious limits on the high-flying life.'

'Oh.'

'So, even though she entered the Club first, I've had more national-ities above 30,000 feet.'

'I see.'

Vera's face tightened. 'But you wouldn't believe what that little bitch did last week.'

'Got divorced?'

'Nope. Brought her husband and her lover on the same flight. Had sex at 9.02 in the first-class toilet with the husband and again at 9.45

171

with the lover in economy class. Never been done by anyone in our group.'

'And this bothers you?'

'Yes!' Vera exclaimed. 'She only did it to show she's sexier than I am. Not that she could ever be, of course. But it's the principle of the thing!'

Giselle sipped her tea.

'And what do you want to do about it?'

Vera stopped pacing and took up the other teacup.

'I want to have sex with three men within five hours on a trans-Atlantic flight.'

Giselle's eyebrows rose almost to her hairline.

'You're shocked,' Vera said.

Giselle shook her head, but had to swallow twice before she could speak. 'No, no. It's just that, uh, it seems to be . . . a rather strange ambition.'

Vera grinned. 'You think I should take a correspondence course in appliance repair instead? Yeah, that will really teach her!'

Giselle watched her for a moment, then laughed. 'You weren't serious about the three men?'

'Yes. Is not only that I don't intend to let her pass me out, you know. I'm not that petty-minded.'

'Well, why then?'

'I just think it's a really wild thing to do.'

'Oh, well once you have a solid reason, what can I say?'

'You don't approve?'

'Do you need my approval?'

'No, but one of your computer programs would be a big help.'

'Why?'

'Well, I've been trying for weeks now to figure out how to get this done. But I just can't work out how to get three of them on board at the same time, in different sections, for a five-hour flight . . . By the time I factor in my work schedules, their work schedules and their destinations, there's always a missing piece. It is frustrating as hell!'

'Sounds like an interesting problem,' Giselle said slowly. 'But I thought you said Tsai-Ann only pulled off her little coup last week?'

'Uh-huh.'

'So why've you been planning this for weeks?'

'Oh, she was boasting about it long before,' Vera said. 'I thought I could pull off a pre-emptive strike.'

'Oh,' Giselle said.

'If I gave you my flight schedules – and Tsai-Ann's – for the next three months between Europe and North America, layout of the jet, and the schedules and financial status of my major squeezes throughout major destinations, you could write me a computer program to select who, and the best times, when I can pull this off without any of them knowing.' Vera grinned. 'Tsai-Ann would have to be on board, of course. It would make her as sick as mud.'

'I can imagine,' said Giselle drily. 'Would you want to have witnesses, too?'

Vera smiled. 'Now there's a sexy idea.'

'Just 'cause I'm a virgin doesn't mean my mind isn't pornographic. But, even so, I think this scheme of yours better stay firmly in the realms of fantasy. Someone has to save you from yourself, Vera, and it looks like it has to be me!'

They sipped their tea in silence for a while.

'It's really a pity you can't write a program to help choose between Robert and Vishnu,' said Vera. 'Emotions are so much more complicated than sex.'

'Pity.'

'What'll you do next?'

'I'm going to play mud mas with a J'Ouvert band.'

Vera's eyes opened wide. 'You?'

'Why not me?'

'Well . . . you've never played mas before.'

'So it's high time I did.'

'But why don't you play in a . . .' Vera hesitated again, and Giselle was amused to realize that Vera was more surprised at Giselle deciding to play mas than she had been at Giselle deciding to have sex. Vera said, 'Why don't you play in a more . . . sophisticated band. I mean, Gis, I just can't see you in a mud band.'

'Why not?'

'I dunno. 'Cause you're not . . . earthy enough.'

Giselle eyed Vera dangerously.

'Was that a joke, Ms Chancellor?'

Vera grinned. 'You really going to do it?'

'Uh-huh.'

Vera threw up her hands. 'Say what! You go, girl!'

Giselle smiled.

◆

But that night she lay awake in bed for some time, thinking. Her conversation with Vera seemed almost surreal. But it made Giselle feel uncomfortable and bitchy. *Vera is really shallow and petty-minded and vicious*, she said to herself. Then she thought, *but she is my friend*. It was like a tiny shock. Eventually, Giselle fell asleep, and she dreamed she was an Indian princess living in the Taj Mahal. Even in her dream she knew that the Taj Mahal was not a palace, but a tomb. Yet this disturbed her sleep only slightly.

Chapter Eleven

Giselle prided herself on her decisiveness. When it came to making up her mind and sticking to a decision, she considered herself to have few peers. For example, she would always remember shopping once in a cloth store in Port of Spain. The management had suddenly announced a reduction in the price of both onion skin (to $20 a yard) and chiffon (to $22.50 a yard) and Giselle had only enough money to buy one kind of material for a dress. While most women would have taken an hour of purest agony to make up their minds, she was out of there in five minutes with three yards of rayon charlait (at $21 a yard) which was what she had come for in the first place. Trivial as it may seem, this incident had always stuck in her mind with a kind of pride.

Yet now, having to choose between two men, instead of three types of material, Giselle found herself *lahaying*, even being *vikey-vy*. That is to say, she was hesitant, uncertain, wishy-washy. And she didn't like it.

Giselle knew, of course, that choosing the right man to spend the rest of your life with is an entirely different proposition from choosing the right material for an evening gown. At the same time, she was aware that most women chose an evening gown with infinitely more care and expenditure of emotional energy than they chose a man. For the majority of women, choosing a man seemed to be largely a matter of circumstances.

Even so, Giselle, for perhaps the first time in her adult life, found herself unable to make a choice.

My only excuse is that I usually know what I want in clothes, she thought. *Wanting a man out of clothes is an entirely new experience for me.*

But which one? The question she faced was the one which has faced good women since time immemorial: what kind of man did she most want to see naked for the rest of her life?

Giselle knew that this was not an issue of mere physical attractiveness. Her view was that there was no person so good-looking who, unless you truly loved him or her, wouldn't look truly horrible when they had just awoken after a long night's sleep. Giselle was a romantic who believed that love conquered all; but she also felt that love *had* to conquer all as long as morning breath was part of intimate relationships.

At one point, Giselle wished she could be like Vera, who – without a second thought – would have slept with both men in order to decide which one she liked better. But, of course, that was utterly impossible for Giselle. She kept weighing all the factors, and was still unable to tip the scales. *The path of true love never did run smooth*, Shakespeare had written, and Giselle suspected he had known what he was talking about.

Giselle might have continued in this way indefinitely, if something had not happened to force a decision on her. So far, she had been able to keep her affair with Vishnu entirely discreet. No one except her mother and Vera knew. And, of course, Vishnu, who had to know. And Vishnu, while he did not speak of marriage as Robert did, did expect Giselle to make a choice. Robert might be in ignorance, but Vishnu was getting tired of being the outside man.

'If you didn't look so fine in tight jeans,' he told Giselle, 'I'd have walked already.'

'I'm sorry,' Giselle told him, and she really was.

'Well, they say suffering is good for the soul. But I think you'd better make up your mind before I grow wings.'

Giselle smiled. 'You? The devil incarnate?'

'Aiy, stranger things have happened.'

'Yeah? Like what?'

'Julia Roberts and Lyle Lovett. Michael Jackson and Lisa-Marie Presley. Deanna Troi and Worf.'

'Well, if Troi could handle a man who has a forehead with ribs, who knows? There might be hope for you yet.'

Vishnu took her in his arms and kissed her long and slowly. Then he drew back.

'I hope so,' he said.

'Talking about strange things, I have a friend who wants to have sex with three men in five hours.'

'Sounds like a more pleasurable version of the triathlon.'

'You ever done anything like that?' Giselle asked, very casually. She didn't want Vishnu suspecting that she wanted to find out just how sexy he was.

'No,' said Vishnu, 'I'm not attracted to men.'

Giselle steupsed. Vishnu laughed, and she ended up grinning with him. Then he pulled her into his arms again and, looking into her eyes, kissed her.

'I'd prefer to have sex with you alone for five hours than have five women in one hour.'

'Not that you could handle five women in one hour.'

'Who'd want to? Vera's fantasy doesn't have anything to do with sex. It has to do with ego.'

'I never said it was Vera!'

Vishnu grinned. 'That's right. You didn't.'

Giselle grimaced. 'Anyway, Vera just wants to make mas.'

She untangled herself from his arms, and took up her bag. He saw her to the door.

'I *will* decide,' she said, turning to him.

'And I'll certainly do everything I can to help you,' he said, leaning forward and kissing her once again.

Giselle said, 'You playing mas?'

'Devil mas on J'Ouvert morning.'

'How appropriate.'

'What about you?'

'I'm playing mud mas with De Earth People.'

Vishnu cocked an eyebrow. 'How inappropriate,' he said.

'Why? And don't tell me it's because I'm not earthy enough.'

Vishnu chuckled. 'No, is just that I can't imagine you dirty, let alone covered in mud.'

Giselle smiled sweetly at him. 'You have no idea how dirty I can be,' she said.

He grinned. 'You must let me find out one day.'

'Maybe' said Giselle. 'There's one thing *I'd* like to know right now.'

'What's that?'

'That time I was here, when you were sick, I saw a calypso called "Phone Sex". Was that yours?'

He nodded. 'A partner of mine does the melody and we sell them.'

'Oh.'

'You want to hear one I just finished?'

Giselle smiled and came back in. 'Sure.'

Vishnu took up his guitar from the corner.

'I've sold this to River Man.'

'Oh, I like him. He have a real nice body.'

'Yeah, well you will see why this calypso would suit him. It's called "Vowels of Attraction".'

Vishnu began to strum a simple calypso melody. His voice was a pleasant contralto:

> As a kaisonian, I have endless women running me
>   down,
> Women of all race, size and age
> And I could tell you what they like about me
>   alphabetically
> But I only have five minutes on stage.

>> Woman does tell me all kinda thing,
>> Things that does leave me blushing still,
>> But since I cyar list what they like about me
>>   alphabetically
>> I will only list the vowels.

> A is for my assets . . .:
> Of course I mean my monetary value, my net worth;
> But I have sense, so the assets in my wallet
> Does never go to any woman who only assets under
>   she skirt.

> I know Jean and Dinah still after the Yankee dollar
> And I does make my money performing in the States;
> But with my assets I doh need to pay
> Any woman for the saliva exchange rates.

> E is for my eloquence and expression
> 'Cause you must always tell a woman how you feel;
> Call her doux-doux and darlin'; and sugar bum bum
> And only then you will find out how she FEELS.
> I have gotten women's favours with mih talk

'Cause women like a man with good lyrics, as
    everybody knows;
But if that doh work, I does take out my guitar
And extempo she out of she clothes.

>   Woman does tell me all kinda thing,
>   Things that does leave me blushing still,
>   But since I cyar list what they like about me
>   alphabetically
>   I will only list the vowels.

I is for my immaturity,
Yes, immaturity is what I said;
You know women does say all man are babies,
No lie: like ah infant, I always want something to suck
    in bed.

O is for my 'Oh', which I does use in conversation
I say 'Oh?' – and you could bet
A woman will always find I am SUCH an interesting
    man
Even though I ain't say a full sentence yet.
And, later in the night, I does say 'Oh' again,
But now is 'Ooh', 'cause talk done,
And with a 'God!' and a 'Yes, darlin'!' and some more
    'Ohs' thrown in,
The woman does always say I have so MUCH passion.

And U is for up
Without which all the other vowels eh no use;
You could have all the other letters in the alphabet
But without a U, high and strong, them woman does
    only steups.

Vishnu sang the chorus again, but had not yet finished:

>   And, finally, I must mention D
>   Which is for *derrière*, which is French for rear;
>   I not illiterate, I know D is a consonant,
>   But ladies look and I am sure you will agree, the D is
>   my best feature.

> Before I go, I would like to say to the men out dey:
> Doh think because I tell you my secret you could get
> Women running you down like they running me,
> 'Cause all I give you was the vowels: I still have the rest
>   of the alphabet.

Vishnu repeated the chorus and, still strumming the guitar, said to Giselle, 'There are extra verses for three encores. You want to hear them?'

Giselle, thoroughly enjoying this, said, 'Of course. The Mighty Vishnu, come again!'

Vishnu smiled and resumed singing:

> How all-you could call me back?
> It only have five vowels, ain't that right?
> They say Trinidadians eight-five per cent literate
> So it must be the other fifteen per cent here tonight.

'More, more!' called Giselle, whistling between her fingers.

> All-you call me again,
> Look, give me a chance;
> Ladies, if you want to hear more
> Come in the back, I will sing about CUNSonants.

'One more time and we will come anywhere you want,' laughed Giselle.

> Listen to me one last time
> I not a great lover, I only all right;
> So doh call me back again, because
> I does only come five times in one night.

Giselle cheered and clapped as Vishnu strummed the last notes.

'That was excellent!' she said.

'Thanks,' he said, putting down his guitar. 'River will do it better. He have all the tones and body language that that kind of calypso needs.'

'Oh, your body language not too bad,' said Giselle. 'And the letter D suits you very well.'

Vishnu grinned. 'Thanks even more.'

'Do you write any calypsos that *don't* refer to sex?'

'Of course. What you think I am, obsessed?'

'Yes.'

'Well, you're wrong. Remember that soca parang calypso by Lord Madman – 'Three Amigos'?'

Giselle frowned. 'Vaguely. I was too busy to get into the Christmas lime.'

'I wrote the lyrics right after Dholak, Basdeo Singh and Bagasse Anthony managed to destroy the *Colony News*. Madman composed a Spanish-sounding melody for it. The song was pretty popular.'

'Well, play it for me.'

Taking up his guitar, Vishnu strummed a Spanish intro so corny it could have come from the soundtrack of any silent-movie Western. Then he began singing in such an atrocious Mexican accent that Giselle burst into laughter from the first line:

> Dees ees de story of three amigos
> Who all were very lame,
> But because of dere strange afflictions
> Got wealth and power and fame.
>
> One of de amigos was a lawyer
> Who deedn't have a spine.
> So since he could not get up
> He used to lie all de time.
> In court, TV or office
> He won hees fights wit'out even trying
> For his enemies could never pin heem down
> Although he was always lying.

The beat of the song quickened as Vishnu sang the chorus:

> So leesten to de story of de three amigos
> Who all were very lame,
> And because of dere strange afflictions
> Got wealth and power and fame.
>
> The second amigo was twisted and bent
> From being *verry* reech;
> You see, 'e learn to beg when young

And when old became a son of a beetch.
So much did dees man love money
Walking upright was an impossible feat
For whenever he smelled hard cash
He would bend over like a beetch een heat.

Giselle, thoroughly enjoying herself, clapped out a rhythm as Vishnu repeated the chorus.

De t'ird amigo was de strangest case
For he only some time was a cripple;
Some time he would have to lie
Especially after hees nightly tipple.
You never knew when he would stand up,
You never knew if he could;
Eet just happened conveniently
So no one ever knew where he stood.
Weeth dees strange affliction
De t'ird amigo used every position
And seence he also had very good diction
Naturally, he became an upstanding lying politician.

So if you are handicapped in your career
You steel can be de very very best,
Lying, bent or standing everywhere:
Amigo! You too can be a success!

Still laughing, Giselle went up to Vishnu and kissed him. 'And you say that's not about sex?'

'It eesn't, I mean isn't. Is just your obscene mind.'

Giselle smiled all through the kiss and she was still smiling, dazedly, when she went out to her car and saw Gemma, the bescarfed and ample cleaning lady from CMC, walking by. Gemma said, 'A-a, Miss Giselle, is you?' and then her gaze travelled past Giselle. Giselle glanced back to where Vishnu stood bareback in his doorway, watching. He didn't even trouble to go back inside before Gemma could get a good look at him, and Giselle later realized that this was quite deliberate.

She turned back to Gemma.

'Hello, Gemma. How you going?'

'Fine, Miss Giselle,' Gemma answered, still gazing fascinatedly at Vishnu. 'I was just going to check out my sister up the road.'

'Oh.'

With some difficulty, Gemma dragged her eyes back to Giselle.

'This is your car?'

'Yes,' said Giselle resignedly.

'I think I see it here before. But I didn't know it was yours – or I would of stop and say hello.'

'Ah. Well, yes, it's mine.'

'Evenin', sir,' she called to Vishnu. 'How things in the yard?'

'Evenin' auntie,' Vishnu called back cheerfully. 'Things in the yard fine.'

'I remember he face,' she told Giselle.

'I could give you a drop up the road, Gemma?' Giselle asked, wanting to end this scene quickly.

'Is all right. My sister living right there.'

'Well, see you at the office, then.'

'Yes, see you, Miss Giselle.'

With a final, searching glance at Vishnu, Gemma walked off. Giselle got into her car and looked at the grinning Vishnu.

'You wretch!' she said, speaking in a penetrating whisper since Gemma was still within earshot.

Vishnu bowed deeply, one arm across his stomach and the other behind his back, like a stage actor, and then went back inside.

◆

Giselle knew that Robert would eventually find out. It wasn't that Gemma would maliciously tell anyone; Gemma wouldn't even think there was anything especially wrong with Giselle having an affair. But it was still too juicy an item not to share: the nice miss from upstairs liming with the nice fella from the yard, even though she does go out with the boss. And, while there was a chance Robert might never hear such talk, Giselle didn't care to bank on it. She already didn't like deceiving him; and she should be the one to tell him the truth.

But should she tell him the truth and then decide? Or should she decide first, which would eliminate the need to tell Robert anything? After all, if she chose him, then he would never believe she had been

183

involved with someone like Vishnu. And, if she chose Vishnu, then telling Robert became irrelevant. And Giselle realized that she didn't mind hurting Robert as much as she minded him having a low opinion of her. Which told her something about both herself and their relationship.

Quite unexpectedly, Giselle ended up making her decision that very night. She had called Robert, who told her he'd be home by nine. It was only seven o'clock, and the thought of a two-hour delay made Giselle feel even more stressed out.

She sat down on the sofa and saw her *Atlantic Monthly* magazine open to the *Midges* story. She was on the last section where Florence had gone off with Wailer to see him spray midges. *And, of course, fuck*, thought Giselle, who now wondered what she had ever seen in Waller's novel. She took it up and began to read:

So now she was in the van of a total stranger, going out to Whitman's Pond. But was he a total stranger? She felt she could control him just by wearing a tight T-shirt without a bra.

'What's your name?' she asked.

'Bob Wailer,' he answered.

'Like Bob Marley.'

'Yes'm, I suppose so.'

She was a bit surprised at his answer, not expecting him to know about the dead reggae superstar. But then she realized she ought not to have been surprised: Wailer was obviously well-travelled – in fact, he probably knew more roads in the county than people whose families had lived in Bradison for generations.

They passed a car heading in the opposite direction.

He said, 'Will it be a problem if people see you in my van?'

'I doh care,' she said, looking at him with a smile which was both pleased and reckless. 'You sorry I come with you?'

He smiled back at her shyly. 'No, ma'am, can't say I am. I'm glad.'

Florence was glad he had asked, though. It confirmed her initial impression: he was sensitive. But she had known that.

'Call me Florence,' she told him.

'Is that your name?'

'I wouldn't lie to you,' Florence said, looking at the speeding, sunlit road. She was surprised at her boldness, but she did not meet Wailer's eyes. Wailer glanced at the woman next to him. He knew something stronger than both of them was developing, like film in a darkroom. But what would the prints show?

This was his habitual way of thinking, in metaphors. On one of his report cards, when he was a boy, a teacher had written, 'Has a remarkably good grasp of the English Language.' He had always felt himself to be precocious, and had begun masturbating when he was eight years old. The maid, a dour-faced spinster in her late thirties, had caught him once and spanked him till his little bum was red and smarting. But she had never told his mother.

He said, 'Where's your husband today?'

So he had noticed her wedding ring. He was so sharp, this Bob Wailer, thought Florence. She said, 'He gone over to Cornfield for the pig show there. He ain't go be back till tomorrow.'

'I see,' said Wailer. Florence wondered what he meant. She had begun thinking even his lightest utterance held a deeper meaning.

They reached Whitman's Pond. Wailer parked on the verge and they got out of the van. He opened the doors at the back and took out a tank which he strapped around his plump torso with easy, practised movements.

'That ain't heavy?' Florence asked.

'I'm used to it,' answered Wailer.

'Hauling that around must keep you fit.'

'I won the 5K race in the Short Fat Men are Sexy Too contest in '87.'

He saw that Florence had begun swatting at the small, black flies which hung like a cloud over the pond. He reached into the van and pulled out a small, glass bottle. Despite the tank strapped to his back, he moved effortlessly.

'Rub that over you, it'll keep them off,' he said.

'Thanks,' she said, moved by his natural consideration. He was sensitive, but she already knew that.

'I want to see you get rid of all dem flies,' she said. 'I never see an exterminator at work on "the leaves of the grass" in the open before.' Florence had read Walt Whitman in her night classes.

'Well, there ain't much to see today,' he replied. 'I'll spray out, but it'll take a day or two for the pesticide to take effect. And I'll probably have to return to do it again. This job is pretty cyclical, like the movement of the stars that wheel in the heavens above us. But I'm glad you're here keeping me company. A beautiful woman makes the time pass quickly.'

Wailer said all this quite casually as he moved about the edges of the pond, spraying softly, with little hisses from his nozzle. Florence hung on the last two sentences, like a coloured silk blouse flapping on the clothesline. He needn't have said them, but that he did showed he was genuinely glad she had come with him.

She watched him move about slowly. There was energy, a strange power in the way he worked. The men she knew seemed hard and hurtful beside him, with big, muscular bodies. Florence looked at how the spray sprayed softly from his dull-gold nozzle and, for the first time in ever so long, she became wet between her legs just looking at someone. Then she realized she needed to pee.

'Bob,' she called, and it seemed perfectly natural to use his name.

'Yes, Flo?' – and that seemed perfectly natural, too. And how often does that happen in life?

'I have to pee,' she told him.

A quick look of concern crossed his face.

'These midges will roast your ass if you try that here.'

'I know,' she said, biting her lower lip.

'Can you hold it?'

She shook her head. Now that she had become aware of her need, there was a burning, urgent pressure in her bladder, like the agony which comes to a wounded soldier when, only after the heat of battle has cooled, he realizes half his face has been blown away and the half which remains is his bad side.

Wailer looked about in a keen, alert way. The black cloud of biting flies still shifted over the pond, like a knell of doom.

He said, 'What did you do with the bottle of repellent?'

'I put it in the van,' she answered.

'Get into the back of the van and wait there. I won't be long.'

Florence did as he ordered, putting her future into his expert hands with complete confidence. She was sure he had faced this kind of emergency before and, though she had no idea what he

186

could do, she knew he had thought of something. His mind worked so much faster than hers. As she got into the van, it occurred to her that he was like some foreigner who had drafted in on the tail of a Concorde jet into her farmhouse. Yet he lived right in the county.

I never knew how extraordinary life could be, thought Florence Nightingale, farmer's wife in Bradison County. I had lost faith.

The doors of the van opened and closed swiftly. Wailer smiled at her. He had taken off the dull-gold tank from his back, but carried a mini-spraying bottle in his right hand. He scanned the interior of the van with keen eyes, and Florence in that moment saw in him the spirit of those far-sighted, wheeling birds which live on insects, as well as the gun-slinging spirit of the Old West.

'I am a man of another age, and of ages that never were,' Wailer once wrote. He was an exterminator and, in that moment, Florence Nightingale understood what this meant in a way perhaps only Wailer himself did. And how often does that happen in life, how often do we understand another human being so clearly?

'Some midges have already got in,' said Wailer. He applied the spray-bottle with gentle but firm squeezes. Then he took up two other bottles he had also brought with him. One was the bottle with insect repellent. The other was a beer bottle. He must use a lot of bottles, Florence thought suddenly, irrationally. But is the attraction between two human beings ever rational and, if it was, would it truly be attraction?

'I thought you could put some repellent on your ass, and then pee into the beer bottle,' Wailer said.

Florence smiled, looking at him with eyes that were bright and, perhaps, a little astonished. It was such a simple, yet effective solution. Yet, at a deeper level, hadn't she expected him to come up with a solution?

She undid the button of her jeans and pulled the zipper down. 'You want to put on the repellent for me?' she asked.

Now Wailer's eyes lit up. 'Sure,' he said, in a husky voice. Florence didn't think so much passion could be injected into that one word.

She turned around and dropped her jeans. Moments later, she felt his soft hand spreading repellent onto her buttocks. And she marvelled that he was able to do this in such an effective, yet gentlemanly fashion.

No midges stung her.

'You have a nice bottom,' he said.

'Thanks,' she answered. 'You have nice hands.'

'I am the artisan and the chisel and all the sculptors' stones which were ever shaped,' he said.

Florence breathed deeply. These simple words, they both knew, said so much more than what they said.

He was using only one hand to put the repellent on and, though she was not looking, Florence knew what the other hand was doing. The connection between her and Wailer was like that: she simply did not need to look at him.

She barely felt it when he entered her, but she ground her hips back against him in that unique Caribbean movement called a 'wine' – a rhythmic rotating motion. Wailer groaned. Florence, her arms braced against the side of the van, looked at the second hand of her watch. She was sure she could make him come inside sixty seconds: and, sure enough, just as the second hand crossed the mark, he did.

Florence drew away from him, pulling up her jeans. On her face was a smile of complete contentment. Jimmy always took at least an hour to come. It was gratifying to make a man come so quickly. Florence felt confirmed in her femininity in a way she had not felt for a long, long time.

◆

Little more remains to be told. Wailer finished spraying, then dropped Florence back home. Several times after that, he sent letters to her telling her about himself and asking for another session in the back of his van. He had, he told her, even bought her a leather outfit, including high-heeled boots. Florence, though clearly moved by this display of ungovernable passion, told Wailer she had responsibilities to her family. 'But I want you to keep on thinking about me,' she wrote. 'You never know what could happen.' She also asked him to fumigate her house.

That Wailer remained loyal to Florence for the rest of his life is clear from the manner of his death, five years later. While watching a pornographic movie, he had a seizure. He had written in his journal the following entry: 'Brown is the Colour of the Gods. It is dark earth, chocolate, the hue of her skin.'

Pinned to his TV set, so its glossy image was always before him, was a photo of Florence's naked bottom.

Giselle leaned back in the deckchair, smiling. The mockery of the story pleased her, and she no longer felt so vicious. Then her gaze automatically went to a box beneath the story, and she gasped as she read what was printed there: '*Richard Kinky is the pseudonym of freelance writer Vishnu Traboulay (who says he's only slightly so).*'

◆

After a few minutes, Giselle got up and went to the phone. She dialled Vishnu's number.

'I want to see you,' she said.

'Again?' he said. 'My fascination growing or what?'

'I'm coming over now.'

Hearing her curt tone, Vishnu said, 'No, don't drive out this late. I'll come by you.'

'All right. You want me to pick you up in St James?'

'No, I'll drive over.'

'All right,' she said, not feeling surprised.

Twenty minutes later, Giselle went out on the corridor overlooking the car park. She had read over the entire story twice. She wanted to see what kind of car Vishnu was driving and, somehow, she wasn't too surprised when she saw it was the Mitsubishi Magna which was always parked in the yard outside his apartment. And when he came up the stairs, a typewriter was swinging from one hand.

'Come in,' said Giselle.

She turned and went inside. Vishnu, using the native intelligence which separates man from the beasts, did not try to kiss her.

'So what's all this?' Giselle said, without preamble.

Vishnu put the typewriter, which still had its cover on, down on the centre table. Then he sat down opposite Giselle.

'Don't waste time getting to the point, do you?' he said.

'Life is too short, I seem to recall you saying once.'

'Yes. Well, I have a confession of sorts to make.'

'That I figured out already.'

'The fact is, I haven't been entirely honest with you.'

Giselle said nothing, but just continued looking at him coolly. Vishnu, meeting her gaze, suddenly swallowed.

'I have to show you some things,' he said. He held up a key. 'The car outside is mine.' He leaned forward and unclipped the typewriter cover. The machine was not merely a typewriter – it was a Smith-Corona word processor.

'What is all this, Vishnu?' Giselle said quietly.

He moved across to the sofa and took her hand. Giselle did not pull away, but she didn't seem too thrilled at being near him, either.

Vishnu took a deep breath. 'Well, you see, Giselle, the thing is – .' He stopped. 'Is like this – ' He stopped again.

'Yes, I got all that,' said Giselle unhelpfully.

Vishnu took another deep breath, then spoke in a rush. 'Look, even though I *am* a construction worker, and have been for the past two years, is not really how I earn my living.'

He did not look directly at Giselle but she stared at him expressionlessly.

He continued. 'I'm actually a freelance writer. I work mostly in the States and parts of Europe. I write articles for various magazines, song lyrics, do a few comic book scripts, commercial scripts, ghost-writing and so on. Is a hustle, but I do pretty well,' he added, as though embarrassed by the admission. 'Two years ago, I sold my first movie script. I decided to use the money to work around the islands, getting material for a Caribbean novel.' He shrugged. 'Or a working man's tourist guide.'

'I see,' said Giselle. Suddenly a lot of things made more sense. She pulled away her hand. 'And you didn't think all this worth mentioning before?'

'I had my reasons,' he said, not looking at her.

'And what, pray tell, might those be?' she said, coldly angry now. 'I would really like to know, if you don't think I'm being fast.'

Vishnu ran a hand round the inside of his collar. 'Phew! This tropical heat really gets to you, doesn't it? Even at night. This apartment have air-conditioning?'

'No,' said Giselle, speaking between clenched teeth. 'This apartment does not have air-conditioning. It never has had any bloody air-conditioning and, as far as I know, there are no plans to install any damned air-conditioning.'

Vishnu smiled nervously. 'Gee, you sound like you belong to the League for the Suppression of Air-Conditioning,' he said.

'What are these reasons?' Giselle said coldly. 'And they better be damned good ones.'

Vishnu looked down at his hands. His fingers flicked against one another. 'You won't like to hear.'

'Please, don't be concerned about my feelings. That shouldn't be too difficult for you.'

He drew a deep breath. 'Look, when we met, I was really attracted to you. And I thought you felt something for me, too. But, if you were, you were holding yourself back. And I figured it was because of what I did, not what I was.'

Now he looked up at her. 'I could have smoothed my path by telling you the truth. You would have found it interesting, of course. It would have put me on your level, in your class. But, as I got to know you, I decided not to.'

'No doubt you were having too much fun play-acting,' Giselle said.

'No. Well, it *was* kind of fun actually, but that wasn't why. It seemed to me that you and I were very well-matched. We got along. But there was another side of you, that I really didn't like: materialistic and bourgeois and superficial.'

'What are you? A bloody socialist?'

'Well, yes but – '

'No wonder you so damn totalitarian!'

'Actually, I believe in Fabian socialism – '

'Vishnu! Do I *look* like I'm in the mood for a political lecture?'

He looked at her. 'No,' he said.

Giselle began tapping the floor with her foot. Vishnu clasped his hands together tightly and continued: 'The reason I am single, Giselle, is because I will not settle for less than I think I deserve. And, despite how attracted I was to you, I couldn't have you unless the side of you I loved – the side of you that appreciated music and books and had a sense of humour and was so kind – was stronger than the other side. And, if I had told you all about myself, I would never have known which side of you was stronger. *You* might never have known.'

Vishnu stopped speaking. Giselle watched him. The expression on her face was as distant as the horizon.

Finally, she said, 'Well, you're a presumptuous son-of-a-bitch, aren't you? Who in hell gave you the right to make all those assumptions about me and decide to make me part of your little psychological game. You – you *man*! All it comes down to is that you lied to me, you deceived me,' she continued. 'I took you because of what I thought you were. You don't know what I went through to make the choice I did. And now I find it was all a lie? What the hell kind of relationship can be built on a lie, *Mister* Traboulay?'

'I didn't lie to you about my life or myself,' he said. 'Everything I've told you was true except that one part.'

'It's funny that with all your perceptions about me, you didn't perceive that the one thing I hate more than anything else is lying.' Now she stood up. 'And it's a pity you didn't have more faith in me because – ' the tears sprang to her eyes and she fought to keep them back. She *would not* let him see her cry – 'we could have had something really good.'

She marched to the door and held it open. Vishnu got up and came forward. There was a deep, intense appeal in his gaze.

'Stop looking at me like a dyspeptic cow,' said Giselle.

'Sorry,' he muttered. 'Can't we discuss this?'

Giselle opened the door a little wider and stood without saying anything. Vishnu paused uncertainly for a moment, then went out.

'I'll call you,' he said.

'I'll call you first,' Giselle answered. Vishnu's expression brightened. 'But you won't like to hear what.'

She closed the door in his dismayed face. After a few minutes, she heard his car start up and drive down the hill.

Only then did the tears come.

After a long while, she sat up and blew her nose and thought, *Oh, grow up, you snivelling bitch*.

She looked at her watch. It was time to go by Robert.

◆

Robert was dressed in a polo shirt and tennis shorts when she arrived – his normal home attire.

'I didn't expect to see you tonight,' he said.

Giselle came in with a bright smile.

'Don't you want to see me? she asked.

'Of course,' he replied.

She came into his arms and kissed him deeply. He kissed her back, and she could feel his surprise at her forwardness.

'And exactly how much of me would you like to see?' she said as they kissed.

Robert lifted his head. His eyes were suddenly intense.

'Everything,' he said.

'Your wish is my command,' said Giselle.

She stepped back and unbuttoned her top and let it fall to the floor. She was not wearing a bra. Robert moved towards her, but she put her hands on his chest and began unbuttoning his shirt. Robert's hands were on her, pushing down her skirt. Giselle, her mind peculiarly clear, kissed him in a kind of fury, and his breath grew ragged.

'Let's go in the bedroom,' he said.

'Why waste time walking all that distance?'

Robert laughed breathily, but took her hand and led her into the bedroom. Giselle was naked now, and the air-conditioning raised goose-pimples on her skin. She lay on the bed, while Robert unzipped his shorts.

As he moved on top of her, she found phrases running through her mind, as though she were reading a magazine story. 'His battering ram rocked the portals of her fortified city, but her walls remained unbreached. Again and again, the ram struck but the city had been well-constructed and the ram had been carved of inferior wood.'

Giselle remembered Florence and Wailer in the back of the van, and thought that perhaps she should change position, but then Robert gave a loud groan and she felt something wet and warm spill on to her groin.

He collapsed on her with a sigh.

'Sorry,' he said. 'You just excite me so much.'

'No problem,' said Giselle.

'It will be better next time.'

'Could I get some tissue paper?'

'Sure.'

He rolled off her and watched as she went to the bathroom.

She came back out after a few minutes and went to the living-room for her clothes. Robert followed her. He had already put his shorts back on.

'You have a lovely body,' he said.

'Thank you.'

She began dressing and he said, 'You not too disappointed?'

'No, I know the first time is hardly ever good. But I'm glad we did what we did.'

He waited till she adjusted her top and then came forward and kissed her. 'So am I,' he said. 'I'm rather worried too.'

'Why?'

'Well, you know the government has been putting a lot of pressure on the Board. And, since the CMC is part of a conglam . . . I mean, a conglomerate, it's affecting business ventures in other areas. So I have to announce some new policy measures to the staff on Monday and it's been preying on my mind.'

'I understand. I'd better go now.'

'I'll see you tomorrow.'

'Yes,' said Giselle.

As she drove home, she looked up at the star-speckled heavens and thought, *Did you have to give me a tough hymen, too?*

◆

Vishnu called her at home the next morning, but she didn't pick up the phone. He left a message on the answering machine asking her to call him. Robert also called, saying he wanted to see her later but had to go to the office. They chatted for a while, and he said he would call her when he reached home.

'I'm anxious for round two,' he said.

'We'll take it slower this time,' said Giselle.

At noon, Vishnu came to her apartment.

'Want to go for lunch?' he asked diffidently, standing in the corridor.

'No,' she answered. She stepped aside. 'Let's talk out on the balcony.'

They went out on the balcony, overlooking the green and brown hills. To the west, a thin plume of white smoke rose from a bush fire. The heat was thin and pervasive.

'You still mad at me?' Vishnu asked.

'No,' said Giselle.

She wasn't angry; but she felt very tired inside.

'I still can't get over how you took me in. I took you for something you weren't. That's hard for me to deal with,' she said.

'I never deceived you about who I was. Just what I was doing.'

'The two things are connected. And it's not only that, anyway. It's the kind of contempt you showed for me by what you did.'

'I never meant to show contempt,' he said quietly. 'I don't feel contempt for you. I respect you more than any woman I've ever known.'

She shook her head sadly.

'How I could believe that now?'

'Just do it,' he suggested.

'I am not a pair of running shoes,' she said coldly.

Vishnu said he knew that, and there was a long silence between them. Giselle looked at the pale sky with its small clouds sailing by with offensive cheeriness. In the distance, she could see the greenish-grey of the sea. The horizon was silver with far sunlight.

Finally, she turned to him.

'Give me some time to think things through.'

He smiled, his face strained.

'I guess I don't have much choice. But, while you're thinking, would you keep one thing in mind?'

'What?'

'One thing I didn't deceive you in – I do love you.'

Giselle sighed. She felt so tired inside. 'You know what the song says. Sometimes love just ain't enough.'

Vishnu said nothing.

◆

When Giselle came in to work on Monday morning, the staff from the editorial department had already begun gathering in the news-room. But all the managers were there as well. To Giselle's dis-pleasure, Vishnu was in the corner with Harry Chan – Harry was

195

showing him a piece of wiring in the wall. Robert came out of his office accompanied by Spengler Payne.

Raising his hands for silence, Robert waited till the murmur of voices had died down and said, 'As most of you know, the CMC is about to establish itself as a major national and, indeed, regional media company. But this task has been made even more difficult than it normally would be because of certain actions on the part of the government, which we have had to deal with. So Mr Payne has once again taken time off from his busy schedule to come and tell you how the Board intends to deal with these issues.'

Robert stepped back, gesturing towards Payne. There was a brief spattering of applause, mostly from the managers present.

'Good morning. I won't keep you long. As Mr Cardinez have just correctly informed you, the CMC is running into some difficulties. But it is a pity that all the information in our newspaper are not so accurate. The other paper I own had the same problems, and I am one man who does not repeat history because I learn from it.

'The question I have for you this morning is this: why does a Prime Minister of this country have to complain that people think he drink his own urine?' There was a ripple of uncomfortable laughter around the room. Payne did not smile, and went on: 'I think this newspaper needs to be more sensitive to people in public life.' Gasps of astonishment came from some of the reporters. Unfazed, Payne continued: 'Nor have the Board of Directors been impressed by the way the conflict between the government and the media have been handled by the paper. One example: before the government have even established a regulatory body, this newspaper have been writing critical editorials and inviting critical comment.'

Giselle looked at Robert as he stood behind Payne. Robert's expression was, it seemed to her, carefully neutral. And then, almost instinctively, she glanced across to Vishnu who, ignoring his repairs, was looking at Payne with undisguised amazement.

'Let me tell you all now: for the sake of the country, the Queres-McBuddy conglamerate have decided to adopt a non-confrontational stance with the government. All of us want the CMC to succeed, especially at a time when jobs are so hard to come by. And, as I told those people in the last newspaper, if you don't like it you could leave. But I know we have good people on board this time, like Mr Cardinez and Mr Budhu, and we will succeed in our grand endeavour in establishing a new media house *and* preserving press freedom.

'In order to make sure we stay on track, one Board member will personally come in every night to check the newspaper before it goes to press in order to ensure the Board's directives are being carried out.'

At this moment, there was a violent buzz and the overhead lights flickered and went out.

'Sorry folks,' said Vishnu in the sudden dimness, 'the printer's devil must have struck.'

Robert said, 'Harry, must that be done now?'

'Sorry, Mr Cardinez, but you know how tight the schedule is,' said Harry. But Giselle was sure he was stifling a grin.

Payne said, 'That is all I have to say, anyway. I hope everybody is clear.'

He turned and left with Robert and, exactly as the door closed behind them, the lights returned.

'Yes, brethren!' said Vishnu with an American evangelist's accent, 'I have *ex-or-cised* the demon!'

There was a sudden, explosive burst of laughter in the room, and Giselle turned away so Vishnu would not see her smile. After all, she reminded herself, she was still angry with him.

But, after that morning, she didn't see Vishnu again, even to glimpse him from afar. It was frustrating. *How's he going to know how vexed I am?* she thought. But Vishnu seemed to have taken Giselle at her word and was keeping out of her way. This only made Giselle more depressed. Why did men listen to women when they laid down the law? It was true that, had Vishnu tried to be with her, she would have behaved like a hypochondriac meeting a leper in an overflowing latrine, but that didn't mean she wouldn't have liked the chance to do so. It was, Giselle felt, extremely inconsiderate of Vishnu to respect her wishes.

Vera, who could have lifted her spirits, was in the island; but she was staying by one of her men friends.

It was only after a week that Giselle, very casually, asked Harry Chan where Vishnu was. 'Oh, he fire the work,' said Harry. Even more depressed at this news, Giselle finally decided to go and see her mother.

Chapter Twelve

When Giselle walked into the house, her mother was with Ronald in the living-room. Giselle picked up on the tension at once.

'I just going to check Ellie first,' Giselle said.

Her mother waved a distracted hand.

'I don't mind the smell of beer alone,' her mother was saying to Ronald, 'but you have to come in here smelling of goats as well?'

'You know how Ramnath like to show off his goats,' Ronald replied. He was sitting reading the newspaper and didn't seemed too perturbed. 'And I could hardly tell the man no when he buying me beer.'

'You men always have some excuse for all-you bad habits. I need to relax after a hard day's work, I forget the time, I was working late, as soon as this show finish, she didn't mean a thing darling, and you have to go in the goat-pen.'

'You never minded before,' Ronald observed.

'Well, I pregnant now. My sense of smell different.'

'Okay, I'll bathe.'

'Oh, don't trouble yourself on my account. This is how you all like to have us: barefoot, pregnant and slaving over a hot stove.'

'I will buy you some slippers first thing tomorrow.'

There was a brief pause, then her mother laughed. Giselle, who had stopped just around the corner to listen, grinned and went on to the back. Fariel was washing dishes.

'Where Tammy?' Giselle asked.

'Went out for a drive with Tony.'

Giselle sat down on a kitchen chair.

'I want your opinion on something.'

'Fire away.'

'Why would a woman want to be with two men?'

Fariel, wiping a plate, considered.

'Are you?' she asked.

'Sort of,' Giselle answered.

'Must be a Karan thing.'

Giselle looked up quickly, but Fariel was smiling.

'Tony's cooled down now,' Giselle said. 'And so have you, if it comes to that.'

Fariel put the last cup on the draining board and dried her hands on a kitchen towel.

'True. But you know how he was.'

'You should have known him in his teenage days. The only girlfriends of mine Tony didn't fool around with were those who were fat, didn't shave their legs, or were religious fanatics. And I'm not so sure about some of the religious ones.'

'So maybe you're going through a Karan phase yourself now.'

'Well, if that is so, it is time to end it. But I don't know which to choose. I like being with both of them.'

Fariel put her hand on Giselle's shoulder.

'It worth the trouble?' she said.

'That is what I have to figure out,' Giselle said. 'I want to talk to Ma. I think I need a dose of practicality.'

'None better than her for that,' Fariel agreed.

Her mother was sitting alone out in the back. From inside the house, Giselle heard the sound of the shower. She sat on the other bamboo rocking chair, and watched the trees sway in the wind.

'How the pregnancy going?'

'Doctor says everything is fine. I feel fat.'

'You look lovely."

'So everybody says. But they always say it as though they're consoling me.'

Giselle smiled. But her mother did look well – softer and more tranquil and younger.

'Mom, I'm having man problems,' Giselle said.

'Once there's a man, there's problems,' her mother said, rocking gently.

'And what about when there're two?'

Her mother raised restrained eyebrows.

Giselle explained the situation as fully as she could, which is to say she left out the details about how far she'd gone with them and said that Vishnu was a plumber. Plumbers, Giselle remembered reading somewhere, earned as much as doctors. Of course, that was in the

United States, but Giselle didn't want to be pedantic. Vishnu did do plumbing, among other things, and she wanted to see how her mother would react to that.

Her mother listened without interrupting until Giselle had finished, then said, 'Seems to me that what you feel for this Vishnu is just a physical thing.'

'I only said that he had a nice physique.'

'Yes, I heard you say it,' her mother said.

'But he's very intelligent, Mom. He makes the most horrible puns.'

'This proves he's intelligent?'

'I like the way he thinks. He just never had the opportunity to develop his abilities. We could have been so, too, if it wasn't for you. Suppose you *and* Daddy had been in that car crash? What would have happened to us? Anthony'd be a mechanic, I'd probably be a hairdresser, Tabitha would have five kids by now, and Miranda would be a hooker.'

'Giselle!'

'Well, you know how Miri is. The point I want to make, Mom, is that Vishnu has done well with what he has.'

'Yes, but you can't talk about what might have been,' her mother said. 'You have to think what is. And what is, is that you and he live in entirely different worlds.'

'Well, so do Robert and I, if it comes to that.'

'Not so different. You can go into Robert's world because there are more opportunities there. But if you go into Vishnu's world, you will be limiting yourself.'

'But life isn't just about opportunities. It's also about chocolate. Forrest Gump had it reversed.'

'Giselle, try to be serious. It is a hard world out there. You have to survive in it.'

'But I am surviving. What I'm talking about isn't that.'

Giselle felt a little upset now.

'Do you like this Robert?' her mother asked.

'Yes.'

'Then I don't see your problem. He can offer you more, and he is obviously more suitable than Vishnu.'

'But I feel differently about Vishnu.'

'I told you. That seems to me to be a physical attraction. And in any case it takes more than feelings to keep a marriage together.'

Giselle blinked. 'More than feelings?'

Her mother nodded. The chair rocked a little faster. 'It takes the right circumstances. It takes the *suppression* of feelings, when you feel you'd like to hit the other person with a frying-pan. It takes a commitment, even when you don't feel very committed. When you have to do all that, and battle circumstances as well, life can be very hard.'

'But,' said Giselle doubtfully, 'if a marriage has to be kept together through circumstances, rather than through feelings, it doesn't seem to me it's worth saving.'

Her mother sighed. 'You always were a romantic child, Giselle. But you're a woman now.'

'Yeah. The boobs and the nice clothes aren't bad, but I could have done without the cramps every month. I remember when dolls used to be my strongest emotional attachments. Those were the days.'

Her mother listened to this outburst, but said nothing. Giselle changed tack. 'So, if Vishnu wasn't just a manual labourer, whom would you tell me to choose?'

'I don't know. I don't know how you feel.'

'The first thing you said you noticed about Daddy was the way he moved on the cricket field.'

'Yes, but I wouldn't have married him on that basis alone. He was making something of himself before he died. That is how you measure somebody's worth, too, Giselle.'

She thought, *But Robert isn't more worthwhile than Vishnu. Robert has power and ambition and lots more money. Vishnu just has talent. But Robert hires Budhu to toady to him and Robert toadies to Bagasse Payne in return.*

Giselle looked at her mother as she rocked in the chair. She loved her mother, but that didn't blind her to the hard set of her mouth which even pregnancy had not changed. Giselle knew the limitations of the way her mother looked at the world. She also knew that those limitations didn't necessarily mean her mother was wrong – the world, after all, *was* basically made of rock.

But even if her mother's other contention was right, about a person making something of himself, Vishnu had also done that. All things being relative, he had done as well, or better, than Robert. And, she thought reluctantly, Vishnu had more *in* him.

Her mother said, 'Robert sounds to me like the kind of man you've always said you were waiting for. He is successful, bright and attractive, even if you think Vishnu is better-looking. Most women would be quite happy.'

Giselle looked down at her hands, which were folded in her lap. Her nails needed cutting. 'Actually, most women would find Robert better-looking, too. He has really nice ties.'

'Well, then,' said her mother.

'The thing is, Ma, I found out something else about Vishnu.'

'What?'

'He isn't only a labourer. He's also a freelance writer.'

Her mother blinked. 'So why is he working as a labourer?'

'Research.'

'What does he write?'

'Articles, stories, calypsos.'

'Does he make money at that?'

'Enough, I think,' Giselle said.

There was a pause.

'Well, it's your choice, Giselle,' her mother said finally. 'You have to do what will make you happy.'

Giselle got up and kissed her mother lightly.

'Thanks for the talk, Ma,' she said.

'Well, I hope I help you make the right decision.'

Giselle went back in to the kitchen to see Fariel.

'Next question, Ellie,' she said.

'Shoot,' said Fariel.

'Why men have such a fixation with sex?'

Fariel grinned and turned off the tap.

'I think you better have a sat.'

They went into the living-room.

'I mean,' Giselle continued, 'I don't understand the way they think about sex at all.'

Fariel laughed. 'Well, that's one of the three most obvious statements anybody could ever make.'

'What's the other two?'

'You know Trinis, when they bounce up somebody – "A-a, is you?" Or when they see you in the morning with your eyes bleary, "You wake up?"'

Giselle grinned. 'Well, I'm sorry for being obvious. But I really don't understand their mentality.'

'I think we women tend to think sex easy for men, mostly because we are told to be moral about it. So we think that, because men have no standards (and, believe me, they don't), they will track anything female, breathing, not too hairy and less than two hundred pounds – because of that, we think sex is no effort for them.'

'Well, isn't that so?' asked Giselle.

'Come on, Gis',' Fariel said. 'Even a cursory look at the, ah, anatomy of the situation will tell you different. I mean, a man who going to have sex must *want* to have sex, right?'

'Well, of course.'

'But a woman who going to have sex don't necessarily have to want to have sex. If a woman want, or if she don't want, all she have to do is lie back and say "Oh God, oh yes" a few times and things cool.'

Giselle grinned. 'You ever do that?'

'Fortunately,' Fariel said, 'I want sex all the time. And that is another thing about men. If a woman not really in the mood, it have signs. We won't get wet, so the man might have a little trouble getting in the door. But you think most men notice? Even when they do, what they say? "Darlin', you feeling tight like a virgin, is just like the first time again" and all the while the woman thinking, "I wasn't a virgin that time either, fool."'

Giselle cleared her throat. '*If* they weren't,' she said.

'If they weren't,' agreed Fariel. 'But you have to understand, Gis, that if a man not in the mood, it is rather hard for him to fake it because things would not be rather hard. Follow?'

'Yes. I'm naive, not deaf.'

'So my contention is that when women and priests suggest men should view sex as an expression of affection, they making impossible biological demands. And, personally, I feel both the women and the priests *know* is an impossible biological demand. But the women want the men to feel emotionally inferior and the priests don't want anybody having sex. It is totally unfair.'

'But I don't understand why you say that unfair? What wrong with sex and affection being linked?'

'Listen, a woman could have sex because she feeling affectionate. A man could only have sex because he feeling horny. Yes, it might happen that he also feeling affectionate, but that is only coincidental. And what you prefer? A man who out to show you he feeling affectionate, or one who out to give you orgasms till you scream for mercy?'

Giselle put up her hand. 'Miss, miss, I know the answer, miss. Orgasms, miss, plenty plenty orgasms!'

'Exactly, young Giselle. So, to answer your original question, that is the real reason men think about sex so much. So they could be ready at the drop of a panty. In fact, I read once that men think about it fifty per cent of the time – Tony say he suppose they does be asleep the other fifty per cent.'

'You really think men think about sex so much?'

'Hear, nah. The only time a man could have sex when he not in the mood is when he now wake up but he not quite awake yet.'

'How come?'

'Because men almost always wake up with a stand. Whenever a man wake up, he does usually find Johnny awake long before him – and I *do* mean long before him. And Johnny does be more awake than any time when the man himself fully awake. Is true the man does normally have a hot pee too, but that could hold.'

'And if his bladder bust, let it bust,' grinned Giselle.

'Exactly,' said Fariel. 'So if a woman want a lil thing in the morning, all she have to do is climb aboard. It don't matter if the feller in the mood. Johnny in the mood, and that is what counts. Even if the feller fall asleep, you don't have to take it personal.'

'Is just biology?'

'Exactly,' said Fariel. 'Of course, if a woman had to rely on that alone, she would hardly be getting as much sex as she needed, unless she had another man – or men, according to her capacities – on the sidelines. Right?'

'As rain,' agreed Giselle.

'So the real question is how to get the man in the mood.'

'Hardly a difficult task.'

'True. I put it badly. The real question is how to keep a man in the mood. And that could be a problem. You see, in this world, you always hear about a man being a good lover. But the most you might hear about a woman is that she 'good in bed', like if we don't like doing it on the dining-room table occasionally. And there's a kind of implication in saying a woman good in bed that she not good in any other way – the old double standards, nah. Anyway, I think we have a harder task than men. All a man have to do is get us excited and, barring psychological hang-ups, women are like propellers on them old airplanes – one spin and we take off. All the man have to do is hold on for the ride.'

'So how do you keep a man in the mood?' Giselle asked.

'There are plenty answers to that question, unless you have a Catholic view on sex education. And the number of answers is part of the reason women have problems with men's attitudes towards sex. Because the assumption is, the more things a man gets excited by, the more perverse he is.'

'Yes, but how do you *do* it?'

'Be a man's fantasy.'

'Oh, I can do *that*,' said Giselle.

'Than you should have no problem.'

'Though I still think a man could think about sex and be affectionate, too.'

Fariel shrugged, and there was a silence.

'Last question,' said Giselle. 'If Tony was poor, would you have married him?'

'I don't know,' Fariel answered.

'If Anton was poor, would you have married him?'

'I don't know that, either.'

Giselle got up.

'Don't worry,' she said. 'It's been that kind of day.'

◆

Vera was at the apartment when Giselle returned home.

'Hi,' said Giselle, surprised. 'What you doing here? I thought you were by . . . I forget his name, the bodybuilder.'

'Sidney. Yeah, I had to leave to give him a chance to recover. He's got muscles, but not endurance.'

'Maybe you should lime with a marathon runner,' said Giselle drily.

'I'm going to the Oval fête with one later,' Vera replied. Giselle rolled her eyes heavenwards. 'Anyway, chile,' Vera continued, 'hear why I really come back. I went and sign up with your mud mas band this morning, so you will have a wining partner.'

Giselle laughed. 'Vera! That's great!'

'Well, you know what they say: two waists better than one.'

'But I thought you were going to play with Poison.'

'I am. Fête at the Oval, come back here to change, mud mas till six, come back home to bathe and sleep for two or three hours and then out again.'

'Oh,' said Giselle. 'Well, as long as you don't overdo it.'

'So you coming to the fête? Bring along Robert or Vishnu. Hell, bring them both – the Oval's a big place.'

'I'll pass,' Giselle said. Not being in the mood for a long conversation, she decided not to tell Vera what had happened.

Vera shrugged. 'Okay.'

'You'll meet me back here or by the band?'

'By the band. I mightn't leave the fête till four and I suppose you going to meet them at exactly two. I have the route map so I must bounce you up. You could save some hunks for me.'

'You not coming with anybody?'

'Aiy, you expect me to go through Carnival without picking up?'

'Sorry, what was I thinking?'

'Anyway,' said Vera, getting up from the sofa, 'Amrit is picking me up at ten so I better get a few hours sleep.'

'Yeah, me too,' said Giselle, yawning.

◆

At two a.m. precisely, Giselle was at the meeting point on Tragerete Road. She was wearing only a skimpy blue bikini, a blue headband and track shoes. And, though she thought she would feel self-conscious, she instead felt perfectly natural. Of course, this was partly because nearly everyone there was similarly undressed. The bandleaders were already there with the containers of mud in the back of a pick-up. People were going over, dipping their hands and smearing themselves and each other liberally. A little hesitantly, Giselle went over and pasted herself. It was real mud they were using, not a cocoa-butter-and-water substitute. It was cool and sticky on her skin. And, as she put on the mud, Giselle became aware of a sudden looseness and ease and carelessness, as if all the tensions of life were lifted from her shoulders. Then, the generator on the DJ truck started up,

Amazon's 'Waiting to See Paul' blared out and the mud-caked bodies began chipping to the rhythm as the band moved down the street.

In the middle of this gyrating crowd, on the dark streets, with the calypso and chutney and soca chutney sounding, Giselle found a joyful exuberance. Strange men – and women – danced around her and, occasionally, some of these people would press against her in a wine which was a simulation of sex. Yet, sexual as it was, it was also understood, a familiar ritual. Giselle threw herself into it, and no man went beyond the dance. When at four o'clock Vera joined the band, Giselle was wining between two men. Vera, eyebrows raised, nonetheless immediately joined to make a foursome moving in perfect unison. And, when those two men moved away, she and Giselle wined on each other. As she played this mas, Giselle for the first time in her life understood why she felt close to women like Vera and Fariel and even Sharma. All of them had an uninhibited, sexual femaleness – the wild side. And they were not afraid to express it. Giselle now realized that this appealed to the same obscene aspect in herself – a side she had always kept bottled up, strictly disciplined, as she lived vicariously through her friends.

I'm like a stripper who keeps on her clothes, she thought in the midst of the music, and she was delightedly aware of her nakedness under the mud.

'You break away, Karan!' Vera shouted above the music.

'And is about time!' Giselle shouted back.

And so the night continued until coming dawn silvered the sky. And it was then, as the band began breaking up and the music played down, that they met Vishnu.

He had horns on his head, was bareback, and wore a pair of trousers so ragged they were nearly immodest. A tin cup hung around his neck. His guitar was strapped over his back. He came through the band straight for Giselle, stopped in front of her and, unslinging his guitar, began to strum an easy, pleasant tune and to sing. Giselle simply stood there. Vera grinned and moved to the side. Vishnu sang:

> Ever since you blank me
> My life has neither song, music nor dance
> So I come to beg for a dollar
> And for jockey shorts to match these pants.

> I really miss your loving touch
> And I feel really sad,
> And as you could see from these holey trousers
> I taking it really hard.

Vishnu looked at her intently as he sang this last line. Giselle looked back at him and, without realizing what she intended to do, slowly licked her lips. Vishnu swallowed and sang the chorus:

> I miss your smell, your smile, your smooch,
> So I've come in rags with my tin cup.
> Because since you been gone
> I find I really hard UP!
> I just want a little help:
> A dime, a quarter, a buck.
> But if you don't have spare change
> I will just take . . . a meal.

Giselle, about to gasp, grinned as Vishnu changed the last word. Passers-by and J'Ouvert players gathered around, some picking up the rhythm with those basic Carnival musical instruments – bottles and spoons. Giselle grinned around, feeling both amused and embarrassed. Then she looked back at Vishnu as his fourth verse threatened to make embarrassment rule:

> I know I doh have to tell you 'bout charity
> Or give you any moral text,
> But I will do anything you want in return,
> Even give you . . . a calypso.

> If you don't have food
> I will take anything you have to nibble;
> Is only because I so hungry
> That when I look at you I dribble.

Giselle ran her hand down her body as Vishnu sang the chorus again. And her expression alone was enough to make his voice crack as he did the next verse:

> Is true I really hard UP!
> But I don't mind going down, nah,

Once it is by your hand
I wouldn't make a sound, except Ahh!

The rhythm of the music now slowed for the final verses:

I have total tabanca,
And I feel totally tootoolbey,
So sugar plum, doux-doux, choonkalunks,
I will call you anything bazodee men does say.

But under all this kif-kif laugh,
The truth is I really come to beg;
Not for money or a meal or sex
But for your heart . . . and a fried chicken leg.

Listen, I only make jokes to win your heart,
You have already won mine . . . and a large Christmas
    hamper;
For I like you very many plenties
And wherever you is I want to be are
For what better basis can there be for true love
Than 'nuff respect, great passion and plenty laughter?

As Vishnu finished, he laid the guitar down on the road, put his hands in her stiffened hair and kissed her. The people watching broke into cheers and claps.

'I haven't forgiven you yet,' Giselle said. 'Where the hell have you been?'

'I quit right after that meeting where you ignored me.'

'Because I ignored you?'

'No, silly. Because nobody who has a choice should work for people like Spengler Bagasse Payne.'

'Even a writer who's posing as a labourer?'

'*Especially* a writer who's posing as a labourer.'

'Interesting ethics.'

'So when will you?'

'When will I what?'

'Forgive me.'

Giselle adjusted her mud-covered bra-top.

'Come to the apartment around ten,' she said and turned and chipped away with a dancing Vera.

Chapter Thirteen

As an ethical person – though not, she now gladly realized, a moral one – Giselle felt she should let Robert know things were over before she went with Vishnu. After all, Robert had nearly been the first. *But a miss is as good as a mile*, thought Giselle as she drove down to Maraval. Vera had gone by one of her men to bathe and sleep.

Giselle had called Robert after she had reached home and showered. He didn't play mas.

'We need to talk,' she said when he answered.

'What's the matter?'

'I'll tell you when I come. But you won't like what I have to say.'

His voice didn't change. 'All right.'

She had always known where her heart – *as well as other body parts*, she thought with a grin – was leading her. But she had resisted. And, although she hated to admit it to herself, the main plank of her resistance had been snobbery. Vishnu was simply not the kind of man she saw herself with in social terms. Giselle was almost glad there was another element of resistance, which Vishnu still didn't know about. *I hope virginity isn't a tougher barrier than social norms*, thought Giselle, then nearly laughed out loud.

Robert opened the door as soon as she pressed the buzzer.

'Hi,' he said. He leaned forward to kiss her, but she swept by him. She sat in an armchair in the living-room. He closed the door and followed her in a leisurely manner. He had a balloon glass of brandy in his hand.

'Can I get you something to drink?' he asked.

'No thanks. Sit down, please.'

'Thank you,' he said ironically. He sat on the sofa opposite her. 'So why are you angry?' he asked.

'I'm not angry,' she said, surprised. 'Why would you think that?'

He shrugged. 'Well, what's the matter, then?'

'I've been thinking,' she said.

He took a sip of brandy. 'I hate it when women say that. It always means trouble.'

'I think we should stop seeing each other,' she said bluntly.

He looked at her calmly over his brandy glass.

'Why? What have I done?'

'You haven't done anything. You've been perfect. I've really enjoyed the past weeks and I thought we might be going somewhere. But I don't think so anymore. It's just me. I don't think we right for each other.'

'I see. Or rather, I don't see. I thought we were getting along marvellously. In what way are we not right for each other?'

Giselle hesitated. 'Our . . . attitudes to life are different.'

Robert drank some more brandy. Giselle realized he was a little drunk. She thought he might have started drinking when she called. 'Come, that's rather abstract,' he said. 'Be more specific.'

'I can't. I just don't think we could have a satisfactory life together.'

'Is there someone else?'

Now his eyes rested directly on her.

'Sort of. But that is not why I'm saying this.'

Oh great Giselle, she thought. *He'll really believe that. Why don't you learn to lie, girl?*

Robert laughed shortly, sharply.

'I hear you've been liming with that carpenter from the construction crew.'

Giselle's eyes widened. She had heard of news travelling fast, but this was ridiculous.

'Where do you hear that?' she said sharply.

He sipped at the brandy again. 'I have my sources.'

Giselle dismissed his sources with a wave of her hand. A moment's thought had told her that Robert must have known about her and Vishnu even before the meeting with Gemma. But she was amazed that he had had an inkling of this and never even hinted at it, either by word or manner. It was as though Connie Chung had been told something juicy in confidence during an interview and decided not to broadcast it on CBS primetime news.

'It doesn't matter, anyway,' said Giselle. 'Who I'm liming or not liming with doesn't change the fact. I'm sorry, because it would have been nice if things had worked out. But I can't see us together.'

Robert emptied his brandy glass and got up and went to the small bar to the side of the living-room.

'You sure I can't get you something?'

'No thank you.'

He returned with his brandy glass quarter-full once again.

'I don't think you've thought this through properly, Giselle,' he said.

'Actually, I have,' she answered.

'I don't think it would be a wise – ' he paused – 'career move.'

'What do you mean?' she said.

'A labourer, Giselle?' he said. His voice rose. 'I know you have humble origins, but please. You can do better.'

'We aren't discussing careers, Robert. We're discussing relation-ships.'

'Sometimes one impacts on the other,' he said.

Giselle shook her head. *You and Mom would get along well*, she thought bitterly.

'I've always thought you very strange, Giselle,' he said. 'Attractive, but strange. You don't quite know how to get along with people. You're too direct, too open. But I thought that was just a matter of youth. Now I see your strangeness goes rather further.'

'I see. So how come you never mentioned my "strangeness" before?'

'Darling, I was trying to build a relationship with you. It wasn't the right time to get into that area.'

'And you still don't see why we have no future?'

'I see your lack of experience, your naivety. And, if you persist in this foolishness, you might find that cured the hard way.'

'You know, Robert, you sound as though you're threatening me.'

'I assure you, that's the furthest thing from my mind.'

But Giselle thought he spoke too smoothly. 'In any case, I'll be resigning in one month.' And, even as she said it, Giselle wondered why she hadn't made such an obviously correct decision before. She had no responsibilities save to herself. *I don't even have a dog*, she thought, vexed.

Robert said, 'You aren't going to claim I forced you to resign, are you?'

Giselle rolled her eyes upwards. 'No, Robert. I don't think like you.'

'Oh. Good,' he said.

Giselle got up. 'I have to go.'

Robert drained his brandy glass in one gulp.

'To your labourer friend?'

Giselle went to the door. Then she turned. He had put down the brandy glass and followed her. She said, 'Robert, I hope we can maintain an amicable professional relationship. There is really no reason why we shouldn't. But my social life is none of your business anymore.'

He reached down and held her wrist. She didn't pull away, not wanting to get into a tussle. But his grip was very strong. She smelled the brandy on his breath.

'I don't think you're thinking this through,' he said.

'I told you I have. Now let me go.'

'You may be thinking, but not with your head. Is that why you've been so coy with me? Because you've been giving it to him?'

Giselle looked at him with utter contempt. There could not have been more disgust in her face if she had been a *cordon bleu* chef and he a maggot in the salad.

'That's probably the first thing you've ever said to me that you really believe, isn't it,' she said with a lash in her voice.

As she spoke, it occurred to Giselle that she was not in a very tenable situation. If he forced himself on her, there was certainly no jury in the Caribbean which would find him guilty. Giselle had gone to Robert's apartment; they had been seeing each other; and he was Robert Cardinez. According to several judges in Trinidad, this would negate any possibility of rape. And, if it came out that she had been seeing another man, Robert could even kill her and only be charged with manslaughter. Trinidadian judges viewed such transgressions with a lenient, even paternal eye, Giselle knew. 'Boys will be boys,' about summed up their attitude.

'Let go of my wrist, please,' Giselle said, very calmly, despite all these thoughts running through her head.

Robert ignored her. 'I'm particularly sorry we never properly got into the, ah, intimate stages of our relationship,' he said. 'You strike me as being a very passionate woman. Perhaps I was too *much* the gentleman.'

'I don't think – ' Giselle began, then Robert leaned down and kissed her on the mouth. Giselle jerked back, coming up against the door, and Robert's hands ran over her breasts. That did it. A white flare of rage exploded in her head and she reached up and grabbed his shirt collar with one hand and hit him in the chest with the heel of her palm.

Robert grunted and fell down. Giselle stepped forward and was about to stamp on him when he shouted, frightened, 'No!'

She stood looking at him, breathing heavily.

'Violence doesn't solve anything,' he said urgently from the floor.

'It might solve your sex life permanently,' she gritted out.

Robert scrambled to his feet. 'Now, Giselle, let's deal with this like rational adults.'

'Where we going to get the other adult from?'

'Ha-ha!' laughed Robert heartily. He eased back in a manner which suggested he hoped Giselle wouldn't notice until it was too late. Giselle's gaze was full of contempt.

Once out of striking distance, he relaxed slightly.

'If you ever try that again,' said Giselle, still speaking through clenched teeth, 'make sure your life insurance is paid up.'

'I'm sorry,' he said, in that tone of voice which really means 'I'm glad', 'but I do find you very attractive. I lost control.'

'Tell it to the women who sleep with you,' said Giselle. 'I'm sure they've told you it's a common problem.'

Robert seemed to experience a brief attack of gas.

'I promise I'll use gentler means of persuasion. The brandy was controlling me.'

'There is no question of persuasion. I am not interested in you.'

'You don't know what you're missing.'

'As far as I can tell, drunkenness, insensitivity and some really bad sex.'

'I'm not giving up, Giselle,' said Robert.

Had she not been well brought up, Giselle might have spat as she spoke.

'This is not the damned Alamo, Robert. Listen, I'll say it in words of one syllable: *I am not in-ter-est-ed.*'

'That's four syllables,' he said, as though catching her out.

Giselle shook her head. 'Leave it, Robert.'

Keeping an eye on him, she opened the door, stepped out, and quickly pulled it shut. Robert did not come after her, but she hurried to her car. As she pulled out of the car park she felt a mixture of relief and fear and anger and, weirdly, a surge of wild humour.

In the end, humour won out and she burst into laughter – perhaps a little hysterically – as she drove round the Savannah, back to her apartment.

Vishnu was outside her apartment when she returned. He had changed and bathed.

'Waiting long?' Giselle asked, opening her door.

'All my life,' he answered.

'Don't get maudlin,' she said. 'It's unbecoming.'

'Sorry,' he said. 'When it comes to you, I certainly want to b-be-becoming.'

Vishnu followed her inside and, when he closed the door, she turned, grabbed the front of his T-shirt in her right hand and pushed him against the door. She stuck her forefinger in his face.

'Don't you *ever* lie to me again!' she said.

He raised his hands in surrender. 'I hear. I swear.'

She released him.

'Fine.'

They sat in the living-room. Looking at him, it occurred to Giselle again how much she had changed and how quickly. He was right, too. Their relationship would not have been the same if he had smoothed her path by telling her the plain facts about himself. Her mother's sudden capitulation had shown that clearly. The strength of the feelings between them now would have been diminished or, at least, have taken longer to achieve. Sometimes, Giselle realized, the deepest truths did not rest on facts.

Vishnu leaned forward and began kissing her.

'Wait,' said Giselle.

'Wait?'

'OK, Dorothy. On what?'

'I have something to tell you.'

'Tell me later,' he said, kissing her again.

Giselle mumbled something, then gave herself more fully to Vishnu's kiss than she had ever done before, except perhaps that first time. His lips pressed softly into hers. Then the kiss was deeper, as if he was seeking to possess her. She felt him pressing more deeply into her, so her head arched back, as he sought some unspoken knowledge of her. The stubble on his face rubbed with pleasant friction against her skin.

She found they had moved on to the sofa, still kissing. Her blouse and skirt were already off. Now Vishnu's kisses were light, exploring humorous. She had not known there could be humour in kissing.

Finally, he moved back, his eyes smiling.

His face was close to hers, his eyes smokily dark. *There is some sort of grey in them, deep down*, she thought.

'The first time I saw you,' he said softly, 'I felt we were meant to be together.'

'The first time I saw you, I thought you had a gorgeous body,' she said.

'I was lying. That's what I thought about you, too,' he said, smiling seriously at her.

She kissed him, not wanting to speak yet. Their hands pressed on each other's bodies, and that was another kind of silent discovery. *It is so strange*, Giselle said in some unconscious flow of thought, *the knowledge there is without speech*. She pressed her hands on Vishnu's arms and she knew their texture and contour and articulation from his shoulders. Or she felt the muscles of his chest, and felt the heavy, dark beat of his heart beneath the cage of his breast, and she knew the strength in him and the flow of his blood. And she was amazed to discover that such knowledge was as important as anything else you might know about a person you loved.

'I love you,' she murmured. She was not sure she had spoken. But it was so simple. She had never been in love before. But that trite saying turned out to be true: when you were in love, you knew. *How strange*! she said in her mind.

They were both almost naked now. Vishnu was intent upon her, as though all obstacles had been removed. Giselle said, 'I'm a virgin.'

There was a sudden, shocked stillness. His voice was as clear as a bell: 'You're a *what*?' It was as though he had never heard the word before.

Giselle sat up. She thought she should be angry, perhaps embarrassed. Instead, she was just amused.

'A virgin. You know, someone who's never had sex. You must have been one yourself some time.'

'You're serious.' His face was still shocked. She felt laughter well up inside her. He said, 'How come?'

'I've never been in love before.'

'Oh.'

There was a long silence while Giselle watched Vishnu and laughed silently.

Finally, he smiled and said, 'Well, I'm pretty sure I'm in love with you, too. And you're only the second woman in my life I've said that to.'

She lay down on her stomach, chin propped on her hand, looking at him with eyes that seemed newly opened. 'Said it and meant it, you mean.'

He shook his head. 'No, said it at all.'

'Are you shocked I've never done it?'

He paused. 'Surprised,' he said.

'Does it change the way you feel?'

'It puts a different perspective on certain things,' he said carefully. 'But it does not change my feelings for you.'

She moved forward and rested her head on his chest. 'Good,' she said.

They lay like this for a while. Then Giselle said, 'I didn't mean for you to stop what you were doing, you know.'

His hand was resting on the small of her back. His fingers moved lightly, restlessly. 'There are things we have to think about.'

'I'm fed up of thinking,' Giselle said. She moved her tongue in a delicate circle on his chest.

Vishnu cleared his throat. 'Giselle . . .'

'Mm?' she said, continuing what she was doing.

'When you say you're a virgin . . .?'

She glanced at him, amused. 'I know. It seems like the kind of story which should be on the cover of the *Weekly World News*, next to the item about the transvestite alcoholic who got pregnant for aliens and found God.'

Vishnu smiled, but still looked a little strained.

'You must have a lot of willpower,' he said.

'Not really. I think when you're Catholic with Hindu forbears, strange things happen to your psyche. You have one tradition where a girl's parents have to pay a man to marry their daughter, another

217

where it's all right to perform fellatio once there's no orgasm attached to it . . . Naturally, a person gets confused.'

'So you think you're no longer confused?'

'Yes.'

'But you can't know.'

'Listen, Vishnu. I've read the *Kama Sutra*. I've watched instructional videos. And, though I've enjoyed it, I'm tired of theory. I'm tired of waiting. In fact,' she looked at him and grinned, 'I'm ready like Freddie.'

'It may be a mistake to rush into anything.'

'You 'fraid I won't treat you gently?'

'No, but . . .'

Seeing his uncertainty, Giselle felt suddenly sorry for Vishnu. 'It's okay, you know,' she said. 'But I sure as hell never thought I'd have to persuade you to have sex with me.'

A smile flickered on Vishnu's face. 'Oh, I intend to have sex with you. I just want everything to be right.'

Giselle looked up into his face. 'A gentleman wouldn't get a girl all horny and leave her like this.'

'But,' said Vishnu, suddenly sounding like he had gravel tangled up in his vocal cords, 'we'll do it very soon.'

Giselle continued looking up into his face.

'Couldn't we just have oral sex for now?' she said sweetly.

Vishnu seemed to collapse a little on the sofa.

'Jesus!' he said.

'Jesus said "touch me not" when he was risen.' Giselle glanced down. 'And risen you may be but you're certainly not Jesus.'

She reached down and stroked him lightly. Vishnu froze. Indeed, except for the drops of sweat beading his brow, he could have been Michelangelo's statue of David.

'My,' said Giselle, putting on the tone usually used for describing the Energizer Bunny. 'It just keeps growing and growing . . .'

Vishnu held his head and groaned.

'If you say not now dear, I have a headache,' said Giselle, 'I'll hurt you.'

Vishnu looked at her. Now his expression was that of one of the damned souls in Minshall's *Danse Macabre*. Giselle moved her hand and hugged him.

'Poor dear. This is very hard for you, isn't it?' she said.

'Literally.'

'Well, at least you can still make jokes.'

He held her face between his two hands and looked into her eyes.

'It doesn't change anything,' he said. 'But give me time to adjust.'

'To what? Me being a virgin? Is it that a big deal?'

'In a way. Give me some time.'

Giselle looked at him intently for several seconds.

'Time's up,' she said.

He stared at her, then laughed. 'I guess patience isn't one of your virtues.'

'I don't feel very virtuous right now.'

She moved closer to him. 'Do you love me?' she asked.

'Yes,' he answered.

'How do you know?'

'I know,' he said.

Giselle liked his answer.

'Will you break my heart?' she asked.

'I don't want to,' he said.

'How about my hymen?' she asked nicely.

Vishnu had a sudden coughing fit.

Giselle grinned up at him.

'Christ, Giselle,' Vishnu said, when he had recovered. 'I can't afford to have heart problems later. You'll kill me young.'

'Only if you have a really big insurance policy,' she said. She snuggled against him. 'And you're talking like if you intend to be around for a long time,' she said warningly.

'I do,' he said.

'What are we going to do?' she asked. She was speaking of practical matters.

Vishnu leaned down and whispered in her ear.

'Oh,' said Giselle.

He lifted her off the sofa and she linked her hands around his neck. She felt as though she were feather-light, on the threshold of a free-flying new world, as he carried her without effort into the bedroom where the sunlight streamed in through the open window.

The sun could hardly know that the bedroom didn't need its heat.